This is NOT

THE

END

MOLLY MORRIS

Chicken
House

2 Palmer Street, Frome, Somerset BA11 1DS
www.chickenhousebooks.com

Text © Molly Morris 2022
Cover illustration © Sarah Long 2022

First published in Great Britain in 2022
Chicken House
2 Palmer Street
Frome, Somerset BA11 1DS
United Kingdom
www.chickenhousebooks.com

Chicken House/Scholastic Ireland, 89E Lagan Road, Dublin Industrial Estate,
Glasnevin, Dublin D11 HP5F, Republic of Ireland

Molly Morris has asserted her right under the Copyright, Designs and Patents Act
1988 to be identified as the author of this work.

Cover and interior design by Helen Crawford-White
Cover illustration by Sarah Long
Typeset by Dorchester Typesetting Group Ltd
Printed and bound in Great Britain by CPI Group (UK) Ltd, Croydon CR0 4YY

FSC
www.fsc.org
MIX
Paper from
responsible sources
FSC® C171272

3 5 7 9 10 8 6 4 2

British Library Cataloguing in Publication data available.

PB ISBN 978-1-913696-21-4
eISBN 978-1-913696-75-7

For Diane Tettamble, who encouraged me to write,
even after I killed her off in each of my stories.

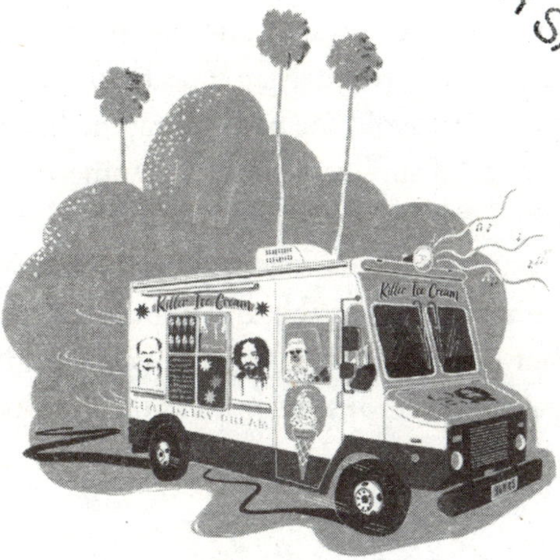
Killer Ice Cream
Killer Ice Cream

Stories with rubbish endings are deeply frustrating . . . but what if your frustration over bad endings grew into an obsession and spilt out into every area of your life? Meet Hugh, our extremely anxious hero, who does everything he can to avoid the bad endings he hates. For Hugh, safe is good. Familiar is good. But somehow he finds himself driving near-stranger Olivia Moon to New York City in this romance-drama-road trip mash-up, a super cool pop-culture feast of the possible and impossible. I love this amazing debut novel, bursting with comedy, friendship and the biggest of questions. Want to know the answers? Read on . . .

BARRY CUNNINGHAM
Publisher
Chicken House

Prologue

The fact that my aunt's front door was unlocked should've been a red flag. Just about every horror movie I'd ever seen featured a stupid, oblivious guy wandering through an open door that definitely should've been locked, only for said idiot to get slammed in the face with a surprise axe. But this was New York City. My aunt's building had a doorman. Wasn't that so she didn't have to lock her front door?

I collapsed on to the couch, sleep immediately creeping around the edges of my vision. Closing my eyes, I tried to remember the last time I'd slept normally. It was before this whole stupid weekend, before I ruined basically every relationship that ever meant anything to me. In fact, I'd probably never sleep again, plagued instead by memories of me attempting to dance like someone that didn't look high on hard drugs, or the way I almost *wanted* Olivia to make fun of me, to be on the other end of her sharp wit, because at least then I knew she cared about me.

At the thought of Olivia, my stomach dropped, cueing the memories of this weekend to start cycling through my head on a never-ending loop.

Olivia, saying goodbye.

Olivia, disappearing through the iron gate of the shady Brooklyn music venue. Alone.

Me, trailing after her, always too late.

Clark and his stupid leather vest.

The way Olivia looked at me when—

A loud thump echoed from down the hall of my aunt's apartment, momentarily breaking me out of my head. It sounded like a towel slumping on to the tiled floor of the bathroom.

I flattened one of the fancy velvet pillows crowding the couch over my head, as if that could shield me from the oncoming sounds of concern and flurry of movement that were almost certainly on their way.

'I've basically had the worst night of my life and if you ask me about it, I'm gonna throw up,' I shouted to my aunt, Karen.

But when she didn't come sliding down the hallway on the balls of her slippery, socked feet, I dragged the pillow off my face and frowned.

'Aunt Karen?'

Only then did I realize how quiet the apartment was, the surrounding silence hard and cold. It was the quiet right before a grenade exploded, as the little metal canister arced through the air and you waited helplessly for the explosion. For the deafening boom. For the blackness.

My feet landed hard on the wooden floor, adrenaline surging up my throat. Somehow, I knew it wasn't my aunt

2

or even an axe murderer in the bathroom. I knew instantly that it could only be one person, that the night could only end one way.

My sprint down the hallway only lasted a half second, but by the time I slammed my shoulder into the bathroom door frame I was already breathless. As I took in the scene, my brain stuttered. The shrunken figure slumped underneath the sink, her trademark white-blonde hair looking green in the bathroom's dingy light.

'Olivia?' I said, barely above a whisper.

At the sound of my voice, she didn't move. But just seeing her like that, I knew. I didn't need to touch her neck to feel for a pulse or see her glassy eyes rolled back in her head.

I knew. Olivia Moon was dead.

1

Four days earlier

THE LORD OF THE RINGS: THE RETURN OF THE KING
Posted in MOVIES by <u>Hugh.jpg</u> on November 10 at 9:13 p.m.

After hours and hours of battles, ghosts, a seriously long journey, quests for honour, glory and orc blood, how did the final movie of *The Lord of the Rings* trilogy close with a pillow fight, a basically silent bar scene and a wedding nobody went to? Even Frodo, equally bored, was like, 'Yo, I would literally rather die than be here right now.'

I could tell by the way she sidestepped carefully along the roof that Olivia Moon had climbed a house before.

'What is she doing?' I said to myself, leaning over the truck's centre console and watching her through the passenger-side window. Then, under my breath, 'The eff is she wearing?'

The last time I saw Olivia Moon — which had to have been a few days before our high school graduation — she'd been wearing nothing but basketball jerseys and shiny leather pants. Now, she was in a beige, oversized Hawaiian shirt and baggy khaki shorts that unzipped at the knees. Looped around her wrists were a pair of thick leather bracelets, ones a kid in our class said made her look like she'd just rolled out of an eighteenth-century porno. That earned him a punch in the mouth that knocked out one of his front teeth, courtesy of Olivia.

The house's second storey had two rectangular windows, each one painted with a white trim I could tell was faded and worn, even from across the street. Olivia glanced up at them, hands on her hips, before kneeling and trying to open one of the windows from the outside. It didn't budge.

I watched in silence as Olivia tried the other window, clenching her fists at her sides when she discovered it was also locked. Even though she was clearly preoccupied, I still hunched down in my seat in case she turned around and noticed me very unsubtly watching her from my sister's ice cream van across the street.

'Is this the part where I do something?' I said out loud, to no one.

Call someone? Text someone?

I picked up my phone from between my legs and stared at the blank screen. But before I could type anything in, a knock on my window yanked me back into my seat. On the other side of the glass was a group of boys that were probably in middle school, their bikes tipped over on the sidewalk.

'Are you open?' said the kid closest to my window.

I waved both hands at them and mouthed, 'Go away.'

Somehow, Olivia didn't seem to notice, her face now pushed against one of the house windows, hands cupped around her eyes.

'Uh, hello?' another one of the kids said. He slapped his flat palm against the glass. 'Can we get some ice cream?'

'I heard you the first time,' I hissed, still waving my hands. 'Get. Out. Of. Here.'

The main kid rolled his eyes and held up his middle finger as the rest of them grabbed their bikes and pedalled off. When I turned back to the house, my mouth went dry. Olivia was standing on the edge of the roof with her hands on her hips, staring directly at me.

'Can I help you?' she shouted from across the street.

This is the part where I probably do something, I thought.

That much, I could figure out.

Shoving my phone in my pocket, I slowly climbed out and edged around the truck, dragging my hand across its metal nose.

'Hey,' I said, drawing out the word so it lasted at least ten seconds.

Olivia was staring at the front of the house again, so she could look up at the tiny circular window on the third storey, which was most likely the attic. On her head was a bucket hat she pushed away from her face, white-blonde hair chunking out underneath and spilling across her shoulders.

'Do you always watch girls out of ice cream vans or

is this the beginning of your creep career?' she asked without turning around.

I didn't really know what to say to that. She kind of had a point.

'Did you forget your keys or something?' I said.

'Not my house,' she said simply.

A memory of Olivia in her backyard surfaced in my brain. Her eleventh birthday party, a rollerblade cake, Miley Cyrus in the speakers.

'You live in Columbia Heights,' I said. The same neighbourhood as me.

'Do you stalk me there too?'

My face flushed red. 'I went to your birthday party in elementary school, the one where we played One Direction on a stage your dad rigged up in your backyard.' I swiped my hand through my hair, toe digging into the sidewalk. 'I don't know how I forgot. That kinda thing scars a person.'

A white drainpipe ran up the side of the house, its plastic criss-crossed with vines. Olivia grabbed on to the pipe and leant back as though she were testing its strength.

'Beats me,' she said, the pipe wobbling under her grip. 'I'm sure your rendition of Harry Styles was truly groundbreaking.'

'Please tell me you're not gonna try to shimmy up that drainpipe,' I said. 'That's how people die.'

'Probably,' Olivia said, stepping backwards. 'But Clark stole something from me and I need to get it back.'

'Shit, this is Clark Thomas's house?'

My head whipped around as if Clark might jump out of the bushes with a machete. Clark was the guy who once put our high school's lunch lady in a chokehold after she called him 'young man', because apparently no one had referred to him as a human before.

Clark Thomas was Olivia's boyfriend.

'Nobody's home,' she said, like this made everything better.

'Yeah, I figured that out by the way you're trying to break in through a window.'

Olivia swiped her hand across the top of her head. She craned her head back so she could see something high up on the house, maybe that third-storey window, which had a slight lip jutting out around it.

'Yeah, well, what Clark took from me is very important,' she said.

She took another step backwards, except this time, she was so close to the edge of the roof that her heel, setting down hard, found nothing but air.

My body went straight. 'Shit, look—' I said, but before I could get the sentence out, Olivia was already tipping backwards, her back curling slightly and her arms flailing as they grabbed at nothing.

Only a single scream echoed down the block, and I wasn't sure if it was from me or Olivia. One leg drifted up as Olivia's body fell, hair floating around her face as if she were underwater. Her back and shoulders crashed into the concrete path just underneath the porch, head bouncing violently like a rubber ball and arms stretched out on either side of her in a limp, perfect T.

Her body sprawled out across the concrete, unmoving. My brain screamed at me to move, to go help her, but everything else in me was frozen, as if it were operating on a five-second lag. Olivia was just lying there as the seconds ticked by. And then, as if something in my head clicked, I darted across the lawn, heart hammering in my throat. By the time I reached her, Olivia still wasn't moving, the brim of her hat pushed down over her forehead and blocking her face.

Up close, her skin was glassy and pale, only her mouth visible underneath her hat. I dropped to my knees and pulled the brim back slightly so I could see up to her forehead. A puddle of blood was already blossoming on the concrete underneath her head, pooling out so I had to edge away from it before it reached my knees.

'Olivia?' I said quietly, afraid if I spoke too loudly, I somehow might scare her.

My voice was almost unrecognizable, small, shaking, faraway. Everything felt like we were suspended in time, the trees swaying slowly on the front lawn, the air warm and still. Even the street was silent, the cars rushing into downtown Washington seeming light years away instead of a couple blocks off.

I couldn't look at Olivia without feeling sick. Her head, clearly flattened into the pavement, the thin trickle of blood leaking from her mouth. Everybody in movies who bled from the mouth or ear ended up dead. And I'd just watched her die.

Turning away from Olivia's body, I fumbled in my pocket for my phone. As I did, there was a rustling behind me, a scraping almost, the sound of tennis shoes swiping against concrete. I turned slowly and widened my eyes cartoon-big.

One of Olivia's fingers was twitching.

I blinked. I blinked again.

'How . . .' I whispered to myself but couldn't finish the sentence.

As if testing the movement and sending the OK to the rest of her body, the other fingers on Olivia's hand began to flex and wiggle, followed by her whole right arm, then her left.

'You can't be alive,' I said breathlessly. 'You can't actually be alive. Your head's inside out.'

As if to prove me wrong, Olivia blinked. Her eyes, glassy and lifeless just a few seconds before, were now bright and darting around the sky as if to assess the situation. Olivia arched her spine, rotated her ankles and unhinged her jaw, the bones cracking loudly back into place.

'Don't get up—' I started to say, hand outstretched in her direction, but Olivia sprung quickly into a sitting position and yanked her hat down the front of her face.

The back of her head was just a flat smear of deep red, the pink squish of her brain pulsing faintly and broken apart by splinters of creamy-white skull.

'Macaulay Culkin,' I said with a gag. 'I'm gonna puke.'

Olivia was still, hands splayed on the ground as her breath came softly, patiently. That's when I saw it; her skull, shattered at the back, was starting to stitch itself together again, slowly filling the gap like a puddle of water spilling backwards. I watched with my mouth open as the skin on her head formed over the newly healed skull, then as hair sprouted and grew until it matched the length of the hair that was still left.

'What. The eff. Is happening,' I said slowly, my voice a supercharged whisper.

Once her head was back intact, Olivia pushed herself on to her knees, groaning with the effort. She tilted her head from side to side, then shook her shoulders as she muttered under her breath and wiped the blood from her mouth.

I must have made a sound because she turned toward me, lips pursed. At the sight of me crouching on the path, she somehow looked even more confused than I did.

Olivia knit her eyebrows together and said, 'What?'

A tidal wave of words and thoughts crashed through my head but none of them made enough sense to put into a sentence. All I could do was stare at Olivia, her eyes fogging over with what looked like anger.

'How did you – what just – I just saw – you're alive,' I sputtered finally.

Olivia stretched her neck again so her bones popcorn-popped. 'Apparently,' she said.

'But I saw you die,' I said. 'Your head was caved in and it looked like – like a crumpled-up Hershey's Kiss wrapper.'

'I think the word you're looking for is tinfoil,' she said.

The image was seared into my brain, repeating itself on a continuous, stomach-turning loop. 'Your head was legit flat. There was so much blood,' I said, picturing it. Now that I'd managed to form a sentence, I couldn't keep them in. 'How did you do that?'

We both glanced down at the pool of blood still fresh at her knees as if to make sure it'd really happened.

Olivia sighed through her nose. 'It's kind of complicated . . .' She gingerly touched the back of her head and winced. 'Hank, is it?'

I swallowed. 'Hugh.'

'Hugh. I'm not really in the right frame of mind to talk about the details. My head is pounding.'

I tried to shift my body so I could see the back of her head again but she turned with me, obscuring it.

'What just happened?' I said, pointing. 'Your head stitched itself back together.'

Olivia jammed her hat back on to her head and tied the straps underneath her chin. 'What're you doing over here anyway?' she said, ignoring my question. 'Don't you live in Columbia Heights too?'

I pointed at the truck across the street. 'Selling ice cream,' I said.

'Oh,' Olivia said. 'Obviously.'

The ladder she used to get on to the roof was still propped up against the house. She stood and wiped her hands against her shorts before reaching for it, then grunted as she tipped the ladder sideways and started disassembling it at the joints so it got smaller and smaller.

'Wait, I'm sorry, can we rewind for a second? What is going on right now?' I said.

A set of stairs hidden behind a big fluffy shrub led down to what I guessed was Clark's basement door. Olivia tucked the ladder there, leaning it against a small window striped with iron bars. Then she skipped up the house's porch steps and yanked out the plastic table and chairs sitting underneath the front window, probably looking for a key.

I blinked, not actually believing what was going on. 'We should go to the hospital so you can at least have a brain scan or something.'

'A brain scan?' Olivia spun around. The laugh that came out of her was sharp and breathy. 'Does my head look messed up to you?'

She tugged her hat up and pointed at her skull, then spun away again so I could see the back of her head, where her hair had been patchy and matted just seconds before. Now it was as if nothing had happened. The new hair even looked brushed. But at the sight of my expression as she turned around, Olivia's face softened from furious to just really annoyed.

'Look, I'm fine. You don't have to do anything except leave me alone.' Olivia gave the front doorknob one last shake, her entire body moving with it, before she stepped back and sighed. 'The one time this family locks their doors,' she said under her breath before thundering down the porch stairs.

'That's probably because Clark knows there's something you want in there,' I pointed out.

Olivia paused as she walked by me and scowled. 'Great observation,' she said.

And then, before I could say anything else, Olivia was on the sidewalk, hands folded across her chest as her shape got smaller and smaller down the block.

'Wait, you're really just leaving?' I called out to her.

Everything about my body was on fire. My fingers, my feet, my neck. Olivia was walking down the street so coolly, so normally, it looked like she was just going to the grocery store instead of away from what felt like something out of a Marvel movie. We couldn't just leave this all here. There were too many questions. I needed more answers.

'Do you need a ride?' I shouted after her lamely.

But Olivia didn't turn around.

After a few seconds, I pushed myself to my feet, feeling shaky and stunned, the events of the last few minutes whirring by so quickly, they fell out of order. Olivia's smashed head. The kids on their bikes. That scream. Not knowing what else to do, I turned away from the house and carefully avoided the pool of Olivia's blood. It was already starting to seep into the concrete, caking into a dried, muddy black. Nagging at me was the feeling that I should still call an ambulance or something, but I wasn't sure where Olivia was going. She'd already turned the corner at the end of the street, leaving as quickly as everything had started.

As I turned the truck back on and felt the engine hum underneath me, there was one thing I couldn't get out of my head. It wasn't that I'd just seen Olivia dead-man drop off a roof, that I was pretty sure I'd never erase the image of her flattened skull out of my head, or even the fact that there was a very good chance I'd either just seriously hallucinated or Olivia Moon was a real-life superhero. It was something so lame, so utterly self-absorbed, I felt almost embarrassed tiptoeing around it.

What bothered me most was that she didn't know my name.

2

DAVID BOWIE

Posted in PEOPLE by <u>Hugh.jpg</u> on July 1 at 7:13 a.m.

I respect David Bowie's right to privacy and to not tell the world he was dying, but I really needed more time to prepare for what was basically the end of music.

'True or false, Lin-Manuel Miranda would kick Marvin Gaye's ass in a sing-off.'

Razz bit into his cherry-blossom doughnut, flakes of white icing dropping on to his jeans. All our windows were down, as Marvin Gaye's 'Baby Don't You Do It' blasted from the ancient truck's tape player, cutting out the sounds of sightseers and businesspeople lining up for tacos and pulled-pork sandwiches at the other food trucks parked nearby.

After picking Razz up from his house and driving into DC later that afternoon, I was doing my best impression of someone who hadn't just figured out his high school's resident weird girl was actually the Terminator. But as we

16

paused underneath the red boxy arch in Chinatown before parking up with the other food trucks at Farragut Square, I could feel my thoughts drifting back to the way Olivia's head had caved in, the way the pool of blood it left behind kind of looked like George Washington's profile on the one-dollar bill. The way she'd looked up at me blankly as though we'd never met before, as though I weren't the only one trying to rewrite the last two years.

'Dude?' Razz said, waving a hand in front of my face. 'This is the part where you debate me fiercely.'

I blinked. 'What are you babbling about?'

'I said, true or false, Lin-Manuel Miranda would annihilate Marvin Gaye in a sing-off.'

I shook my shoulders, getting rid of the nerves. 'False,' I said. 'A thousand times false. Marvin Gaye is the king of Motown. Lin-Manuel Miranda is basically a Disney character.'

Razz blinked his eyes wide as though he couldn't believe what he was hearing. 'You do know insulting LMM is blasphemous,' he said, adjusting the black beanie balanced on the back of his head, 'punishable by death in New York City. The man is a genius.'

I nibbled around the edge of my brown-butter dough-nut and its thin sugar crust. 'I'm not doubting he's very good at making Disney and Broadway gold. But when it comes to out-singing Marvin he's got absolutely no chance. Marvin Gaye bled soul. And like, if we're being honest here, I bet Lin-Manuel Miranda would agree with me. He'd probably fanboy the eff out if he met Marvin Gaye.'

'Only one way to find out.' Razz set his doughnut on the counter and swapped it for his phone. The screen lit up Twitter blue as he typed out his tweet. 'If Lin-Manuel Miranda actually answers, you have to spend Thanksgiving in California with me.'

'If Lin-Manuel Miranda answers you I'll move to California, period.'

'Deal.'

If I just pretended to focus on the groups of people lining up beside the truck for ice cream, there was a chance I could get through the afternoon without spiralling into a mental breakdown. Ordinarily, I told Razz everything. But if I casually mentioned to him I'd just witnessed Olivia Moon's head reverse explode, I was pretty sure he'd gently usher me to the nearest insane asylum. Besides, I still wasn't sure what exactly I'd seen. A real-life Marvel hero? Or the beginning of a movie where a bunch of human-mutants sue a power plant for empty-ing toxic waste into the water supply and causing everyone to hallucinate?

Because it was nearing the last weekend of summer in DC, the city was mercifully busy. Last-minute tourists were still flooding the sidewalks on their way to the National Mall, cramming in museum visits before the crisp blanket that was fall fell over the district.

'Do you have any Cherry Garcia?'

Standing at the front of the line just beneath the counter's metal edge was a little girl in flamingo-pink sunglasses and yellow Dr Marten boots.

Razz sighed. 'If you want Ben and Jerry's or something shaped like Spongebob Squarepants, you'll have to go somewhere else,' he said. 'There's a CVS off Dupont Circle.'

'You,' the girl said, pointing a glittery fingernail at him, 'are a terrible businessman.'

It was my turn to sigh. 'Whipped Cream Wuornos has strawberries in it, plus marshmallows and rainbow jimmies.' It was one of the phrases I'd become so familiar with that summer, I practically had it tattooed on the inside of my eyelids.

'What about Banana Bundy? Is that named after the killer guy?'

My eyebrows disappeared into the mop of thick black hair my sister Ellen called 'the swamp'. 'You know who Ted Bundy is?' I said.

The girl fixed her hands on her hips and said, 'I have HBO.'

'Touché.' I pointed to the menu painted on the inside of the doors that were propped out against the sides of the truck. 'All our ice cream flavours are named after killer guys. Or girls. Whipped Cream Wuornos is named after Aileen Wuornos.'

Generally, the mugshots of Charles Manson and Dennis 'BTK' Rader stencilled on the side of the van got the point behind 'Killer Ice Cream' across, but where kids and the generally naive were concerned, it was both a blessing and a curse that they didn't know who people like Richard Ramirez or John Wayne Gacy were. Ellen suggested that when questions came up, I should just be honest, so long as I didn't say anything that would haunt anyone's dreams, but some of the questions people asked meant our conversations could get pretty weird.

'What about Green River Mint Chocolate Chip?'

'That's named after Gary Ridgway, the Green River Killer,' I said. 'He's one of my sister's favourites.'

The girl's eyes widened to the outside of her sunglasses, mouth dropping slightly open. She shot a glance to who I assumed were her parents, waiting in line for pulled-pork sandwiches a few trucks down.

I coughed. 'And when I say favourites, I mean—'

'I'll have a scoop of that,' the girl said, swallowing, 'with chocolate jimmies.'

In a cup, she clarified, as Razz slid open the freezer door and leant down to scoop ice cream from the plastic tubs inside. As sunlight poured in through the window, so did the day's unbearable heat, sticky, thick and 10,000 per cent humidity. I swiped my forehead before exchanging the ice cream for five dollars and giving the girl her change.

Razz and I continued serving customers, two robots on autopilot, until the line for the truck eventually died down. It was nearing two o'clock, which meant the lunchtime rush was almost over, leaving long, awkward pauses between us where I'd normally say something witty about Will Smith or *Buffy the Vampire Slayer*.

Instead, I said quietly, 'I saw Olivia Moon fall off a roof today.'

The words were out before I could swallow them back.

Razz turned toward me slowly, his eyes widening in surprise. 'What did you just say to me?' he said. 'Was that a joke?'

'No.'

'And you're only just telling me this now?'

'I mean, she was fine,' I said. Because she was fine – after her brain stitched itself back together. 'She was breaking into Clark Thomas's house.'

'Of course she was,' Razz said. 'And did you ask why she was breaking into the home of baby Charles Manson?'

'Apparently he stole something from her.'

'Why is that the least surprising part of this story?' Razz rolled his eyes and slammed both doors to the truck's window shut. 'Dude, let's get out of here,' he said as he scrambled into the passenger seat. 'All these fanny packs and "I Heart DC" T-shirts are making my eyes water. Whoever said fanny packs are fashionable again is genuinely deranged.'

The streets were heavy with people despite it being a Thursday. I guided the truck through the maze of tall office buildings and on to Constitution Avenue, where the street opened up, lined with big leafy trees that cast wide nets of shade over the sidewalk. We crossed Constitution and curved up with 15th Street so that a pool of grass stretched out on the right side of the truck. Spiked up in the middle was the Washington Monument, its off-white sides zigzagged with scaffolding. The grass surrounding it was packed with tourists, picnickers and dudes throwing

Frisbees as Segway tours and packs of kids with adults at the front holding signs on sticks streamed along the pathway. On the left side was the National Mall, its brown-green grass framed by faceless museums and the Capitol building at the end, its marshmallow dome poking up into the endlessly blue sky.

Seeing the familiar history-book streets of DC brought to my chest a warmth and easiness I hadn't felt since before watching Olivia Hulk-smash her head on the sidewalk. I liked DC. It was about ten square miles in size, so you only really needed the Metro to get between it, Virginia and Maryland. Sometimes, while lying in bed at night, I could hear gunshots in the distance, coming from the direction of the Shaw or Petworth neighbourhoods, but it was just what you signed up for here. It was the soundtrack to the city. I knew all my neighbours, mostly because a lot of them practically lived on their porches, watching the street for anyone that didn't belong. They'd been in their houses their entire lives, their parents having done the same. There was a good chance I'd end up like them one day, and I wasn't sure how I felt about it yet. But DC was the only home I'd ever known. The only place I really felt comfortable.

We crept slowly behind a long train of traffic held up by a red light. Out to the right, the Lincoln Memorial was just visible in the distance, Abe a tiny blip in what looked like a concrete shoebox. The long, rectangular reflecting pool stretched out in front of him, the blue-brown surface glassy and flat.

As we passed a family in matching pink T-shirts with 'CONNOR FAMILY VACATION' plastered on the front, Razz wrinkled his nose. 'God, what is wrong with these people?' he said. 'Why would you choose a literal swamp for a vacation? It's like forty million degrees out there.'

'Maybe if you didn't dress like a goth pillowcase, it wouldn't feel so hot.'

At this, Razz glowered at me through a gap in his long purple-black hair. It was true, though; Razz rarely left his house without wearing at least three layers. They generally consisted of a T-shirt – usually black, usually of some horror-movie-looking band – and some kind of flannel button-up, also either purple, black or the occasional dark red. This was then coupled with black jeans, heavy black leather boots and a black beanie he somehow kept just exactly balanced on the back of his head so his manga-style hair waterfalled down his face.

Once we made it to the end of 15th Street, the red-brown spires of the Holocaust Museum rising up on our right, I flicked on my turn signal to loop back up past the White House before heading home to Columbia Heights, but Razz tapped my shoulder and shook his head.

'Go left,' he said, pointing to the Mall.

'Don't you have to finish packing?'

'I've still got time to go through my record collection,' he said. 'I need you to distract me with whatever outfit phase Olivia's in these days.'

A half-smirk crossed my face at the thought. 'She was

23

wearing a giant Hawaiian shirt today, with parachute pants and this bucket hat she actually like, tied under her chin.'

'So, what you're saying is she's dressing like a couch.'

I snorted. 'Pretty much.'

'Sounds like a step down from her days as a basketball groupie.'

'But a big step up from preppy moron.'

'Hey, you used to be one of those preppy morons,' Razz said, looking at me. His hair fell across his nose. 'You were practically their leader.'

I shuddered at the memory. 'You were one of them too.'

He batted his eyelashes. 'That was many moons ago,' he said in a far-off voice, one hand clasped over his heart. Then he smiled, revealing a set of perfect chalk-white teeth. 'Remember freshman year when Olivia had her religious girl phase? That one only lasted a few days, until she started dating that senior with a mohawk.'

I frowned. 'Is the religious girl phase when she wore all those turtlenecks?'

'No, that was her art critic phase, hence the beret.'

'Of course it was,' I said. 'She was at least wearing those bracelets today, the ones that look like handcuffs from *Game of Thrones*.'

'Well, god bless her for consistency.'

In the thirteen years we'd gone to school with Olivia Moon – we were what our yearbook dubbed 'lifers', which meant we'd gone to the local elementary, middle and high schools together – she'd been through no less

24

than fifteen phases, most of which didn't pick up until high school. Some lasted days while others lasted years. There was the art critic phase, the emo kid phase, the soft-ball girl phase and the alt kid phase, which probably lasted the longest. Then there was the theatre girl phase and even a brief, but interesting, hockey phase, for which she wore a bunch of vintage Washington Capitals jerseys.

I wasn't sure what to call this new phase. Florida-dad phase? Trailer-park-guy phase? It was a weird one, even for her.

'Do you need to go home before coming to my house tonight?' I said. 'I'm not letting you borrow my boxers again.'

Every Thursday night was *Survivor* night in the Copper household, which meant Razz slept over in the summer. The familiarity of this tradition made my heartbeat slow to somewhat normal, because unlike Olivia magically un-bashing her head in, this was something I could predict.

'Dude, I told you like a million times, tonight is my last official family dinner until Thanksgiving,' Razz said. 'Then tomorrow I'm going to Richmond to see my grandma till Saturday afternoon and when I get back you're sleeping over so we can watch all *The Hobbit* movies and eat ourselves into a coma until it's time for me to hit the open road to California. I already bought every single type of Oreo Giant had.'

I let out a frustrated sigh and glanced over at the gold-ish dome of the Natural History Museum across the Mall's crunchy grass, before stopping for a red light.

'I keep forgetting you're ditching me on Sunday for a bunch of communist hippies,' I said.

That was a lie. Before Olivia, Razz leaving for Berkeley was all I thought about. But the more I joked about the fact that Razz was going off to college and I was staying in DC, the more I hoped it looked like I could actually acknowledge it was just part of the circle of life and not something that actively gave me heart palpitations.

'I feel like I should've called an ambulance today,' I said quietly, almost without meaning to. 'You know, with Olivia.'

'What, so they could tell the cops you'd just watched as she tried to break into somebody's house? That's called aiding and abetting.'

I rolled my eyes. 'Hardly.'

The light turned green and we were off. As quickly as it started, the National Mall ended again, spilling us out into the tangle of streets making up Capitol Hill. We stopped at another red light, falling into silence as Razz looked out his window and I tried desperately not to think about Olivia Moon and inevitably only thought about Olivia Moon. Because while I clearly wasn't worth remembering to her, I was pretty sure two years ago, she'd saved my life.

3

THE DARK KNIGHT RISES

Posted in MOVIES by <u>Hugh.jpg</u> on February 25 at 9:19 p.m.

Christian Bale, you are dead. I'm sorry but you just are. You flew a helicopter with a bomb into the middle of the ocean and therefore, you are dead. So how do you end up in an unidentified cafe making stupid nods at Michael Caine? How, Christian? HOW?

I stared into the blank textbox on my computer screen, trying to figure out what exactly I hated about the ending to the movie *Interstellar*. For the most part, the movie was incredible. It was one of those films that felt like an achievement, like by watching it you were witnessing history or science or whatever being made.

But the ending? Less than satisfying. Or even sense-making.

With only the marshmallow-looking suit on his back, Matthew McConaughey travelled solo through a black hole, where basic logic says he should've been sucked into deep space and withered away, but instead, he was miraculously recovered by a passing spaceship just in the nick of time. There was a big reunion, the movie came full circle.

Blah, blah, blah.

Because honestly, what were the actual chances he would survive? I get that the movie was sci-fi, but his rescue left something missing. The ending was too clean, too neat. I couldn't help but feel like Matthew McConaughey's character was one of the few in this world whose deaths would've actually made more sense than what really happened.

I started to type my thoughts into the empty post, deleting and rewriting sentences as new ideas floated through my head. When writing a new post, I tried to keep them short, more just a quick summary of my feelings rather than an essay. That way, my words were a start to the discussion rather than the discussion itself, leaving room for the rest of the posters on Spoiler Alert to think for themselves.

Since I started Spoiler Alert two years ago, the website had grown to nearly 1,200 posts, all of which were devoted to bad endings. Managing the posts was what I did most afternoons following ice cream shifts, and most mornings and most nights, when the rest of DC was asleep. The posts were commented on by a community made up of, by my last tally, around 700 users. Very few people but me had permission to start a thread, but I took suggestions and gave editor access to some of SA's loyal followers who'd been around since the beginning.

Sometimes Razz helped out too, mostly with subjects like books by dead British authors and the entire catalogue of the *Evil Dead* films.

The site was divided into five sections: books, movies, TV, people and misc., for things like bands and wars, and in each of those sections were individual threads for specific subjects with bad endings. Good endings and all their fake neatness didn't interest me. Most of the time, they left behind a sour feeling that was like a slap to my internal organs.

Underneath each post was a list of comments where the discussion ensued, some longer than others. The *Dark Knight Rises* post had more than 300 comments, while nobody really cared about Oasis. You didn't necessarily need to have even seen, heard about, or read the subject of the thread to comment. While others in the SA community disagreed, I didn't think this was the point. A bad ending was a bad ending regardless of whether or not you'd watched it play out up close.

But what made an ending bad? That was another thing Spoiler Alert users couldn't agree on. To me, there was a very definitive list of what made a cringe-worthy close:

- Endings that were too long (*The Lord of the Rings: The Return of the King*)
- Endings that meant nothing to the overall story (*War of the Worlds*)
- Endings that were just kind of lame (*The Matrix*)
- Endings that came out of nowhere (Led Zeppelin)
- Endings that were too short (the season ten finale of *The X-Files*)

• Endings that made no sense (Buddy Holly)

The list went on and on, constantly growing as I watched, read and researched. I was always discovering reasons why I didn't like a particular ending, and I searched for new ones obsessively, my outrage over their stupidness growing and growing. Which was ironic, because as I found worse and worse endings, the other ones started to not look so bad.

After pressing 'publish' on my *Interstellar* thread, I clicked through to the finished page and leant back, scanning the post. It wasn't my best. The thoughts were a little scattered, my points gummy around the edges. Because every time I tried to imagine Matthew McConaughey sitting on his recreation porch in space, speaking in his long southern drawl to that sarcastic box robot, Olivia Moon's face would appear in the window behind him. I tried to focus my thoughts on the frustration I'd felt when Matthew McConaughey woke up in that hospital bed after surviving the black hole, but I couldn't get Olivia out of my head.

As soon as I'd gotten home that afternoon, I scoured Olivia's Facebook page until my eyes crossed. I scanned through all her pictures and posts, going all the way back to when she first got an account in middle school. Unsurprisingly, there weren't any videos of her chopping her arm off and growing it back, or crushing her foot underneath something heavy, only to have it look perfectly fine. On the surface, everything about her was frustratingly normal.

Olivia had 587 Facebook friends – nearly double the number of people from our graduating class – but I supposed that probably happened when you'd been a part of almost every single clique Mount Luther High School had to offer. Her last post was from February 13, just a single cryptic line attached to a picture of the frontman from the band The Killers:

If ur not Brandon Flowers you can't be my valentine!!!!!!!!!!!!!!!

On second thought, it wasn't that cryptic. It was actually pretty straightforward.

But besides that, there were only photos other people had taken of her, the latest of which was one of her in the same shirt she'd been wearing today, the Hawaiian one whose sleeves went past her elbows. In the photo, she was standing in front of a tall bush, one hand reached up to brush her hair out of her face, but she'd moved at the last second and blurred her features into a smear of peach and white. Where her nose, dark eyes and mouth were supposed to be was just a shock of electric-blonde hair. There was something about the photo that left me feeling vaguely uneasy, like I was looking at the last picture taken of someone before they died.

I opened Facebook again and stared at the posts on my timeline absent-mindedly, trying to remember what I knew about Olivia Moon. So far, it could be summed up as:

- She lived in Columbia Heights, same as me.
- She had been (but was most likely no longer) dating Clark Thomas.

- She currently shopped primarily at thrift stores for men.
- We were once kind of friends in that superficial way people are friends when they're twelve (AKA we were not actually friends).
- Two years ago, we shared a weird experience that basically meant the entire world to me but clearly nothing to her, an experience we both never acknowledged afterwards and that she apparently forgot about.
- She could heal her broken body with . . . what? Her mind? The force of the universe?

Basically, it was nothing and everything at the same time.

I clicked back to her photos, this time scrolling all the way through to the beginning. The very first one was a picture of Olivia in a sky-blue T-shirt, her hair tied up in a ponytail on top of her head and her smile so bright it was practically blinding. Something like real happiness glowed in her face, nothing like the white-hot annoyance that radiated off her that morning. What had changed?

In the picture, Olivia's arms were wrapped around two other people: on her left was my neighbour across the street, Becky Cayman, while Razz was on her right, a soccer ball balanced under his foot. All three of them were wearing matching uniforms, black face paint streaked under their eyes.

'Razz played soccer?' I said to myself.

Middle school was mostly a blur peppered with blips of

sneaking into the Chinatown Regal to see *The Hobbit* and fantasizing about meeting Cara Delevingne at Shake Shack, but I felt like I would've remembered Razz playing a sport. Razz, who I once had to spoon-feed ice chips to after we walked from the Chinatown Metro Station to the White House, which was less than a mile away.

At the very least, it made for an interesting development. Because while I knew he and Olivia were more or less friends when we were kids, this was proof they did more than just sit together at lunch; they hung out outside of school too, before Razz and Olivia split away from the group.

When we were younger, me and Olivia were part of the same gang, along with Razz and Becky Cayman. We were one of those lazy boy-girl groups that mashed together like two different colours of Play-Doh. Becky and I were sort of bound together by proximity, as we'd been neighbours for our entire childhood, and when you're a kid, that kind of thing is a big deal. But while we all sat together in the same general area of the cafeteria at lunch, went to each other's birthday parties and sometimes hung out in Meridian Hill Park on the weekends, we didn't have much of a friendship. At least not until high school, when the realization sank in that the whole group thing wasn't going away and we might actually be friends. But by then, Razz and Olivia Moon were long gone.

After scrolling through the rest of Olivia's photos, I clicked back to her wall and blinked my eyes into focus. A new post had jumped to the top of her page, posted only in the last few minutes by a person whose profile picture was of a chihuahua wearing a gold party hat.

Regina Smalls > Olivia Moon
August 24 at 5:02 p.m.
Hi doll, we R all thinking about U this weekend. Miss U and God Bless love, Grandma Reggie

I clicked through to Regina Smalls' page, but it was locked down so tight, all I could see was her profile picture.

Returning to Olivia's page, I stared at the new post and frowned. Her grandma was thinking about her? That meant there was something specific to think about. But what? Maybe there was more going on in Olivia's life than even her risking getting charged with breaking and entering suggested. Something sad, maybe. Or exciting. It could've been one of those, 'We're all thinking about you!' notes, like out of encouragement. But encouraging what? A quick recovery from her fall? But then that would only have been if Olivia *had* gotten hurt, and news travelled incredibly fast to the land of wherever chihuahuas wore party hats.

'Nope,' I said to myself. 'Still nothing.'

It was impossible not to feel frustrated. How could I not know anything about someone I'd sorta hung out with for a few years? It wasn't like we went to each other's houses outside of birthday parties or anything, but we still stood in the same general vicinity of the hallway in middle school. Did that not count for anything?

As I was about to close the lid of my laptop, a box popped up in the bottom right corner of my screen. It was a message, just six little words that sent my entire body cold.

Olivia Moon

I think we need to talk

4

MARVIN GAYE

Posted in PEOPLE by <u>Hugh.jpg</u> on November 29 at 8:24 p.m.

On the brink of a comeback after a very weird, self-imposed exile, Marvin Gaye – one of the greatest soul singers of all time – was shot and killed by his father, who then served approximately zero years in jail for his crime. Because that's justice for you, ladies and gents.

Sometimes my house felt frozen in time. Most of it was exactly the same as it had been two years ago, as if somebody'd pointed a remote control at each room, every corner and every slice of firewood stacked in the basket beside my dad's leather lounger, and pressed pause. Almost every surface was filled with something: porcelain dog figurines my mom found at garage sales, books stacked from floor to ceiling on elaborate shelves my dad built when he went through his random carpentry phase. There were school pictures, family pictures, concert posters, certificates and even pictures of people we didn't know – again, garage sales – covering the walls of each room, which were already painted in various colours so bright they resembled the set of a kids' TV show.

Mom used to call it organized chaos. Ellen called it a circus.

Our house wasn't dirty or anything. Mom had tried her best to shake off the military cleaning habits my grandma had pumped into her DNA, but she couldn't get rid of everything. She vacuumed and dusted religiously so that even though our house was crammed with a million tiny things, they were at least a million tiny clean things. And despite the clutter, we still knew where everything was; that was why Ellen and I never changed anything after our parents died, because even though our house was the definition of crazy, it still made sense to us. It was our home, mine and my sister's.

Upstairs, Olivia's message still sat unanswered on my computer. At the sight of it, of the little green dot in the message window showing Olivia was online, I'd slammed my laptop closed and stood staring at it, chest heaving, as though I'd just watched a video of someone driving into a wall. It was like that green dot was her, there, staring at me, waiting for me to move. That's when I realized Olivia would see my little green dot fade to grey, and know immediately I was a giant wuss. But by that point, it was too late.

When my sister Ellen arrived home that night, shoulders weighed down by reusable grocery bags, I'd been collapsed on the couch for nearly an hour watching the *Buffy* episode where some students become human-hyenas and eat their school principal.

'So, you do have your phone,' Ellen said, nodding her head at my cell, which was resting on my chest. She heaved the grocery bags on to the kitchen island. 'I've only been calling you for the last two hours. Now Dan's on Chinese food duty for dinner tonight.'

I swallowed and stood, trying my best not to show the nerves zigzagging up and down my arms. My brain had been too overwhelmed with thoughts of Olivia Moon to answer any of my sister's calls.

'Why are you so obsessed with me?' I said.

'Hughcifer, you are my everything, you beautiful baby boy child,' Ellen cooed. 'Guess who I ran into at Cafe Front Lawn?'

She gestured her long, tattooed arms out to the front of our house. Since the population of our home dropped from four to just me and my sister, our neighbours lingered for suspiciously long stretches of time in our front yard, making sure we still knew how to bathe and feed ourselves.

'Who?' I said, craning my neck to see if the mystery person was still lurking.

Ellen flicked her hair over her shoulder. 'Mrs Cayman,' she said. 'Apparently, they're having a going-away party for Becky before she leaves for college tomorrow, and she wanted to know if we'd join.'

'And you said, "hey girl, get a life"?'

At this, my sister cracked a smile. Mom used to say when Ellen and I smiled at each other, it was like we were looking in a mirror. We were built like our dad, tall and noodle-shaped, but looked like Mom, pale, with black hair and eyes that were a weird mixture of grey and frostbitten blue.

'I said I'd ask you first.'

I plucked out a new pack of Doritos from a bag on the counter and avoided my sister's gaze. 'Well, colour me declined,' I said. 'The last thing I need right now is to sit on Becky Cayman's porch pretending to sneak sips of stale beer while talking to people I have nothing in common with any more.'

'Ah come on, I'll go if you go,' Ellen said. 'We've lived across the street from the Caymans since birth. Becky was your first little girlfriend.'

A blush spread across my face. 'Little girlfriend?' I said, feeling the heat all the way in my hands. 'We went out for two days, Ellen, and it was only eleven years ago. It's too soon to talk about it.' I pretended to wipe my eyes at the thought of Becky throwing the bag of Sour Patch Kids I bought her at 7-Eleven into the gutter outside our elementary school.

Ellen swatted the back of my head and laughed. 'We could always go after *Survivor* if you change your mind.'

I chewed a Dorito slowly and nodded, the crunching loud in my skull. The thought of telling Ellen about Olivia briefly slipped into my head, but I shook the idea away. Admitting I'd a) been anywhere near someone getting severely hurt, b) been anywhere near someone that maybe, possibly, probably could regenerate their broken body parts, or c) actually thought this was real and therefore was admitting I was clinically insane put me at risk of unleashing Worried Ellen, a version of my sister I still hadn't gotten totally used to. Worried Ellen was convinced I'd get carjacked if I drove the truck past six at night.

As if reading my mind, Ellen said, 'So, how'd the truck do today?'

She was cramming a loaf of bread into our broken breadbox and trying to wrangle the door closed. By the time she'd jammed it down, she was mildly out of breath and had to run a hand along her forehead to wipe away a line of sweat.

I brushed Doritos dust down my shirt, leaving behind a smear of yellow-orange. 'I got into a weird conversation with a child about Ted Bundy,' I said.

'All conversations about Ted Bundy are weird, regardless of how old you are,' Ellen said.

'True.'

Killer Ice Cream had only been in operation for just under a year, but it was already ranked as one of the best food trucks in DC and had been profiled by a load of local magazines and websites. They mostly talked about the fact that Ellen had dropped out of Boston University only two years in, forgoing her business degree for the real thing. To them, she was a born entrepreneur, but she rarely talked about her real reason for moving back home, which was that she had to look after her orphaned little brother.

Serial killers had always fascinated my sister. Not necessarily their crimes, she would lie, but the psychology behind them, which wasn't actually a total lie. When we were kids, she read every true crime book she could get her hands on. Instead of Wonder Woman and Katy Perry, Ellen's hero was John Walsh, the host of *America's Most Wanted*. She used to lurk around the Crime & Punishment Museum every Saturday when they filmed the TV show, in hopes that she might catch him going into the building, as if he'd just use the front door. What her third-grade teacher called a 'worrying hobby' eventually became Killer Ice Cream, a business she ran out of the van. She'd worked at Cold Stone in high school, and her love for ice cream stuck around, while singing for tips did not. During the week, she was a bartender in Dupont Circle, but on the weekends, she invented ice cream flavours named after the Zodiac and Edmund Kemper. Over the years, she'd taken a lot of shit for the concept, ranging from well-researched conversations to the occasional picket line. One guy even threw a napkin dispenser at my head, convinced I had to be one of those weirdos that worshipped the Night Stalker and had decided to glorify him with chocolate ice cream. But nobody was more repulsed by serial killers than Ellen. And besides, a little notoriety wasn't bad for business.

Once the grocery bags were empty, Ellen shoved them in the gap between the stove and the sink.

'Where's Razz? Is he taking the Metro over?'

'He's not coming tonight.' I tried to hide the bitterness in my voice but mostly failed. 'It's his last family dinner at home, this is my new normal, blah, blah, blah.'

'Is he all packed for school?'

'Basically,' I said. He'd already carefully folded his clothes into oversized suitcases and peeled down his death metal posters to reveal equally black walls. 'His mom is driving him to California so he can bring his entire record collection.'

Ellen wrinkled her nose. 'What's that, like a hundred albums?' she said.

She rooted through the cabinets beside me and pulled out a jar of peanut butter, tearing off its foil top in one easy slice. I grabbed two spoons from the silverware drawer.

'Try five hundred.'

The image of Razz's bedroom, empty of records, all his books, his weirdly obsessive Spider-Man figurine collection – essentially everything that made his room Razzy – left my stomach in knots. Every time I thought about how I would say goodbye to him, the visual in my head went straight to black. Just an empty, impossible void. We could hug. Say we'd keep in touch. Any way I spun it though, things would be anticlimactic and dumb and never the same. The way I saw it, we'd probably stay friends for a few months but eventually he'd realize I was just his lame home friend who, in the last two years, had barely Google Imaged life beyond DC, much less actually entered it.

'If I were going to college, you'd have a cake walk,' I said. 'I don't have anything to take, so it would've just been like me showing up in America with some stamps and a Fruit Roll-Up to my name.'

My whole life consisted of about six Marvin Gaye records, ten T-shirts and a mediocre-sized comic book collection, but unlike Razz, I wasn't going anywhere, so none of it really mattered.

Ellen set the peanut butter jar on the counter with a thud. 'There's still plenty of time for you to change your mind about college.'

I barked a laugh. 'Hardly. Most classes start next week, and even if I wanted to go, there wouldn't be any spaces left. I'd have to take, like, Intro to Pencil Sharpening. Plus, you know I'm not leaving DC.'

'Why are you so weird about leaving DC?' Ellen said. 'It's not Manifest Destiny times any more. Bandits and smallpox aren't waiting behind the bushes to massacre you the second you leave the district.'

'Yeah, but there could be sea monsters. Cults. Born-again Christians.'

Ellen lifted her eyebrows.

'OK, fine,' I said. 'But I'm still not going.'

Even though I wasn't actually afraid of getting jumped by born-again Christians, I still hadn't left DC since my parents died. Outside DC was the land of the unpredictable. The unfamiliar. Too many possible bad endings.

'Hugh.' Ellen gripped the edge of the counter, her face suddenly serious. 'You told me you wanted to take a year off school. If leaving DC is the problem, then just go somewhere local. Hell, do something online. Do you want to go to college? There's probably still time to sign up for junior college classes.'

43

'I also told you I wanted to take Rihanna to prom freshman year, but sometimes when we're young, we just don't know what's good for us,' I said.

But Ellen wasn't buying my lightness, not after all our arguments about 'my future'. Somewhere between the Doritos and peanut butter, Normal Ellen had walked out the front door, making room for Worried Ellen to officially arrive.

My sister's jaw tightened. 'I just think even a computer class or something would be better than you sitting around all year,' Ellen said.

'I'm not sitting around, I've got the truck,' I said.

'Yeah, but what if you didn't have the truck?'

I squinted at her. 'Why? What's happening to the truck?'

'Nothing – just, well, nothing,' Ellen said. 'I mean, nothing right now. But you never know, the truck could fall into a sinkhole, or get abducted by aliens, or fall into a sinkhole created by aliens . . .' She could barely look at me, her brain spiralling into what I could already tell was going to be a full-blown tirade.

I pulled in a deep breath, preparing myself for the inevitable. For situations like this, Ellen and I had a specific method of diffusion called the 'Oldies Distraction'. Some people (Razz) thought it was unorthodox, but it hadn't failed us yet.

Clearing my throat, I set a hand on my sister's shoulder. Then, I sang: '*Here I am on bended knees, I lay my heart down at your feet, now . . .*'

44

I stopped, waiting for my sister to finish the line as the last note hung in the air. It was from Frank Wilson's 'Do I Love You (Indeed I Do)', one of Ellen's and my favourite songs. The idea behind the Oldies Distraction was that if someone could get the angry party to join in on singing an oldies song, the odds were, they could be distracted from the argument long enough to either stop caring about the issue altogether, or to at least shelve it. Our dad was of the mindset that Motown music could cure anything.

But apparently today, my sister wouldn't be so easily shaken. Where me and college were concerned, Ellen didn't like to back down.

'Come on,' I said, nudging her. '*Here I am on bended knees, I lay my heart down at your feet, now . . .*'

Ellen bit her lip. For a second, I was starting to think this might be our first failed Oldies Distraction, but then my sister surprised me with a low tune under her breath.

'*Do I love you,*' she sang back begrudgingly.

In the end, she couldn't make me go to college and she knew it.

I squeezed her shoulder. 'That wasn't so hard,' I said. '*All you have to do is ask, I'll give until there's nothing left, now . . .*'

'*Do I love you.*'

She sighed, and just like that, the tension in the air dropped away.

'Indeed you do,' I said to my sister just as she rolled her eyes. 'All hail the Motown gods.'

Ellen and I kissed our fingers and raised them to the sky.

We finished the bag of Doritos and made it halfway through the jar of peanut butter before a single headlight shone through the kitchen window above the sink, drenching the countertops in a blindingly white light as the sound of a husky engine echoed across the alleyway behind our house. I dropped my spoon into the sink as Ellen retrieved a stack of plates and forks from the cabinet, and sorted them into a neat pile on the kitchen island.

Just over the squat fence bordering our backyard, a man in an oversized leather jacket was wrestling a motorcycle upright, pounding his foot on the kickstand and swearing loudly when the bike teetered into him. It was obvious just by looking at him that, whereas some people went backpacking through Asia, this man's quarter-life crisis involved fixing up his uncle's old Harley-Davidson. Even from a distance, you could tell he reeked of desperation, Taco Bell and Abercrombie & Fitch cologne.

It was Dan, Dan the Tax Lawyer Man. Ellen's idiot boyfriend.

He came in balancing plastic bags on either arm and bringing with him the sweet, slightly sharp scent of General Tso's chicken. Dan was wearing a white button-up shirt, grey pants, a candy-cane-striped bow tie and polished leather boat shoes, his blonde-brown hair gelled backwards like Christian Bale in *American Psycho*.

'Please tell me I'm not late,' he said, huffing.

'Seven fifty-six,' Ellen said, stealing a look at the little green digits on the microwave clock. 'You're just in time.'

I glanced backwards at the *Survivor* season two box set sitting on the coffee table in the next room. 'Dan,' I said, pressing my hands together at the fingertips and resting my chin on top of my nails. 'I'm not sure if you understand how DVDs work, but I'll take this one slow for you. They don't follow a schedule like the TV, so you can play them whenever you want.'

Ellen grabbed my face between her hands and planted a kiss on my forehead. 'He's a genius,' she exclaimed.

'I know how you guys like your routines,' Dan said, dropping the bags of Chinese food on to the counter. 'I got the "friendly reminder" email after I showed up seven minutes late last week.'

I smirked at the memory. I'd even attached a picture of a flaming bag of dog poop as a warning.

'Survivor Thursdays are serious business,' my sister said as she unloaded the little white cartons of food from the bags and spread them out evenly for inspection.

Survivor Thursdays had been a family tradition since season two first aired, not long after I was born. They were generally accompanied by takeout food from the Little Dragon, a lot of screaming and sometimes a few tears. For the most part, me and my sister had given up watching the live seasons because – though it wasn't something we admitted out loud – watching *Survivor* episodes our parents had never seen didn't feel right.

'Is there beef and broccoli in there?' I said, craning my neck.

Dan shrugged his jacket off and draped it on the back

of the couch. 'I also got the menu in the mail, in case of emergencies. Emergencies being, Hugh doesn't answer his phone.'

'I'm a busy person, *Dan*,' I said.

'Did you put stars next to our favourites?' Ellen asked me.

'He marked them with little Post-it notes shaped like arrows,' Dan said.

My sister ruffled my hair. 'Good boy.'

'Where's Razz?' Dan asked.

'He's a traitorous deserter and we will not speak his name,' Ellen said. Her arms windmilled toward the food. 'Now come on, come on. We've got two minutes until showtime.'

The three of us scooped Chinese food on to our plates, the greasy, sauce-soaked meat pooling out in curvy shapes. Ellen poured cups of Diet Coke and brought them through to the living room. As I settled into Dad's chair, Ellen and Dan sat on the couch, the blanket Mom made by sewing Ellen's baby clothes together draped across their laps.

'OK, before we begin, a summary of last week's episode.' My sister pointed her fork at me as Dan fumbled with the remote. 'Hugh, will you do us the honours?'

The sound of croaky didgeridoos suddenly hummed in the air as the *Survivor* title screen flickered on to the TV. I cleared my throat and set my plate on my knees.

'*Survivor*, season two. Setting: the Australian Outback. When we last saw them, the Ogakor and Kucha tribes had

48

merged into one, Barramundi, ending in Jeff's devastating exit. This left five former Ogakor members over Kucha's four. As the evil Jerri and her sidekick Alicia plot to overthrow Colby and his crew, will crowd favourites Elisabeth and Rodger save their skins, or will the Kucha tribe be picked off one by one like Outback Steakhouse shrimp cocktail?'

'Wait, which one's Alicia?' Dan said, his mouth half full of egg fried rice.

'Short, braids, super ripped,' Ellen said.

'I thought that was Amber,' Dan said.

I swallowed a piece of chicken. 'No, Amber's the one that marries Boston Rob in *Survivor: All Stars*.'

'They get married on the show?' Dan said.

'What?' Ellen said. She looked at me, her face a mask of incredulity. 'How would that even make sense? Who would perform the ceremony?'

I shook my head. 'Yeah Dan, keep up.'

'No, they meet on *Survivor: All Stars* and then they get married *eventually*,' Ellen said.

'Amateur hour,' I muttered under my breath.

Dan liked to 'joke' about the fact that he had to ask Ellen out approximately eleven times before she relented, and that was only so he'd leave her alone. No matter how hard I tried, I still couldn't wrap my head around it, around him, in our house. With my sister. Ellen had been to South by Southwest like four times. Her arms and most of her legs and shoulders were covered in tattoos of cats and *Alice's Adventures in Wonderland* quotes. She liked the

Smashing Pumpkins and her favourite movie was *Man on the Moon*. Dan worked in his dad's Georgetown law firm, had been on at least four Caribbean cruises with his fraternity brothers, and his favourite musical acts were Coldplay, Twenty One Pilots and Jimmy Buffett, in that order.

He had a tendency to pout, something he was doing a pretty good job of as his Chinese food went cold. 'I haven't watched this show a million times like you guys,' Dan said as he pushed a mound of beef and broccoli around his plate with his fork. 'Sometimes it's like you're speaking your own language.'

Ellen kissed his cheek. 'We'll teach you,' she said before reaching over him and pressing play on the remote.

The *Survivor* opening song buzzed to life. It was a strange mix of guttural tribal chanting and the sound of somebody strumming a popsicle stick against an old-timey washing board. I sang along with the music just like me and my sister always did, but when I glanced over at her, Ellen wasn't even looking at the screen. She had her arm slung around Dan's shoulders, her mouth pressed to his ear. As she whispered something I couldn't hear, Dan's own mouth curled up into a shy smile. I shot my eyes down to my lap, pretending not to see. I missed the last set of words flashing across the screen: *One survivor*.

5

PRINCE

Posted in PEOPLE by <u>Hugh.jpg</u> on July 6 at 3:32 p.m.

The fact that the world suddenly lost Bowie and Prince in the same year is a cruel joke and I will have none of it.

Alicia was voted off that episode. Next week, it would be Jerri, then Nick, Amber, Rodger, Elisabeth and Keith, leaving Colby and Tina in the finale. It was never really a contest, though. Tina would take it in the end, crowned the Sole Survivor of the Outback. Ellen and I had watched season two no less than three times all the way through, and she still cried every time the tribe voted Rodger off.

I escaped upstairs as Dan and Ellen loaded our plates into the dishwasher, their voices replaced with the sound of an old Kanye West song and more voices, a small crowd of them. Through a crack in my curtains, I could see the house across the street, its porch illuminated by the light of red and white paper lanterns. The fuzzy glow barely reached the people crowded around a small glass table, but I knew who they were without even seeing their faces. Becky Cayman was seated in the porch swing next to someone who was probably Lily; Dexter was resting on the porch railing, his legs dangling underneath him; Quinn was loitering on the stairs while Sam sat in the plastic chair by the front door, where I would've sat if I were at Becky's going-away party. I knew without a doubt Sam would've taken back his spot on the stairs next to Quinn if I showed up, and that Becky would tease me the entire time about the fact that I was wearing a hat even though it was dark outside.

As I watched them, my phone buzzed from my pocket. At first, my heart stopped at the thought that it could be another message from Olivia, but once I saw Razz's name flashing on my screen, I let out a long breath. On the other end of our FaceTime, he was standing in front of his record player as a synth beat came through his video.

'My mom says I can only take three boxes of records to Berkeley, and I think it might actually kill me,' he said. 'How do you decide between Sufjan Stevens and Kurt Vile?' He held up two records like I was supposed to know who either person was. 'It's basically impossible. Why can't I just be like Gigi Hadid and have my mom get me like, a massive apartment with a room I can store all my records in?'

'You keep saying these names like I know who you're talking about,' I said.

Becky was looking at something on Lily's phone as she

lifted her cup to her mouth and took a drink. The image of Olivia with her arms draped around Becky and Razz floated into my head.

'Did you play soccer with Olivia Moon?' I said suddenly.

'Oh god,' Razz groaned, 'don't remind me.'

'Did she ever—' I didn't know how to phrase the next part without sounding completely ridiculous. 'When you were with her, did you ever see something that didn't make sense?'

Razz's eyebrows shot up. 'What, you mean like the movie *Armageddon*?'

'No, like,' I squinted at the wooden frame encasing my window, 'did Olivia ever get hurt, but then, you know, she wasn't . . . hurt?'

'You'd have to go to practice to get hurt,' Razz said. 'She barely ever showed up, and even when she did, she didn't talk to anyone except Becky.'

'If she didn't show up, why'd she join in the first place?' I said.

'Olivia didn't actually like soccer. None of us did,' Razz said. 'We just did it because Becky Cayman demanded we join what she deemed a socially acceptable sport for her quote-unquote friends. I mean, look at how Olivia shapeshifts. She isn't actually into basketball or hockey or musicals or whatever. She just goes for what she thinks is cool and then becomes them which, in Becky's case, was an idiot in Skittles-flavoured lip gloss.'

Back across the street, Becky tucked her legs up against

her chest and dropped her chin to her knees. She always did that when she was tired; I'd keep an eye out for it at parties and then flick her leg whenever she accidentally fell asleep so nobody else would realize. In high school, me, Becky and the rest of our friends had our own routine we cycled through every weekend for nearly two years. I knew my seat around the table at Ben's Chili Bowl and how many beers it took for Becky to start complaining about how hot it was in her basement almost as well as I knew the freckles on her shoulders.

'You talk about Becky like she's an evil dictator,' I said.

'That's because she *is* an evil dictator,' Razz said.

I watched the group for a few seconds as they joked about something Sam had said and then, as if she could sense me, Becky glanced up at my bedroom window. Even through the dark, I could see her half-smile, her fingers flexing into a wave that almost wasn't there.

'Your friendship with Becky was completely different to mine, or even Olivia's,' Razz said as I disappeared again behind the curtains. 'You couldn't even remember I existed until high school and we went to the same birthday parties for seven years.'

Even though Razz and I technically met in middle school, we *met* met outside our high school counsellor's office two years ago, after Razz had been transitioning for about a year and Ellen found the post-parent shedding of my usual group of friends slightly worrying.

'Yeah, but I still know Becky better than that,' I said. 'She can be kinda pushy sometimes, but she's not Kylo Ren.'

'Says her ex-boyfriend,' Razz muttered under his breath.

'We were seven years old,' I said. 'If a relationship happens before puberty, it doesn't count.'

'Well Olivia thought she sucked too,' Razz said. He rifled through his records, peeling back their uneven cardboard edges until he found what he was looking for, some album with a robot appearing through a sheet of purple-grey mist. 'Olivia quit soccer the summer before eighth grade anyway, when her mom died. Becky was so pissed Olivia turned in her uniform without having it dry-cleaned, that apparently Olivia took it back and threw it in a puddle outside her house. It sounded epic.'

At this, an alarm went off in my head.

'Wait, what?' I said. 'Olivia's mom died?'

A few days before eighth grade meant it was likely August, roughly five years ago. That must have been what Regina Smalls was posting about on Olivia's Facebook wall, why she was thinking of her. It was coming up on the anniversary of her mom's death.

'Yeah,' Razz said slowly, watching me. 'Why do you look like you just swallowed glass?'

I let out a long breath. 'Nothing,' I said. 'I just – I can't stop thinking about Olivia falling off the roof this morning.'

Razz sighed. 'Look, she's weird and Becky's the worst. That's childhood friendships for you. Vaguely disappointing and generally bizarre.' Razz collapsed on to his bed and dragged his beanie down over his face so all I could see was his mouth. 'Ugh, I should go. If I don't start making some serious progress on my record collection before I go to Richmond tomorrow, I might just burn my entire house down out of spite.'

'Wait, but,' I started to say, feeling embarrassed at the sudden wave of desperation sweeping through me, 'what's happening tomorrow night?'

'What do you mean? You're coming over, we're eating ourselves into a processed-food coma. End of story. I'll call you when we're leaving Richmond.'

He hung up, his face disappearing from my screen. Part of me was annoyed at the sudden exit, at his inability to see I was clearly losing my mind about this whole Olivia thing, but the other part, the quieter, mopey part, said I'd better get used to it. When Razz moved to California, this would be my life. Bored. Mostly friendless. On the sidelines. Unless.

Unless.

Phone still lit up in my hand, I thumbed through to Facebook and found Olivia's message, questions racing through my brain. For years I'd talked to barely anyone outside of Razz and Ellen, at least about anything important. What if I said something embarrassing or completely bizarre to Olivia? She'd already been able to forget about me once; maybe instantly erasing weird people from her brain was another one of her superpowers.

But to wuss out of this would mean potentially wasting the opportunity to find out about one of the craziest things I'd ever seen. To prove to myself that maybe I could still somewhat talk to other people in a vaguely normal way. No matter how nervous I felt, I couldn't risk missing it.

Sucking in a deep breath, I typed out the only thing I could think to say:

Hugh Copper
Hey

Then, I waited.

6

Yes, I'm a dude and I read the *Twilight* books, and the ending was AWFUL. I'm sorry, but I didn't just endure all kinds of crap and read 1,000+ pages promising this big, epic vampire battle only to have said rival vamps finally come face to face, shrug, then go . . . nah nvm. Those are forty-eight hours of my life I will never get back. EXCUSE ME, WHERE CAN I APPLY FOR THOSE HOURS? STEPHENIE MEYER, I DEMAND THOSE HOURS.

Thankfully Olivia's response was almost instantaneous.

Olivia Moon
What's yr number?

I froze, fingers hovering over the screen. The idea of Olivia Moon wanting to talk to me on the phone after what'd happened that morning seemed as impossible as Marvin Gaye rising from the dead and asking for our

Wi-Fi password. And yet here she was, requesting my number.

With shaking hands, I typed out my phone number and watched in horror as my screen went black again within seconds, an unknown number flashing across the top.

'Hello?' I said, swallowing.

The voice on the other line was low and whispery. 'I need you to do me another favour.'

Blinking quickly, I smoothed down my hair. 'What was the first favour?'

'You successfully left me alone when I asked you to. Good job.'

This left me at a loss for words.

'Now, it gets a little more complicated,' Olivia said, filling the silence. 'Clark took something very important from me, and I need your help to get it back.'

This was enough to jolt me back to life.

'Me?' I said, not really believing her. 'Why me?'

'Oh, don't play dumb,' Olivia scoffed. 'We both know what you saw today. We're basically blood brothers now.'

I sat up straighter, feeling my back strain. 'So that was real? I didn't hallucinate?'

Olivia paused. I could almost picture her pacing around her bedroom, contemplating admitting the truth we both already knew.

'No, you didn't hallucinate,' she said eventually, sounding annoyed.

Even though I knew this, it still felt as though Olivia

had arranged to have a watermelon drop from fifty storeys up and explode between us, leaving a pink, pulpy mess splattered all over our faces. Now that I knew it was real, there was so much to break apart. So much to ask.

'But how?' I said, combing my fingers through my hair. 'Does anybody else know? Are there other people who can—'

'Whoa, whoa, whoa,' Olivia said, cutting me off, 'not so fast. If you help me, I'll play twenty questions with you. That's the deal.'

Everything about my body felt nervous and jittery. I jumped to my feet and began pacing around my room, ping-ponging over the faded brown carpet.

'Help you how?' I said. 'You don't even—'

Before the words could fall out, I stopped myself. *You don't even know me*, I wanted to say. Though I knew that wasn't technically true. Because whether she realized it or not, we were connected in another way, one I fought thinking about every time Olivia passed me in the halls. One I didn't want to remember.

'That's kind of the problem,' Olivia said. 'I don't really know yet. Clark took my stuff and then he sorta disappeared. First, I need to find out where he is, then we make a plan. I mean, the most we're talking about here is you being bait while I sneak into wherever he is and grab my stuff.'

'Bait?' I said. 'So, the swap is, you tell me more about what I already know and Clark kicks the shit out of me?'

'Nobody's kicking the shit out of you,' Olivia said.

'What kind of stuff did he steal? Is it of the priceless artefact kind, or is it illegal?' I swallowed. 'Both?'

'This is sounding a lot like twenty questions . . .' Olivia said.

'Just give me this one,' I said. 'I can't commit to something that might get me arrested.'

Olivia sighed. 'Fine. It was a crate full of all my mom's stuff,' she said, 'at least the stuff I managed to save before my dad got rid of everything else. Inside was like, records, tapes, pictures, some books, home movies, her seashell collection, notes. Everything that was important to her.'

I stopped pacing and squinted into the darkness. 'He just took it?' I said. 'Are you sure he didn't like, stash his weed in some compartment and he's going to bring the crate back tomorrow?'

'Nope,' Olivia said. 'He wanted to get back at me, and this time he went for gold.'

'But this is like, next-level cruel. This suggests Clark Thomas has more brain cells than a goldfish, and I'm not sure I'm ready to believe that.'

'There are two sides to every brain-dead coin, Hugh. Haven't you heard that before?'

With Clark Thomas, I doubted it. But I had to give him credit. If that really was his intention, he wasn't half the moron I thought he was. He was sadistic.

I could barely look at the framed pictures of my parents I'd taken down and hidden in shoeboxes under the stairs after they died, much less walk into their bedroom, where their sheets were still the same ones they'd slept in the night before they were gone. The whole house reeked of them, sure, but not all mementoes were created equal. Ellen and I kept their bedroom door shut, cornering off the important stuff, where every time I touched something, my fingers burnt as sharply as if I'd just stuck my hand in a hot oven. The idea of somebody rifling through my house and stealing my parents' things made my insides shrivel.

'OK,' I said, slumping on to my bed. 'I'll help you get it back.'

Olivia exhaled in one long breath. 'Good,' she said simply.

'Can you at least say why Clark took your mom's stuff?'

'Because he's a dick.'

'Yeah, but there's gotta be more to it than that.'

A series of rhythmic clicks came through from Olivia's end, like fingernails tapping anxiously against plastic.

'I found out he was cheating on me, so I beat up his car with a lamp.'

'Jesus,' I said. 'A lamp? Why not just call him out online like a normal person?'

'Boring,' Olivia said as she pretended to yawn. 'Social media is for reputations and reputations don't matter.'

'Yeah, so instead you obliterate a perfectly good lamp? That makes sense.'

Olivia's laugh was breathy and unexpected. 'It was the first thing I could think of when I found out about Casey,' she said. 'Casey is Clark's ugly bassist, AKA the other woman.'

'Clark's in a band?' I said.

'Of course he's in a band. He's an asshole.' Seconds ticked by as Olivia breathed quietly into the phone. 'I wanted to ruin something important to him.'

I didn't know what to say.

'But it's whatever now. The important thing is getting everything back.' Olivia cleared her throat. There was the sound of what might've been bed springs groaning, then the faint noise of music. 'I'm going to do some serious internet stalking tonight, and I'll call you tomorrow with what I find. Then you help me and I answer your dumb questions. In the meantime, you can't tell anyone about my head. Deal?'

I kicked up my legs so they sprawled out across my bed, bare calves suddenly going cold as the air conditioning box in my window let out a breeze. This was all moving so fast. One second Olivia didn't know my name and the next she was asking for my help. We hadn't talked in years, not since that night. That night her name appeared in my DMs, a few days after my parents died.

Every time I saw her it just brought back memories of the way I felt, sitting motionless at my parents' funeral, how everything about me ached in a way I couldn't describe, to the point where I actively avoided her. To see Olivia Moon meant reliving all those feelings. That emptiness. I couldn't deal with it, and when I did accidentally slip up and pass her, it seemed like she couldn't deal with it either. Her eyes always immediately snapped to her feet, mouth swallowing down the conversation with whoever she was hanging out with that week until she just ended up mumbling into her chest.

Now, here we were plotting to steal from Clark Thomas, Mount Luther High School's head juvenile delinquent. The guy who put eighty goldfish in the school pool but forgot it was chlorinated, so the first PE class of the day just found a giant pond of rotting fish. But if Olivia was worried about Clark, or even nervous about talking to me again, she didn't show it. So, I couldn't either. Not now.

'Deal,' I said.

7

THE HANDMAID'S TALE
Posted in BOOKS by Hugh.jpg on January 29 at 4:29 p.m.

What? Wait, what? Did that just – wait, what just happened?

As I probably should've guessed, pretending to have a normal day while waiting for Olivia Moon to call with a plan to steal something back from her future serial killer ex-boyfriend was basically impossible. Usually I'd take the truck out on my same old route, circling through Columbia Heights down to Petworth and then looping back up to Shaw, but Ellen had taken the truck that morning for purposes she hadn't specified. Razz was already in Richmond visiting his grandma, so hanging out with him was out of the question too.

It was almost as if the universe was conspiring against me, so I had no choice but to sit and stare at my blank phone screen and wait for Olivia to call.

Outside my bedroom window, a crow was skipping up the oak tree whose branches scraped along my house. It hammered its beak into the bark, pulling back thin strips of brown that flaked down to the ground below, before flying over to the house across the street and landing on its roof. That's when a thought occurred to me.

I picked up my phone and waited as it rang. Using my phone now was a risk – what if Olivia called? – but the thought of waiting any longer by myself was equally undesirable.

'You're lucky I'm answering after you didn't come to my party.'

She was trying to sound mad but I could hear the smile in her voice. I looked through the window at the house over the road, tall, red brick and with a white picket fence cutting between the lawn and sidewalk. Standing in the top window, one hand on her hip and the other pressing her phone into the side of her face, was Becky Cayman.

'You didn't invite me,' I said.

'Mom said she told Ellen,' Becky said.

'Yeah, that's not you,' I said. 'And also not me.'

I could practically see Becky roll her eyes. 'Details,' she said. 'You don't have to make stupid excuses about avoiding us. Sometimes we all just hang out. You know, sober.'

My eyebrow quirked up. 'You're a bad liar, Cayman.'

Becky turned away as the curtain in front of her window closed. 'Well, I've kinda got a lot of packing to do, so I should probably go.'

This was the part where most people would start feeling nervous. Becky, using her bored voice. Becky, the

66

girl that always had more important things to do. But I knew her better than that.

'When are you leaving for Rutgers?'

'Tonight. I've got orientation on Monday and my parents want to make this whole trip up to New Jersey a family vacation with Emma and Sydney. Because what would my last weekend before college be if they all weren't trying to torture me?'

Becky didn't exactly get along with her younger sisters. They were ten-year-old twins, born long after Becky'd grown used to the idea of being an only child. It didn't help that they were not only miracle babies, but basically matching child prodigies, too.

I leant my head against the window and blinked down at my lawn, the grass too long and speckled with yellow weeds. Sometimes Becky forgot I would give anything for my parents to embarrass me in front of strangers, or have them break up an argument between me and Ellen, but I didn't hold it against her.

'Well, since I didn't come to your party I kinda feel like I owe you,' I said. 'I don't want you to go to Rutgers hating me.'

'I don't know, Hugh.' Becky sighed. 'I'm sorta busy. These hangers aren't gonna throw themselves into a box.'

My mouth turned up in a smirk. 'Just give me five minutes,' I said.

Becky laughed. 'It better last longer than that.'

'Seven minutes. Eight, tops.'

Her curtain snapped open and Becky reappeared. She

was wearing a white shirt, giving her body a ghostly shape in the window.

'Fine,' she said. 'But don't expect me to like it.'

I tapped my fingers against the glass. 'I can guarantee you won't.'

As Becky pulled her shirt back over her head, the glow from the afternoon sun outside cut through my curtains and caught the smooth, silky streak of her hair. For a second, I saw it smeared with blood, jagged edges of skull emerging through the brown, but when I blinked again, it was gone. No blood, no skull. Everything was intact.

Most guys from our class were intimidated by Becky, by her sarcasm, her never-ending string of comebacks and the way one of her front teeth stuck out a little farther than the other so it caught on her bottom lip. But I'd seen her cut by that same soft light in my bedroom so many times, I couldn't help but imagine her always framed that way whenever her name came up.

There was nothing scary about her. She was just Becky.

The whole thing between us started at the beginning of senior year, when Becky and I were partnered together for a physics project. By that point, I hadn't been hanging out with our group for about a year. They were all still telling the same jokes, doing the same thing on the weekends. It was exhausting. But sitting in Becky's basement again, in that same spot by her dad's treadmill, left me feeling like I'd stumbled into a forgotten dream. Our assignment was to build a boat made out of paper, paint and a few pieces of wood, but what started as a brain-storming sesh for our boat's theme ended pretty quickly when Becky leant across the couch and kissed me.

'You look like a porn star from the seventies,' Becky said from the end of my bed.

She scooped her hair into her hands and began smoothing down the frizzy pieces with her fingers. I glanced down. It was too hot for my comforter so I was just sprawled out on my bed in my boxers, bare chest half covered by a sheet.

'How do you know what a porn star from the seventies looks like?'

A hairpin was wedged between her teeth so when Becky spoke, she had a lisp. 'OK, you look like *what I imagine* a porn star from the seventies looks like.' She spat the hairpin into her hand. 'Better?'

Once her hair was secured into a ponytail, Becky climbed back into bed next to me and propped her head up on her hand.

'You gonna miss me when I go to Rutgers?' she said.

I rolled my head over in her direction, feeling indescribably warm. I knew I was supposed to like the sex part better than lying in bed, but there was something about having Becky next to me that made me feel safe. I'd never done anything like this with anyone before – the whole 'hooking up' thing – and the fact that we kept coming back for each other made me wonder if there was something more between us I wasn't admitting. Something more I was feeling that I couldn't put my finger on.

'Meh,' I said with a lazy shrug.

Becky made an annoyed sound and nudged me with her free hand, but left her fingers resting on my chest. She ran them along the freckles scattered across my collarbone and smiled when goosebumps prickled up in their place.

Nobody knew about us. Not Razz, not Ellen. But I knew what they would say. Razz would be weird and pissed off. Ellen, giddy. Maybe Lily knew, because she was Becky's best friend, but I was too afraid to ask. I didn't know what exactly we were doing, but it wasn't a relationship. That was pretty clear by the way we only snuck into each other's houses when we knew the other person was alone.

I caught Becky's fingers in mine and lifted her hand up so I could see the lines criss-crossing her palm. 'I can't believe you're leaving the nation's capital for America's armpit,' I said.

This thought settled in my stomach, sending a wave of uneasiness swelling through me. Just like Razz, Becky was leaving too.

Becky laughed through her nose. 'If my sisters aren't there, New Jersey can't be that bad,' she said. 'At least I won't have to work a boring job in the city just to get away from them.'

'You quit Forever 21?'

'No, I'm going to come down from New Jersey for my shift every night.' She laced her fingers through mine and squeezed. 'Obviously I quit my job. If you'd been at my party, you would know that.'

'I know, I know,' I said, sighing. 'But everyone's leaving for college and I don't want to be this lame comeback kid who shows up at the last second and is like, "Hey, don't forget to leave some jobs for me after you graduate!"'

No matter how much I didn't want to go to college, it still made me uncomfortable admitting it to people out loud. Declaring I wasn't going down the universally accepted path for success was like admitting I drank pee.

'I think it's cool you're not going to college,' Becky said. 'College isn't for everybody. I would've skipped it except my parents would probably disown me. That, and the fact that staying here with my sisters would be like actual death.'

I did my best to swallow a cringe and attempted a smile instead. That was the other bad part about telling people I wasn't going to college: having to listen to them justify to me why it was totally acceptable.

'Do your parents still want you to be a doctor?' I asked.

Becky let her head flop on to the pillow as she groaned. 'Yes, obviously. I tried explaining to them I'm horrified by blood, but they won't listen. I've been looking it up and I think I want to major in Communications.' Her face emerged from the pillow, red and framed by frizz again. 'I mean, ideally I'd major in English, but at least with Com I can actually have a career that doesn't involve having to sell meth on the weekends to make ends meet.'

'Is it that, or is it because you don't want people to know you can read?'

Becky narrowed her eyes at me. 'I'm fine keeping my

Jane Austen collection a secret, thank you very much,' she said.

Not many people knew Becky Cayman spent most of her summers rereading *Sense and Sensibility* in her back-yard tree house. But then most people didn't know her like I did, or see past her tiny shorts and long hair.

My room was suddenly flooded with Motown music, the jangly beat soft at first before rumbling up to the opening line of the Four Tops' 'It's the Same Old Song'. My phone. I grabbed it before Becky could see the name I knew instinctively was flashing across my screen.

Becky sat up next to me. 'Who is it?' she asked as I stood and paced over to the end of my bed, carefully wrapping my fingers around my phone so she couldn't hear.

I glanced at her and held up a hand. 'Just give me a second,' I whispered. 'Hey, hold on,' I said into the phone. Becky rolled her eyes and flopped back on to my pillow as I shuffled out of my room and into the bathroom.

'OK,' I said, sitting down on the toilet. 'What's the plan?'

'He's in New York,' Olivia said quickly. From the way she spoke, it was almost an explosion, like she'd been hold-ing the words in for days. 'His band is playing in Brooklyn tomorrow night and Sunday night at some place called the Cabinet.'

'Clark is in New York?' I said. 'I'm sorry, but how does someone just schedule a last-minute show in New York?'

'You're asking me like I'm supposed to know,' Olivia said.

'You're the one who dated him.'

'Yeah, but that doesn't mean I understand him. All I know is, I need you to drive me to New York tomorrow so we can sneak into the venue and get my mom's stuff back.'

'How am I supposed to do that?' I said. 'I don't have a car.'

'You have a truck.'

I scratched my fingernail against the roll of toilet paper attached to the side of the bathroom sink, trying to piece together what she was saying.

'That's my sister's van, and she'd never let me borrow it,' I said.

'She let you borrow it yesterday,' Olivia said, 'when you were stalking me.'

'I wasn't borrowing it, that was to actually sell ice cream,' I said. My right foot drummed against the bath mat, shaking my whole body. 'And I definitely wasn't stalking you. I just happened to be on Clark's street.'

'Then sell ice cream on the way to New York. I don't care what you do so long as we get there this weekend. His band's next show is in Toronto and I don't have a passport, so if I miss him now who knows when I'll get the crate back. He'll probably leave it up there just to spite me.'

I bit my lip and considered this. 'Look, even if I wanted to take you to New York, I can't. I've barely ever driven the truck outside DC, and I don't even know if it'd make it that far. It was made in the eighties, so in terms of

73

engineering, it's basically on the same level as a covered wagon.'

'The eighties gave us cell phones,' Olivia fired back. 'The truck can't be that bad.'

'That's not the point,' I said. 'My sister would never let me take it that far.'

'Then don't tell her.'

I furrowed my brow. 'Are you suggesting I steal my sister's truck?'

'I'm suggesting you do whatever you have to.'

Springing to my feet again, I stepped nervously from the shower to the sink, towel rack to the toilet. This was what I wanted, right? A window into Olivia Moon's life? But I didn't expect it to come at the cost of my sister's truck. Why couldn't Olivia just ask for a ride to Arlington or Alexandria? We could do that in like, half an hour. I knew those routes in my sleep, including which gas stations didn't charge to let you use the bathroom. But New York? I'd never driven that far by myself, or on streets that packed. DC's comparatively plus-sized streets were practically like Luigi Raceway in *Mario Kart*. New York City was Rainbow Road.

'Why don't you just take the bus?' I said. 'I've taken the Megabus to New York from here and if you don't use the bathroom, it's surprisingly not as disgusting as you'd think. There's the train, too, or you could get a Zipcar.'

'Amtrak equals expensive. My driver's licence equals non-existent,' Olivia said. 'Don't you think I would've considered all this before calling you? Look, Hugh' – there was a shuffling on the line, as if she were doing some pacing of her own – 'my only option is getting a ride up there from somebody else. You said you'd help me.'

'Yeah, that's when I was just supposed to be bait. You didn't say anything about leaving DC.'

Up until yesterday, Olivia couldn't even remember my name. And now she was asking me to get her to New York? It still wasn't making any sense. Plus, I could already see how this would all pan out. The ending to end all endings, where I accidentally fell head first down an open sewer grate and died. My sister would still be pissed off and Razz would be too busy in California to go to my funeral, so my urn would just sort of sit outside the church in a cardboard box until a hobo took said cardboard box to make a sign and my ashes sat there alone for all eternity.

As much as I wanted to understand how Olivia could do what she did, to keep my word, to give her back what I owed her after that night two years ago, I couldn't just steal my sister's truck and go to New York.

'Olivia, I'm sorry,' I said reluctantly, 'but I can't.'

'You said you would,' she said.

'I know, and I want to, but—'

'Fine,' she said suddenly. 'Never mind.' There was a crash on her side, like glass exploding. 'You can run away now.'

Then the phone went dead.

The walk back to my bedroom felt like a swim through sand. Becky was sitting on the edge of my bed, her phone in her lap. When I appeared in the doorway, she looked up.

'Who was that?' she said.

I swallowed, not sure if what I was about to say was a mistake. 'Do you remember Olivia Moon?'

Becky squinted. 'Olivia Moon called you?'

'I saw her trying to break into Clark Thomas's house yesterday,' I said as I sat next to her. The next lie came easily. 'Someone else saw her too, so now the cops want to talk to me. Apparently, I'm a witness or something.'

'Olivia is so unbelievably weird.' Becky lay back down on my bed and sighed, as if Olivia had scaled Clark's house expressly against her wishes.

'Didn't you used to be best friends?'

As if detecting bad smell, Becky's nose twitched. '"Best friends" is a little strong,' she said. 'We were good friends, maybe, until she showed up to school freshman year dressed like a nun. You know, long skirt, long sleeves. She even had her hair braided. It was like eighty degrees outside and she was wearing cashmere.'

'How does everyone remember the religious phase except for me?' I said. 'Razz got that one too.'

'Razz?' Becky's forehead creased. 'Oh, you mean – yeah. I always forget she's a he now.'

I frowned, not sure if she was joking. 'I'm pretty sure it's a little more complicated than that,' I said, my fingers instinctively tightening into fists.

Becky, sensing the sudden stiffness in my shoulders, nudged me with her elbow. 'I'm obviously kidding,' she said quickly, her face breaking into a smile. 'But seriously, it doesn't surprise me Olivia would try to break into

76

someone's house.' When she looked over at me again, her voice dropped. 'She is low-key crazy.'

My frown deepened. 'Crazy how?' I said.

'Let's just say she's not the safest person I know.' Becky made a slicing motion across her thigh, pretending to cut her pinkie finger into the soft part of her flesh. 'Once, she actually cut herself in front of me with the edge of a seashell. She tried to play it off like it was an accident, but I knew she did it on purpose. The cut wasn't that deep, thank god, because when she showed me her leg again it was practically gone.'

It would've been, if Olivia's body could repair itself quickly.

'When was that?' I said.

'Eighth grade, maybe?' Becky pulled both shoulders into her ears and sighed. 'She was always doing stuff like that, U-turning every five seconds. Everything would be totally normal, we're just like, watching *Teen Mom* after school at my house, and then the next second, she's yelling at me because I went to get custard from Rita's with Lily and didn't invite her.'

I had a hard time picturing this version of Olivia. Needy. Sensitive. Anything other than the hard-faced one from yesterday, the one that was so eff you to all the consequences of her lamp-hurtling actions.

'My mom said it was probably because she wanted attention, because her parents sucked,' Becky continued. She sat up again. 'Sometimes she got so mad, she'd just explode. It really freaked me out, but I stuck around because I thought I could help her. We might not have been best friends but she was still at my house all the time. My mom was always asking about her, telling me to invite her to sleep over. I think she felt bad for her.'

'And then you guys stopped talking when Olivia started dressing like a nun?'

Becky's eyes narrowed ever so slightly. 'Judgemental, much?' she said. 'I didn't stop talking to her. She stopped talking to me. And I don't mean she slowly started hanging out with other people. She literally ignored me and Lil every time we tried to talk to her. It was like all of a sudden we didn't exist.'

I bit my lip. That was the thing about Olivia; it was almost as if she could shed her skin whenever she felt like it, starting over in a place and with people she'd known her entire life. A weird part of me admired her for it. Most people saved makeovers for college or new cities. Olivia just decided when to end a chapter in her life and start a new one, even if it meant closing the door on everyone around her for no apparent reason.

Without another word, Becky leant in and kissed me. She let her mouth linger against mine as she said, 'Can we not spend my last few hours in DC talking about Olivia Moon?'

I nodded slowly, the warmth from Becky's mouth spreading down my neck and into my chest as I shut my eyes. With Becky this close, her breath on my face, Olivia Moon started to feel farther away, her white-blonde hair fading into the back of my head.

At the sound of a door creaking, my eyes snapped open again, bringing my room back into focus. Suddenly everything felt hot and too bright, as though I were seeing my room through a neon filter. As I swung my head around, breath heavy in my chest, I realized with a jolt that somehow I wasn't actually in my bed any more. I was sitting at my desk, the dark screen of my computer in front of me like a square black lake. Becky was gone. Outside, the sky was cold and grey, the oak tree bordering my window reduced to mostly twiggy branches with a few brown leaves straggling behind.

Over my right shoulder, the floorboards underneath the carpet groaned. Ellen stood in the doorway, her eyes swollen and too big for her face.

'You ready?' she said, hands playing nervously with the slick fabric of her black dress.

'Ready for what?' I said, my voice hoarse.

Ellen frowned. 'We're supposed to be at the church in ten minutes,' she said.

'The church?'

I glanced down at my lap for the first time. I was wearing black pants I didn't recognize, their slightly wrinkled fabric hanging loose off my thighs. I frowned. The pants were clearly way too big, almost as if they were—

'Oh my god,' I whispered under my breath.

A growing sense of horror crawled up my neck as my hands groped along the collar of my black suit, the silver-striped tie cinched way too tight around my throat. The pants were practically parachutes around my bony thighs.

They were too big because they weren't meant for me; they were meant for my dad.

This whole stupid suit, down to the tie, belonged to my dad.

I dug my nails into my palms as I leant my head on to my desk and tried to keep breathing. It felt like my chest was caving in, like the room was squeezing into a tight fist, as the reality of what had happened crashed around me.

'It was all just a dream,' I said, knowing it was impossible. But somehow, it wasn't.

All of it. Everything. Everything with Olivia, the last two years. Graduating, Razz, Ellen and Dan, all those times with Becky. It was all just a dream.

Today was the day of my parents' funeral.

THE END

. . . 'Can we not spend my last few hours in DC talking about Olivia Moon?'

I blinked, my fingers closing in around Becky's wrist. The microscopic hairs on her arm were soft and fine.

'You're real,' I said without meaning to.

Becky was real. This whole moment, the last two years – it was all real.

She frowned. 'Um, obviously?' she said. Her eyes searched my face, squinting and concerned. 'Why are you being such a weirdo today?'

Oh, you know, I wanted to say. *I just saw a girl's head crack open like a freaking egg and then stitch itself back together and I'm pretty sure I've either been plunged into some* Inception-*style coma or miscast as a really pathetic sidekick in a Marvel movie. No big deal.* But instead, I pulled Becky back into me and kissed her, relaxing into my pillows as the image of Olivia, of me disappearing into my dad's suit, escaped my head, if only for a few more seconds.

When Becky went home half an hour later, adrenaline still buzzed in my veins. I paced across my bedroom floor, feeling the nerves bubbling under my skin. Ever since my parents had died, my brain had started writing its own endings, which was partially the reason I never left DC. Every time I did, I couldn't stop picturing myself smashed up against a dashboard, the windshield fractured into a billion tiny pieces. But this ending with Becky – this one had been worse. Because this time, I was freshly submerged in the black hole that was the days after my parents had died, the same dark, numb place I thought I'd never escape.

Only one person had tried to save me then, and that was Olivia.

The thought of driving to New York might've made me want to cut out my insides and string them up like Christmas lights around my house, but no matter how I looked at it, I owed Olivia. That night – it meant everything. Plus, it was already hard enough living with myself on an average day without having to add to the list the fact that I'd had a chance to make it up to Olivia and instead chose to completely screw her over.

Hands shaking, I typed out a text on my phone and pressed send.

Hugh: OK, I'll drive you to New York. But we HAVE to be home by 9 pm

Nine seemed like a reasonable hour. Most bad things happened after nine. Plus, that still gave me enough time to sleep over at Razz's house before he left on Sunday.

Eventually, Olivia replied:

Olivia: Done
Olivia: We ride at dawn
Olivia: AKA 6 am Your house. Be there or be SQUARE

I cocked an eyebrow at her responses, then set my phone face down on my nightstand. Olivia Moon was kind of a dork, unless this too was all just part of her latest phase. Then, something occurred to me.

Hugh: Wait how do you know where I live?

Hugh: Olivia?

Hugh: ?????

Olivia: Resources

Olivia: I have many, many resources

I sighed and set my phone down again. Stretching back out on my bed, I folded my hands across my chest and waited for the end, for my brain's newest invention of how Olivia and I would crash head first into impending doom. I closed my eyes, my breathing calm and patient. But nothing came.

8

OK, so two of the easily best characters in this show sacrifice themselves for all the dork humans in the big bad battle at the end, and all Buffy cares about is the fact that the mall got blown up? I'm sorry, did I just have a stroke?

The plan was simple. I would sneak outside to meet Olivia at six in the morning, and we'd head north to New York. What actually happened was not so simple.

When I crept downstairs, the kitchen light was already on. Spread across the dining table was a half-eaten bowl of Cocoa Puffs, the keys to the truck, a pile of papers and pamphlets, and Ellen's open laptop, the screen glowing yellow-white. A rustling sound came from the other side of the closed bathroom door, a line of light showing from underneath.

I pocketed the truck keys, my eyes lingering on the pamphlets. They were all from the bank, their titles staring up at me in tall, serious letters. There were at least four or five of them, each accompanied by pictures of one or two people either laughing, smiling at each other, or staring pensively into the distance with their heads balanced in their hands.

The toilet flushed. My hand instinctively snapped to my pocket, touching the outline of the keys through my jeans, but a flash of words on Ellen's computer screen caught my eye. I leant over and scrolled through the open email. I'd never snooped through my sister's stuff before, but the first few lines had made the hairs on my arms stand up.

To: ellen@killericecream.com
From: sarah.reno@giantfood.com
Subject: Monday
Date: August 25

Hi Ellen,

Great! If you just ask someone at the bakery counter, they'll bring you back to the office. I know we've been over this before, but I wanted to confirm that we'll need to see the following at our meeting:

- Tub mock-ups
- 3–5 sample ice cream flavours
- Any ideas for new flavours (??)
- A press kit

Plus anything else you'll need for your pitch. FYI, I've had Killer before and I'm in love with the brand. I think you'll do great.

I also wanted to check, are you still considering selling the truck? I know it's only a minor point, but Rachel's going to want to know Giant will be Killer Ice Cream's exclusive stockist. It's something to think about.

If you've got any questions for me ahead of our meeting, let me know. Otherwise, I'll see you Monday!

All My Best,
Sarah

When the door to the bathroom opened, I barely registered it in time for me to step away from the dining room table. My head was swimming, the contents of the email shooting up like fireworks in my brain. Ellen had a meeting with Giant? The grocery store chain? And more importantly – she was selling the truck?

'Macaulay Culkin!' Ellen exclaimed at the sight of me, a hand shooting up to her forehead. 'You scared the crap out of me. What're you doing up?'

That's what all the weirdness about me losing the truck must've been about.

'I–I—' I stammered, groping for an excuse. At six in the morning, there weren't many. 'I'm meeting Razz at the Lincoln Memorial to watch the sunrise. He's being really sentimental about this whole Berkeley thing.'

'You're kind of late,' my sister said, glancing at the window above the sink.

The sky was just turning a pinkish yellow, illuminating wisps of cotton candy-clouds that floated over the trees.

'I was supposed to wake up at five, but my alarm didn't go off,' I said, then eyed the clock on the microwave. 6:07. 'I gotta go.'

The email. The truck. Olivia. It was too much at once, sending the gears in my brain spinning out of control. If I wanted to get to New York, I'd have to do what I always did: bury my feelings down so deep, I basically tripped over them.

'Are you taking the Metro?' Ellen called after me as I darted out of the kitchen and slammed the front door. 'Be careful!'

But I was already down the porch steps and halfway across the lawn, too far gone to answer.

My sister might not have seen me swipe the truck keys, but she'd definitely hear the truck's engine choke to life before we pulled away. Once I turned the key in the ignition, I had maybe a minute max before Ellen figured out what was going on.

Olivia was leaning against the Killer truck's driver-side door, big pink wads of bubblegum expanding from her mouth. She was wearing khaki cargo shorts again, along with a scratchy beige button-up that was meant to be short-sleeved, but because it was so big, the sleeves fell down below her elbows. Even though the sun was barely up, half her face was hidden behind red heart-shaped sunglasses and a cream-coloured bucket hat, her hair sticking out from underneath the rim in tufts of white blonde.

'Where've you been?' she said at full volume.

At the sound of her voice, I instinctively hunkered down into a crouch and held a finger to my lips. 'Be quiet,' I hissed. 'My sister's awake.'

'At six in the morning on a Saturday?' Olivia said. 'Is she a sadist?'

I unplugged the cord connecting the generator in the truck to a power source in our house and fumbled for the keys in my pocket. Once I finally jammed the right one into the lock, I swung the driver-side door open and slid into the front seat.

As Olivia stepped in, she slung a brown leather bag on to her lap and watched me, the sunglasses and hat obscuring her expression. Key plugged into the ignition, I started to turn on the engine but stopped and stared down at my hands instead. Was I really going to do this? Steal my sister's truck and drive it to New York for Olivia Moon? Somebody I barely knew? Over my left shoulder stood my house. Still exactly the same as it had been two years ago, with icicle-shaped Christmas lights strung around the gutters, dark blue front door and black wrought-iron table and chairs on the porch. But inside, everything was about to be different, and for the first time in two years, there was nothing I could do about it.

I glanced at Olivia. She stared back at me over the top of her sunglasses, mouth open and gum dangling dangerously over the edge of her teeth.

'Well?' she said. 'Is the New York Express leaving the station or what?'

Without answering, I turned the truck's key, ignoring

the white-water rapids of blood rushing in my ears. Then, I cranked the gear into drive and let the wheels roll forward.

No matter what I did, everything around me was changing. Now, it was my turn.

Minutes after the truck started moving, my phone rang. This continued so solidly that, by the time we'd reached the edge of DC and got on to the parkway, I had, by my calculation, around sixteen missed calls. I flinched instinctively whenever my phone began chiming, but Olivia didn't seem to notice. Her whole body was twisted in her seat, eyes glued to the passenger-side window like she'd never seen anything past Columbia Heights before.

When we reached the turn-off for College Park and the University of Maryland, my phone mysteriously went quiet. I poked it nervously, more than a little worried human contact would bring it back to life again.

'Do you have any music?' Olivia whirled around in her seat, bug-eyed sunglasses fixed in my direction.

I pressed play on the tape player so that Martha Reeves and The Vandellas instantly flooded every corner of the van, commanding everyone, everywhere, around the world, to start dancing in the street.

'And, you have a tape player,' Olivia said. It sounded as though nothing in her life had ever disappointed her more.

'This van's so old, we're lucky it didn't come with a gramophone,' I said. 'Ellen had to pay a fortune to get a tape player installed.'

Olivia pushed her back into the seat but this time faced forward. 'In that case, why not just get a CD player?'

'Because we're purists,' I said.

'Or you're just hipsters,' Olivia muttered. 'Plus, the sound quality sucks. Nobody who had to listen to tapes because there wasn't another option listens to them any more. And do you know why that is? Because tapes are stupid and shitty.'

'Have you ever rewound a tape before?' I said. 'It's so satisfying, it's like cracking the top of an icy puddle with your shoe.'

Olivia rolled her eyes. 'You are so weird.'

I nodded my chin toward the glove compartment on the other side of her knees. 'There's more music in there, if you want to pick.'

The glove compartment door fell open with a snap. Inside wasn't Ellen's and my entire tape collection, but it had the highlights: Marvin Gaye, The Jackson 5, The Temptations and Tammi Terrell. Olivia strummed her fingers along the tapes' plastic edges and mumbled each band or singer to herself.

'They're all oldies,' she said finally.

Her presence was a welcome distraction from the fact that my sister was most likely plotting my murder and life as I knew it was self-imploding. I could feel my hands softening around the steering wheel, my heartbeat returning to normal.

'There's not much after 1990 that's worth listening to,'

I said. 'With the exception of Michael Jackson's *HIStory*, obviously. "Earth Song" can bring any man to his knees.'

'You've clearly never listened to Nirvana,' Olivia said.

I glanced in my rear-view mirror. '*Nevermind* is pretty good, I'll give you that,' I said before turning right. 'And Kurt Cobain easily had one of the worst endings of the 1990s, which makes the band's story all the more interesting, but in terms of soul, everything pretty much died in the early eighties. We have Marvin Gaye's dad to thank for that.'

'Kurt Cobain's *ending*?' Olivia said. In spite of her sunglasses, I could see her eyes, wide and confused. 'You talk about him like he's a board game or something, not a living, breathing person.'

'The shotgun blast to the head did that, not me,' I said. At the sound of her incredulous scoff, I tried to backtrack. 'I'm not trying to be insensitive,' I said, fighting a stammer. I flicked on my turn signal to weave around an old man who was hunched over his steering wheel trying for dear life to see the road over his dashboard. 'I talk about everyone like that.'

'And their deaths as endings.'

'Well, yeah, basically,' I said. 'When you, you know—' I swallowed. Sometimes I couldn't even say the word. *Die*. 'That's it. You're over. The end.'

Olivia gave a breathy laugh and shook her head.

I pressed my mouth shut, back teeth chewing my tongue. Even though I had Spoiler Alert, I didn't like to talk about endings. Not in real life. Razz was the only person I'd actually told about the hundreds of threads knotted up in the internet, while Ellen only had a vague sense of their existence. The other people I met through the discussions found the site on their own, because they were fellow enders like me. But, I reasoned, if I wanted to figure out more about Olivia, opening up the Chinese food carton that was, well . . . me, might help.

I swallowed, eyes fixed on the road and the vast network of mini-malls sprawling out on either side of us. 'I started this website called Spoiler Alert, where we talk about endings. You know, the endings to movies, books, people. That kind of stuff.'

The sentence came out of me in one long breath, like I'd just told her my deepest, darkest secret.

'You only talk about the endings?' Olivia said. 'What about everything else?'

'Endings are the most important part.' I adjusted my hands on the steering wheel so my grip was at eleven and one o'clock. 'The worst ending can overshadow even the best middle. Look at Buddy Holly. Even though he was only twenty-two when he died, he was so major that John Lennon, Paul McCartney *and* Bob Dylan all cite him as being one of their musical influences. But most of the time, all anyone remembers is the plane crash that killed him. I mean, think about how many people know the line "the day the music died", and then compare that to how many people know "Peggy Sue".'

Olivia looked like she couldn't decide between laughing or yelling at me. Her eyes were squinted and her mouth was in a half-grimace.

'So, you're saying everything he did in the middle is completely pointless.'

'Not pointless,' I said. 'But it all gets diminished.' I could feel the frustration radiating off her, shoulders tense underneath her fringe of hair. We were not getting off to the start I wanted. 'That's just how it is sometimes, I'm not saying it's right.'

'Oh, definitely not,' she said. 'You just went and made a whole website about it.'

'I just –' I began, struggling to say something I could barely articulate in my head – 'I feel like if I can map out the endings, I can try and see what went wrong.'

'Mapping out what went wrong doesn't do you any good,' she said. Her face was almost touching the glass of the passenger-side window, her reflection melding into the real thing. Nose touching nose, lips on lips, so there were two Olivias. 'It still doesn't change the middle.' She laughed darkly. 'Or the end.'

As we crossed underneath the Patapsco River, the sudden orange-tinted darkness of the Baltimore Harbor Tunnel sent me deeper into a thought-spiral I'd been wrestling with over the last few weeks about the ending to the book *Ender's Game*. Razz had recommended it to me a few months ago, and I was only just nailing down why the final chapters annoyed me so much. It wasn't that there were whole chunks of the book that made absolutely no sense, or even that when Orson Scott Card reveals the big twist at the end things somehow make even less sense. It was the fact that the twist was so unbelievably lame and textbook terrible, that when I did finally reach it, I was confused *and* pissed off.

'You took the wrong exit.'

The van was flooded with sunlight again, the tunnel long behind us. Sunglasses pulled down to the tip of her nose, Olivia stared at me, forehead wrinkled. Instead of crossing past Baltimore I was somehow forking into the Inner Harbor, the sharp spikes of skyscrapers jutting up over the dashboard.

'Shit,' I said, flicking on my turn signal and crossing into the right-hand lane. 'Can you look up on my phone how to get back?'

Olivia reached down for my cell, but just as she brought it into her lap, the phone rang again. From the corner of my eye, I could see Ellen's name flashing on the screen. Olivia pressed ignore.

'Twenty-six missed calls,' she said, holding up the lock screen so I could see the notifications. 'Does your sister not have a life?'

'She has a life, we're just sitting in it,' I said.

Just as Olivia started to open Google Maps, my phone screen went black again as another call came through. ELLEN. Even the letters of her name, white and tall, looked angry.

Olivia dropped the phone in her lap and let out a frustrated growl through her back teeth. 'That's it,' she snapped.

Her arm became a circling blur as she wound the

passenger-side window down, Marvin Gaye's soulful voice disappearing into the rush of air. Then, before I could reach out for her hand, I watched as Olivia dangled my cell over the edge of the window and dropped it, her face expressionless as my phone slipped away.

After a few beats, Olivia calmly rolled the window back up and sat facing forward in her chair.

'There,' she said as she smoothed down her hair and took a deep breath. 'That's better.'

I felt like I'd been punched in the stomach.

'You—' I started to say, but the words could barely reach my throat. 'You just – you threw my phone out the window. You actually just threw it out the window.'

My phone had already disappeared in the gravelly distance, probably crushed underneath a grey-black wheel.

'You clearly weren't answering it,' Olivia said.

'I was going to eventually,' I said, my voice sounding strangled. 'It's illegal for me to answer my phone while I'm driving.'

Olivia narrowed her eyes. 'Wow, your life must be a real risk factory,' she said.

A swallow inched down my throat. 'I do all right,' I said, though we both knew I was lying. 'That phone was my birthday present. I don't have an upgrade for another year, and an iPhone without an upgrade costs the same as a kidney. What am I supposed to tell my sister?'

'Tell her I threw your phone out the window,' Olivia said simply. 'She doesn't know who I am.'

'And that's going to make it way better.' The more the situation sank in, the higher my voice went. 'Not only did I steal her truck for somebody she doesn't know, but now you're the reason my phone's gone too.'

We were fully in a tangle of the city by then, buildings rising up in every direction so both the waterfront and highway were no longer visible. I could feel the grey edges and shiny windows tightening in on us, caving in like a deflating balloon.

'I planned it so we could use my phone for directions on the way up and yours on the way down, so I hope you brought your charger,' I grumbled.

'Me? I don't have a cell phone. iPhones without an upgrade cost the same as a kidney,' Olivia said, doing a surprisingly respectable impression of me.

As I slowed the van down for a stop light, I turned to face her, open-mouthed. Olivia looked back at me, bright-eyed, as if we were deep in the throes of an argument about her favourite movie. She looked like she was finally having fun.

'Then how,' I said, trying to keep my breathing even, 'are we supposed to get to New York? I've never driven there before. Jesus, I've barely left DC in the last two years.'

'Why is that not a surprise,' she mumbled, then nodded at the newly green light. 'Then I guess we'd better get a map. There's a gas station two blocks up.'

9

SIGNS
Posted in MOVIES by <u>Hugh.jpg</u> on January 3 at 6:14 a.m.

On the whole, *Signs* does a pretty good job with the creep factor. There are crop circles and weird sounds picked up in baby monitors when there's nothing there. It can't be actual aliens terrorizing Earth, because that would be too predictable for M. Night Shyamalan. Except . . . it is. And it doesn't help that these aliens are basically the lamest ones in the galaxy, who essentially take one look around Earth and go, 'Yeah, no thanks'. The Shyamalan twist here is that this movie just sucks.

The gas station was sandwiched between a vacant lot and an abandoned house with boarded-up windows, its stoop occupied by a sleeping man with a trash bag tied around his head. Somehow, we'd managed to choose the sketchiest-looking corner of an otherwise busy city, the gas station's lifeless, one-roomed snack hut sitting in the back-right edge of the parking lot. Almost half the letters on the gas station's sign were burnt out, so instead of

EASY MART it just said S MAR. The pumps were almost completely empty except for a woman in a bikini who was sprawled out on the blacktop in between the parking spaces like a human X guiding in planes for landing.

Avoiding the woman, I pulled into a parking space and waited as Olivia disappeared into the snack hut without a word. We hadn't spoken over the last few blocks, and I couldn't shake the feeling we were somehow in the middle of a fight. Technically I was the one who should've been mad, seeing as I was now phone-less, but with Olivia more or less ignoring me, my own annoyance just felt gratuitous. Becky's words from the day before kept trailing in and out of my head: *Olivia is low-key crazy.* Though Olivia wasn't bouncing off the walls or anything, I was starting to worry I might be in way over my head.

Down by the street was a phone booth whose glass panels were spray-painted a powdery black. From where I sat in the truck, it wasn't clear whether it was a working phone booth or somebody's house, but seeing it made me even more aware of the distinct, phone-shaped emptiness in my pocket, and the inevitable plank walk I knew I had to do. I could imagine what Olivia would say, but letting my sister know I was alive – totally and completely unreachable, but alive – would only take a few seconds.

When I knocked on the phone booth's inky glass and didn't get an answer, I opened the door a crack and found it empty. The tiny space reeked of pee and old cigarettes, the floor crowded with wadded-up newspapers. Scrawled on the walls were various phone numbers, each one promising either a 'good time' or 'death', and dangling from the payphone was a phone book with giant chunks ripped out.

Swallowing deeply, I typed in one of the few numbers I had memorized by heart and waited, the phone's dull ringtone humming in my ear. There wasn't a time I could remember ever being so nervous to call my sister. We were all each other had. We could say anything, do anything in front of each other. But now, with the truck stolen and Ellen's big secret unveiled, I wasn't sure where we stood.

'Hugh,' Ellen said to my uneasy hello. 'Please, please, *please* tell me you have the truck.'

'I can confirm the truck is with me,' I said.

Ellen sighed. 'Oh, thank god. Why didn't you just tell me you were driving Razz to the mall?'

I opened my mouth to respond, but paused. This thought never occurred to me. I didn't have to tell Ellen about New York. For all she knew, I was just driving Razz around on an indie bookstore tour of DC. At the end of the night, I could find someone that would wind back the truck's odometer like they did in the movie *Matilda* and Ellen would never have to know.

'I-I just got kinda flustered. Sorry.'

'Are you gonna be home soon? We really have to talk and I need the truck.'

I swallowed. 'Razz and I are going to sell ice cream down by the White House,' I lied. 'And then I'm going to his house for dinner.'

'Well, look, I need the truck tonight, so just forget

about selling ice cream and bring it back. I'll pay for you to Uber to Razz's house.'

The newspapers flattened under my feet were from years ago, their words faded to almost nothing. I kicked at them with the toe of my shoe, tearing their edges and uncovering a little orange-pink patch of what I prayed wasn't puke on the floor. Clearly Ellen was desperate to get the truck back because of this meeting on Monday. She'd probably stashed the notebook where she listed all the reasons she wanted to ruin my life under the driver's seat.

'Why do you need it back so bad?' I said.

If she wanted the truck back, she'd have to start telling the truth.

'Because I just do, OK?'

'You just do,' I said slowly. 'You just . . . need it to drive cross-country to flee rogue vampires? To do doughnuts in a Nebraskan field to help perpetuate the myth of crop circles?'

Ellen breathed out through her nose. 'I just need it.'

My hands clenched into fists. I'd never caught my sister in a lie before, and if I hadn't seen that email maybe I never would have. What else had she lied about? Why couldn't she just tell me the truth?

'Why can't you just tell me you're thinking about selling the truck?' I said finally, my patience flying out into the hazy Baltimore air.

There was a pause as my words hung between us. Ellen pulled in a deep breath before saying quietly, 'I was obviously going to tell you.'

'But when? When I went outside one morning and the truck was just gone?'

'I've got this meeting on Monday, and if it—'

'Yeah, I know,' I said. 'I saw your stupid email.'

'You read my emails?'

'Can we not act like that's the actual issue here?'

'It seems like a very actual issue to me,' she said. 'Look. OK. I'm sorry I didn't tell you about the meeting or about the truck. I don't even know how it's all going to go and I'm being weird and nervous, and I screwed up.'

'Yeah, no duh,' I said.

'Yes, yes, Ellen bad, Hugh good,' she said. 'But now that you know, I need my ice cream back. I have to put those flavours in these tubs I've mocked up, so the buyer can actually taste-test the product. I mean, I could ask her to imagine eating Happy Birthday Charlie Manson, but she'd probably picture something that tastes like LSD.'

Her attempt at a joke fell flat between us. I swallowed, a rock-hard lump forming in my throat.

'But why does that mean you have to get rid of the truck?' I said.

'Because, it'd be obsolete,' she said. 'You don't see Ben and Jerry out there pounding the pavement.'

'But what am *I* supposed to do?'

'Oh, come on,' Ellen said, sounding hopeful for the first time during our conversation. 'You won't have time for the truck any more.'

'Because I'll be so busy doing absolutely nothing?'

'You won't be doing nothing. Look, it was unfair of me

to ask you to drive the truck in the first place. You didn't really get to hang out with your friends senior year and I feel bad. I want you to get that time back.'

'You and I both know after this weekend, I won't have friends,' I said.

'Don't be a drama queen.' Ellen cleared her throat. 'I want you to have time for yourself again. You can work on your weird website or get a job with people that aren't your sister. I thought you'd love this.'

'Oh yeah, is that why you didn't tell me?' I said. 'I didn't go to college so I could help you with the truck. What am I supposed to do if there's no truck?'

At this, Ellen groaned. 'Please tell me that's not why you're skipping college.'

'OK, that's not the reason,' I said, waving the thought away. 'But thank god I'm not, if I'm just gonna be an heir to an ice cream fortune.'

My sister huffed a laugh. 'You're not an heir to anything yet. Dan thinks—'

At the mention of Ellen's lame, Coldplay-loving boyfriend, I could feel my blood heat up again. 'You told Dan about all this but not me?' I said.

'His dad has a business degree from Georgetown, so he's been giving me advice,' she insisted. 'He's been help-ing with my pitch, and he agreed having the truck doesn't make sense if—'

'I've been driving that truck since you started Killer,' I said. I held out my hand and began to count on my fingers. 'I know all the best routes, I know where to avoid, and when. I even know what songs to play in each neighbourhood. For instance, playing "Wheels on the Bus" in Shaw will get your tyres slashed.'

'Look, I didn't want to get you worked up over nothing. Kind of like what you're doing right now.'

I raised a hand to my chest. 'Pardon me if I'm a little annoyed you're completely upending everything in my life,' I said.

'I'm not upending everything in your life. This doesn't have anything to do with you outside of the fact that I'm your sister and this could be good for me. Things change, like you suddenly having a life that goes beyond trolling the streets of DC for overheated middle schoolers.'

There were so many nuances to driving the Killer truck, so many things I'd picked up in the last year. It was where Razz and I listened to Marvin Gaye on tape as we drove to Alexandria for doughnuts; where I'd escape if Becky Cayman had Sam and Lily and all them over when her parents were gone for the weekend.

'*This old heart of mine.*'

The song, clear and sharp, soared through my train of thought. It was the Isley Brothers' 'This Old Heart of Mine'. I knew the next line, and Ellen knew I knew, too. *Been broke a thousand times*. But it felt like the roof of my mouth was coated in peanut butter, my throat tight and dry.

'Hugh, come on,' my sister said to my silence. 'Nothing's even happened yet. The people at Giant might just think I'm part of the Manson Family. Finish the song, please. *This old heart of mine . . .*'

The truck, gone. Razz, gone. Becky, gone. The thought played in my head over and over and over again until it completely drowned out the noise from the street outside.

'I can't,' I said at last. I hated the way my voice sounded, choked and small, powerless in the confines of the dusty black phone booth as heat radiated through the darkened panels.

Ellen started to speak again, her words panicked and hurried, but I couldn't hear them. I hung up, the sudden quiet in the phone booth punctuated by my slow, steady breathing.

As it turned out, Motown couldn't cure everything.

For the first time ever, the score was Reality 1, Oldies Distraction 0.

10

JERRY LEE LEWIS'S CAREER
Posted in PEOPLE by <u>Hugh.jpg</u> on May 17 at 8:34 p.m.

A good general rule of thumb for rock stars (or basically anyone) is to not marry your thirteen-year-old first cousin once removed. Kinda makes it hard for people to like you or your music any more. To paraphrase Jerry Lee Lewis: Goodness gracious, great balls of WHAT IS WRONG WITH YOU.

G iant might not want Killer Ice Cream in the end, but that didn't stop me from panic-obsessing over what my life would be like without the truck.

- No truck meant no routine which meant no hobbies except for Spoiler Alert. This would ultimately lead to me either becoming the uber-evil nerd in *South Park*'s World of Warcraft episode or the utterly horrifying human vegetable in *Se7en*.
- Without the truck, I'd need to get some other job. Everybody knows it's easiest to get a job through nepotism, so I'd have no choice but to take a mail gig

at Dan's dad's law firm, where I'd shotgun so many beers, I'd eventually just turn into a giant can of Natty Lite.

- Killer Ice Cream would be so successful in stores, even Target would carry it. The founder of Target would be like, 'Yo, let's rename Target to Killer Target,' and Ellen would make so much money, she'd finally buy us a mansion in Potomac, one of DC's most expensive neighbourhoods, except we'd each have our own wings of the house and I'd never see her again.
- Post-parents, I had the truck. I had Razz. No truck + no Razz + no parents = the end of Hugh as I knew it.

It was me back at square one. And I didn't know if I could do square one again.

Olivia had re-emerged from the gas station with a map of the entire United States and an armful of snacks: a sharing bag of Starbursts, two Cokes, a bag of Cheetos and a pack of fudge-topped Berger cookies. We'd spent the last twenty minutes in silence as Baltimore faded into suburban Maryland, the crunch of Cheetos between Olivia's teeth and the low, constant hum of the generator in the back the only sounds in the truck.

'What does it feel like when you,' I glanced sideways at Olivia, desperate to get out of my head, 'you know?'

The sound of her reply filled me with relief.

'Bone-stitch?' she said.

'I didn't know it had a name.'

She nibbled the end of a Cheeto. 'It's not exactly the

WebMD diagnosis, but that's what my mom called it.'

'Does it hurt?' I said.

'Not really. It's more tingly and gross rather than painful, kinda like when paint dries on your hands and that first time you flex your fingers, your skin is all tight and crackly.'

Overhead the clouds had split, revealing the kind of bright blue sky that reflected off the dashboard in a blinding cloud of gold.

'When did you first figure out you could do it?' I said, swiping at my watering eyes.

'Is this the part where we play twenty questions?' she asked.

I shrugged.

'I don't know,' she said. 'That's like trying to pinpoint when you first figured out you could breathe.' She licked the Cheeto dust off her fingers. 'I've never really had to think about it. I could always do whatever I wanted. If I was running around with scissors, it didn't matter if I accidentally stabbed myself because I knew whatever happened to me would heal on its own.'

I tried to picture a tiny Olivia running around on the playground like a maniac, her mom standing somewhere on the outskirts of the sandbox not really paying attention because she didn't have to. But imagining a life with a complete and total non-fear of accidentally stabbing myself with scissors and slowly bleeding out near the monkey bars was basically impossible.

I knew how this next question would sound, but I had

to ask it anyway: 'Are you part of the X-Men?'

There was a long pause as Olivia thought this through. Then, finally, she said, 'Did you just ask me if I'm a superhero?'

I leant my head back against my seat and chewed the inside of my cheek. 'They're not really superheroes,' I said. 'The X-Men are more of a weird gang.'

'I'm not an X-Man, or whatever,' she said. 'I'm not a superhero, I'm not a circus freak. I don't know what I am.'

'Then how do you do it?'

'I don't know. It's something I've always been able to do. My mom could do it too.'

'But I thought your mom died.'

Olivia gave a toothless smile. 'Everybody has their weaknesses,' she said.

'What's yours?'

'Jeez, Hugh, not on the first date.'

Biting my tongue, I tried to push away the desire to know. We still had hours of driving ahead of us, which meant there'd likely be other chances to figure out the inner workings of Olivia Moon.

'Has anybody seen you,' I paused, not knowing how to phrase it, 'get hurt like you did falling off the roof?'

'Like that? Not really. Just you and Clark.'

'Not even your dad?'

'It's hard to see things in DC when you live in Atlantic City.'

I frowned. 'If you don't live with your dad then who do you live with?'

'I don't really see what the answer to that has to do with anything, but I'll give you a bonus. I do live with my dad, but he's in Atlantic City five days out of seven.'

That admission deserved forty questions of its own, but I got the sense I was hitting a dead end. I curled my toes into my feet and flexed them again, cracking the little knuckles in my shoes.

Once she finished the Cheetos, Olivia rifled through the snacks at her feet and frowned. 'I went about my snack selection all wrong,' she said. 'I want something chocolatey, but a Berger cookie is gonna be too thick. Wash that down with a Coke and I'll basically go into a diabetic coma.'

'You can have some ice cream if you want,' I said. One scoop wouldn't totally deplete Ellen's supply for Monday. 'The Night Choccer has chocolate ice cream, marshmallow and fudge.'

Olivia's eyes widened. 'Bingo,' she said.

She unclicked her seat belt and leant over the headrest as she groped for the ice cream scooper stashed in a well next to the freezer.

'You're not gonna reach the ice cream from there,' I said. 'Just go in the back.'

'I'm too lazy,' Olivia said. 'And reckless.'

As if to prove her point, Olivia, balancing precariously on the chair's arm, tipped forward and fell into the back of the truck with a yelp, her feet swinging up and almost hitting me in the head.

'Macaulay Culkin!' I shouted. 'Are you OK?'

'Ow, ow, ow.'

Olivia pushed herself up to her knees and slumped against her chair, her hand cradling her chin. A single line of blood trickled down her neck from a centimetre-long cut on her lip.

'What the actual shit are you doing?' I said as Olivia slowly climbed back into her seat. By the time she was there, feet on the floor, the cut had already disappeared, leaving in its place a smear of blood that was drying into the neck of her T-shirt.

'Calm down,' Olivia said. She flicked down her sun visor and examined her bloody face in the mirror. 'I'm fine.'

'Yeah but like, you do get you could do less stupid shit and not get hurt in the first place, right?'

Olivia looked at me, eyes glinting. 'Where's the fun in that?'

I shook my head. 'Am I supposed to find that cool?'

'Clark thought it was.'

'Well, I don't think getting hurt is cool. In fact, I think it's the opposite of cool.'

'Yeah, I heard about your thrilling relationship with endings.' She swiped at the blood on her chin and neck with her T-shirt before snapping the visor back into place. 'You and me, we're like the perfect rivals,' she said. 'I don't feel anything and you feel too much.'

'I do not feel too much,' I grumbled.

Olivia glanced over at me. 'What happened to your parents?' she asked.

At my widened eyes, Olivia tried to shrug.

'What?' she said. 'I've answered your questions. Can we just agree it's my turn?'

Her face, now blood-free, was a mask of curiosity. In that second, it was somehow clear to me she wasn't trying to taunt me or even just ask about my parents because she knew she had to, like Becky and everyone else did after my mom and dad died. The only thing on Olivia's face was a question mark.

'They got in a car accident,' I said.

For the most part, her expression stayed frozen and focused, but I thought I might've detected a wince.

'Ouch,' Olivia said eventually. 'Did the other guy die too?'

I opened my mouth to answer, but swallowed down the response. It never occurred to me that Olivia might not actually know how my parents died. For a long time, it felt like it was headline news in our neighbourhood, as though someone had sent out an email chain that threatened eighteen years of bad luck if people didn't forward it to at least thirty other people. It was alive in everyone's faces at school, too, as they watched me in the hall, in Spanish class. But depending on who Olivia was hanging out with that second, maybe it somehow hadn't reached her.

'No,' I said slowly, my eyes trained on the distant line where the sky met the road, 'it was, uh, kind of a crazy story.' My heart was pounding, the story tasting rotten in my mouth. 'They were driving on the Woodrow Wilson Bridge, you know, that crazy big one in Virginia.'

Olivia nodded.

'They were driving and it was really dark. All of a sudden, this car is coming down the wrong side of the road; I don't even know how it happened, but the other driver was drunk. My dad is driving, and the car is coming straight at him and he goes to swerve out of the way, but there's a school bus next to him. The only way to survive is by hitting these kids, but if he does that, they'll probably die too.' Now that I'd gotten started, there was no way to stop. My brain was spinning in circles as the story poured out of me, the image of my parents making that split-second decision as real to me now as Olivia sitting next to me. 'So instead of hitting them, my dad just kept going straight until the other guy crashed into them head on.' I cleared my throat, my eyes stinging with tears at the image of my parents crushed up like melted Barbie dolls on the dashboard. 'They died instantly.'

For once, Olivia seemed at a loss for words. There was no sarcasm or bite. But while Olivia was quiet, something inside my chest unlocked. Getting this story out, telling her this about my parents, left me feeling weirdly lighter.

'Damn,' she said after a few seconds of silence. 'That's horrific.'

'It's OK,' I said quickly, even though it wasn't. 'It was their twentieth wedding anniversary.'

'Oh,' Olivia said, then added, 'so no big deal. But I guess if you're gonna go out, that's a pretty badass way to do it. Saving a bus full of kids.'

I weighed up her words. She kind of had a point. 'I mean, I guess,' I said. 'But they still died suddenly. And horribly. And needlessly, all because some stupid asshole thought getting hammered and going out for a joyride was cool.'

The lightness in my chest was replaced by a swelling anger at the thought. How hard would it have been for him to just get an Uber? To take the Metro?

'So now you live with your sister?' Olivia asked.

I nodded. 'And her idiot boyfriend,' I said. 'Mostly.'

It was Olivia's turn to nod.

'What about you?' I said cautiously, pretending to look in the rear-view mirror at the little red car behind us. 'Your mom . . .'

'Dead,' Olivia said. When she lifted her hand up to push her hair out of her face, one of the brass buttons on her wrist cuffs caught the sunlight. 'D-E-A-D, dead.'

'Does that mean you don't want to talk about it?' I said.

'Ding, ding, ding,' Olivia replied.

I shifted in my seat and coughed, trying not to think about the fact that however Olivia's mom died, it would have to have been really gruesome. Gruesome enough to kill someone that couldn't die. And that Olivia may or may not have the same fate.

'Well,' I said slowly, pushing the thought away. 'I'm really sorry.'

Olivia tilted her head against the window and said into the glass, '*C'est la vie.*'

The solid line of trees edging up along the highway suddenly fell away, swapped for an endless stretch of river.

Down below, the water was a muddy brown, but because of the way the sun stretched across it, it almost looked silver, waveless and glassy, reflecting the craggy surface of the clouds. The only thing separating us from the water was a concrete wall that, if I were standing next to it, wouldn't even reach my waist.

In the passenger seat, Olivia had fallen asleep. Were we still fighting? Had we been fighting in the first place? Now, she was so quiet and still, the calmest I'd seen her over the last few days, so much so that she almost looked like a completely different person.

It was in that moment that I recognized the look on her face. The slumped cheeks leading to slack shoulders and hands that were palm-up on the chair, fingers loose. It was the face of somebody that was finally relaxed, somebody that worked so hard, day after day, to look one way, when they really felt another. It was the face of somebody that was, even for just a second, letting go. I knew that face because I'd worn it so many times before. Or, if I hadn't actually worn it, I'd felt it melt across me in a similar sort of way, slinking down the rest of my body until I was just a spineless puddle of goo.

After my parents died, every day became a constant battle to seem OK. I hated the way my teachers, my neighbours and especially my friends looked at me, the way conversations stopped whenever I walked into a room. That was the worst part, the way they all just stopped, as if time paused, hiccupped, and then picked up again on its train ride to eternal OK-dom. And any time I actually did let the face – the 'I'm super cool about literally everything, why would you even ask?' face – drop, the vibes in the room would go from zero to excruciating in three seconds flat. People knew I was in pain and acted like I was in pain, but if I actually admitted to said pain, I was somewhere on the same level as Kanye West and Satan, in terms of who would you least like to hang out with.

So instead of dropping the face, I dropped everything else. It seemed easier at the time to surround myself with people who if, god forbid, the face dropped for a second, wouldn't act like I'd just burnt a bunch of books. And for the most part, I was realizing, Olivia did the same. She'd dropped everyone around her. Her friends were on a constant rotation, looping around and around on the record player that was Olivia's social life. But for whatever reason, she was still wearing the face, only letting it slip when she gave herself permission to sleep. Or maybe she'd just gotten so used to wearing it after her mom died, she forgot it was even there.

A half hour or so later, Olivia blinked awake.

'Do you ever wonder why people pay to eat spaghetti in a restaurant?' she said softly, twisting in her seat so her spine cracked. 'That's basically the easiest, cheapest meal you could possibly make at home. That's like paying for a PB&J sandwich, which, by the way, people also do.'

I turned to look at her, my mouth open. She was staring out the window at the endless line of trees.

'Do you—' I started to say, but stopped.

Because she did. She remembered that night, our conversation from two years ago. The night Olivia saved my life. That was exactly how it started, with a completely random, bizarre question.

I'd never told anyone about that night because it wasn't something I liked thinking about. In fact, it was something I was actively trying to forget. I didn't want to remember the way I'd felt, the way I stared into my darkened computer screen and recognized myself in its empty reflection. Everything about me was numb, a deep, bottomless void that, no matter what I did, I knew would eventually swallow me whole.

It was the night of my parents' funeral. I was still in my suit, tie cinched so tightly into my collar I ran the risk of decapitating myself. I'd slept-walked through the entire day, following my sister at the cemetery, then back to the house where what was left of my family, friends and some of my parents' co-workers wandered around my living room looking as lost and out of place as I felt. I couldn't bring myself to talk to any of them because there was nothing to say. All I did was sit in my dad's lounger, shrinking into my suit and praying I would disappear every time someone told me how sorry they were.

Once everyone left, I could actually hear the thoughts in my head again. Or really, the silent space where my thoughts were supposed to be. Everything about me felt heavy, dazed and unpredictable, and that was what scared me the most. Not that I was going to kill myself right then or even die, but that anything could happen. And for the first time, I was acutely aware I didn't necessarily have any control over it.

That was when my phone glowed. A message from Facebook had popped up on my screen, just a single line.

Olivia Moon

Have you ever seen dog poop on the sidewalk and thought, good gawd, that dog really needs to go to the vet?

I peered down at my screen for at least thirty seconds, trying to make sense of what she'd said. I hadn't spoken to Olivia Moon in years, and there was nothing in our non-existent interactions that suggested we so much as thought about each other.

My computer screen came to life with a touch to my mouse. I clicked through to Facebook and found her message.

Hugh Copper

What?

Olivia Moon

Have you ever wondered why more people don't use umbrellas when it's snowing? It's all water coming out of the sky

I still didn't know why I answered. The effort it took to type that one word felt like the same needed to push a car over a cliff. Olivia Moon was weird. Everyone knew that.

But this sounded like the babbling of a crazy person, and not just because I barely knew her.

Hugh Copper
I genuinely have no idea what you're talking about

Hugh Copper
Really not a good time

Olivia Moon
Sometimes I just like to spit out my thoughts about the universe back into the universe. It helps them make sense and then it's not on me any more, you know?

Olivia Moon
Where do you keep your thoughts?

Hugh Copper
. . . in my head, usually

Olivia Moon
Ooooh, that's not healthy, you gotta get that shit out before it poisons you

Olivia Moon
Come on, this is your cue, give me your weirdest thought

Olivia Moon
I promise not to judge you

My fingers stuttered on the keys.
My thoughts?
Now that my parents were gone, I was only just starting to realize I had more going on in my head than who

would buy the Malibu for Becky's next party. And it was this realization that paralysed me.

Hugh Copper
OK

Hugh Copper
Do you ever look around sometimes and think, I always thought there'd be more than this?

Olivia Moon
Go on . . .

Hugh Copper
Like, I always thought I'd be cooler than this?

Olivia Moon
Oh, Hugh

Olivia Moon
Every fucking day of my life

We talked like that all night. Beyond those first few lines, I couldn't remember the specifics, but our conversation swerved into the farthest corners of my brain so that by the end of it, we'd seemed to practically cover our entire lives until that very second, minus the whole body-part-regeneration thing, apparently. I might not have known Olivia Moon before, but now she knew everything about me. We didn't talk about my parents, but we didn't need to. I didn't want to. Instead we talked about everything else, carefully sidestepping the one subject that, in that moment, was close to tearing me apart. By the end of our conversation, the numbness wallpapering my lungs was still there, but I was too exhausted to think about it, much less fear it. Instead, I peeled off my suit and fell asleep.

It was the closest I'd ever come to an ending. And Olivia Moon had pulled me back.

Sitting next to me, Olivia was stroking the fabric of her shorts, her face still giving nothing away.

Then I said, 'That night you messaged me. How did you know my parents were dead?'

There was a long slash just below her right shorts pocket that was so big, she could fit her whole hand into it. Olivia poked at it, grabbing the little scruff of fabric edging around the cut.

'Mount Luther was so incestuous, it was kinda hard not to know,' she said.

This stung. I watched the yellow paint on the road in front of us disappear beneath the van at lightning speed, trying to ignore the way my eyes were filling.

Everyone might've known about my parents, but Olivia was the only one who'd said anything. At least anything that wasn't just a bunch of mumbling or hollow apologies.

'And you didn't know how they died?' I said quietly.

Olivia shrugged. 'I didn't want to know.'

'But when I saw you fall off Clark's roof, you didn't know my name.' Even the memory of it made me cringe. 'You called me Hank.'

Olivia laughed through her nose. 'OK, OK, I knew who you were,' she relented. She turned her body to face me. 'I'm going to tell you something very weird and you have to promise you won't think I'm a stalker.'

'I'm not sure I can make that promise,' I said.

She folded her arms across her chest. 'Fine, then you're not gonna know.'

'Fine, I promise I won't think you're a stalker. What is it?'

'OK, so,' she glanced at me through the corner of her eye, 'I may or may not have been basically, more or less, keeping tabs on you over the years. You know, ever since I stopped hanging out with Becky.'

I couldn't help but let the horror show on my face. 'Tabs?'

'You said you weren't going to think I'm a stalker.'

'I don't think you're a stalker,' I said. 'I think you're a straight-up axe murderer.'

Olivia laughed. When she did, the hairs on my arms stood straight, prickling my skin with goosebumps. I quickly smoothed them down, hoping Olivia wouldn't see.

'I don't want to skin you alive, OK?' she said. 'I just always knew you were different. Sam and Becky and all them were just like everybody else, all brainless and boring and acting like the only people who mattered were the ones at their lunch table. But you were interested in other stuff. Like, I remember one time you were arguing with Becky about something dumb, like the best TV show ever made, and you were losing your mind over the fact that nobody had seen *Buffy the Vampire Slayer*. You weren't embarrassed you were the only person who knew about it; you were furious, and I liked that.'

'It *is* the greatest show ever made.'

'Obviously,' Olivia said. 'My mom had all the seasons on DVD and we watched the entire show at least once a year.'

'Who's your favourite monster of the week?' I said.

Each season of *Buffy* always had a general storyline running through each episode, but sometimes they were peppered with totally random monsters that had nothing to do with killing the Big Bad.

'The Gentlemen, duh,' she said.

I groaned. 'Oh my god,' I said, thinking of who were undoubtedly Joss Whedon's creepiest creations: a bunch of bald, smiling dudes that ripped out people's hearts and made it so they couldn't scream for help. 'Please tell me you're not a giant *Buffy* cliché. The Gentlemen are like everybody's favourite villains.'

'What, so you'd rather I lied?'

'I'd rather you weren't so basic.'

Olivia rolled her eyes as she fought off a smile.

'Although that said, *Buffy* does have one of the worst endings of all time,' I said.

'What?' Olivia's eyebrows shot up. 'No, it doesn't. It has the best, most amazing, Buffiest ending ever.'

'Are you kidding?' I said, remembering the final scene. 'The two best characters in the whole show sacrifice themselves in the name of the human race and Buffy and her pals just like, make jokes about the fact that the mall blew up.'

Olivia snorted. 'Every single moment of *Buffy* is a constant stream of insane banter.'

'Well yeah, I guess,' I said. 'But the ending, it just – it just felt really lame.' My words weren't coming out right, my throat closing in around them as I struggled to think. 'It just sort of . . . I don't know . . . it . . .'

'Ended?'

I shot Olivia a glance. 'Well, yeah. Kind of.'

Olivia faked a smile and gave me a look that said, *duh*. 'That's because it was over.' She shook her head and laughed quietly. 'Did you ever think that maybe you don't like the *Buffy* ending not because it's a bad ending, but just because it's an ending? Period?'

'I . . .' I said slowly, my train of thought tying itself up into knots. I'd never really thought about it like that.

But before I could pause on it longer, Olivia waved away our tangent with her hand. 'Never mind,' she said, her wrist cuffs cutting through the air. 'Back to what I was saying, before I was so rudely interrupted.'

'You're right, you're right,' I said, blinking away the thoughts. 'You were explaining why you stalk me.'

'That's *stalked*, past tense,' Olivia said. 'Like, I don't know. You didn't belong with that group, so I guess I was just waiting for you to figure it out. You know, I'd keep an eye on you to see when you finally woke up, if that makes sense.'

I nodded. 'And then I did, after my parents died.'

'Same,' she said. 'I know this sounds stupid, but it kinda

felt like fate that you would see me fall off Clark's roof. Like, after all those years of watching you, you had to be the one to help me get my mom's stuff back.'

My fingers ached as I flexed them over the steering wheel. I hadn't realized I'd been gripping it so hard. Olivia and I had so much more in common than I thought. Razz never complained about answering my phone calls at four in the morning, but he didn't actually understand what I was going through. Losing a parent broke you. Your whole life they were the best proof you had that you would grow up, and when they died before you realized they could, it felt like losing your future. Nothing could ever be certain any more.

'You should've talked to me before that,' I said.

'Yeah, maybe,' Olivia said. She scrunched her shoulders into her ears. I could see through the gap between her sunglasses and face that her eyes were shut. 'But I messaged you that night because I knew what you must've been feeling. Nobody did that for me, and I always wished they had.'

I bit my lip and nodded again. 'Well, thanks,' I said.

Olivia tilted her mouth up into a slight smile. 'You're welcome.'

11

TOYS 'R' US
Posted in MISC. by <u>Hugh.jpg</u> on October 8 at 2:04 a.m.

And there goes the last shred of my childhood. Thanks a shit ton, Amazon.

It was somewhere on the New Jersey Turnpike that I realized the inside of the truck had gone completely silent. Which wouldn't have been that worrying, except for the fact that the truck was *too* silent.

I tilted my head on my shoulder, wondering why the quiet felt so off. As unease crept over me, the reason flashed into my brain with neon colours: the generator powering the freezer in the back wasn't humming, which meant it wasn't running.

In my panic, I swerved the truck to the side of the highway, cutting off two grey cars whose drivers each responded with rage-fuelled honks. As I mumbled apologies under my breath, panic expanded in my stomach like a sponge.

'What're you doing?' Olivia said, swivelling her head.

I was too frantic to answer. Only when I'd put the truck in park, the swells of air rocking us as other cars sped past, did I say, 'The generator isn't running any more.' I scrambled into the back, tripping over my seat and almost diving toward the freezer. 'How?' I said as I rubbed the sore spot on my elbow where I'd slammed it into my chair's armrest. 'How how how how how?'

After buying a second-hand freezer from an ex-ice cream guy on Craigslist, Ellen had rigged up her own generator to power it when the $400 freezer's internal motor died two days later. It was connected by a tangle of colourful wires whose purposes I had absolutely zero knowledge of, except that they shouldn't be frayed and disconnected. Which they were.

'All the wires are unplugged,' I said breathlessly as I felt the freezer's white metal side. Ordinarily it ran pretty hot but now it was only lukewarm. 'How does that even happen?'

'Maybe they came loose,' Olivia said, appearing at my side. She opened the freezer's top and peered down at the tubs before removing one of the lids. Her expression flattened into a grimace as she let out a long, low whistle. 'It's not looking good in here, doc,' she said.

I sprung to my feet and peered down at the ice cream. The top edge of Whipped Cream Wuornos was a pinky liquid line that was just starting to drip.

'It's not totally melted yet,' I said, not quite believing my own words. 'We have to get these tubs into a freezer like right now if we want to save them.' If there was no ice cream, there'd be no meeting for Ellen on Monday. I couldn't deny this thought brought me a teeny-tiny fraction of comfort, but I shook it away. 'Ellen needs this ice cream for Monday, or else she's gonna totally bomb.'

Olivia watched me carefully. 'I literally have no idea what you're talking about.'

'My sister, she's got this stupid meeting on Monday to see if Giant wants to stock her ice cream. No ice cream means nothing to sample.' I slapped the freezer lid closed. 'Don't open that again. We need to keep the cold sealed in.'

'Where are we supposed to get a freezer?' Olivia said. 'Can't you just fix it?'

'I don't know how to fix a freezer. I still eat Chef Boyardee out of the can.'

'Oh my god, wow,' Olivia said. 'We'll come back to that later.'

I knelt down to look at the wires again. At least ten of them were disconnected, their thin silver ends fuzzy and splintered.

I rested my head on the freezer's lid and groaned. 'I'm pretty sure we're being punished,' I said.

'Punished for what?' Olivia asked.

I stood up as far as I could and edged my way back to the front seat. 'For stealing my sister's truck,' I said. 'This is the universe's way of telling me I'm the shittiest little brother ever.'

'Are you still talking about that?' Olivia crawled over the armrest of the passenger seat. 'You didn't steal her truck. She's your sister, so what's hers is yours.'

'She's my sister, not my sister-wife,' I said. 'She spent all the money our parents left her on this truck. It's, like, everything she has.'

At least until it wasn't.

It took every ounce of me not to flinch at the cars rushing by my window. It wasn't hard to imagine the wheels running over my head, brain oozing out of my ears in an orangey pulp.

'We really need to get out of here. Can you look on your phone for—' The memory that we were missing all things phone or GPS hit me and I gritted my teeth. 'Crap,' I exclaimed, then buried my face in my hands. 'Oh, god. How are we going to find a freezer?'

'How does she not have back-up tubs?' Olivia said.

'I mean, she's got a couple, but not the entire stock. There's nowhere to put it in our house; my parents were practically hoarders, so the place is a walking disaster. She usually has to make stuff as and when we need it.'

'Then can't she just make more?'

'Ice cream takes time,' I said. 'You have to pasteurize it and then cool it all back down and' – I shook my head – 'it doesn't matter. But she's trying to get ready for this meeting, she doesn't have all this time to make like eight new batches of ice cream.'

'We need to get to New York. We're only like, two hours away. Max,' Olivia said. 'Besides, this ice cream'll probably be fine until we get there and then you can just hijack some bodega's freezer.'

'These tubs have maybe an hour left,' I said. My fingers

ran across the truck's keys and jangled them as though they were wind chimes. 'If I don't save them, my sister will think I did this on purpose and then she'll actually kill me, and that's not even an exaggeration. She will literally skin me alive and become one of her own ice cream flavours.'

As I said this, the truth to my words sank in. If this all went the way it was heading, not only would I have stolen Ellen's truck, but broken it too and totally screwed her ice cream. Even though she was more or less actively ruining my life with this whole Giant plan, I couldn't just let that happen. I wasn't Loki. All those hours concocting new flavours, all those interviews she gave to gross food bloggers whose final questions always revolved around her plans that night, would be for nothing.

Olivia slid her sunglasses back on to her face. Propping her elbow up on to the base of her window and nestling her knuckles into her forehead, she let out a long sigh.

'I know somewhere we can go,' she said. She pointed to the sign hanging from the highway overpass up ahead. 'It's in Ocean City, AKA the Jersey Shore.'

Images of beefed-up orange dudes and girls with spaceship-shaped hair from MTV took over my head. But the sign above us said Ocean City was only sixty miles away.

'I can work with the Jersey Shore,' I said. 'What's at the Jersey Shore?'

'Maybe something, maybe nothing.' Olivia shrugged. 'There's only one way to find out.' She sat up suddenly and pointed her finger in my face. 'But once we get there, we have to get in and get out. No hanging around. I want to get to New York before I'm forty.'

'I can do that,' I said. 'We'll drop the ice cream wherever we're going and get the truck fixed. This place has a freezer, right?'

'Like I said, maybe.'

Maybe or not, there wasn't a better option. The clock on the dashboard said it was only eleven, and the ice cream could survive if we moved quickly, didn't hit any traffic and sped for all sixty miles. If I did it right, I could get the truck up to seventy miles per hour, but it was going to take a lot of concentration.

My breathing came back slowly as we returned to the Turnpike and I pushed the truck so hard, the back end rattled. The whole time, all I could think was there was still a microscopic chance my sister wouldn't have to murder me after all.

'The Little Sandy Inn?' I said, eyebrows now permanently fused to my hairline. 'This is where we're supposed to put the ice cream?'

The one-storey motel, on a run-down corner of Ocean City, New Jersey, was made of aqua-blue wood with cake-yellow windows and a roof that looked like it would cave in if so much as a seagull landed on it. It was a miracle it was still standing, seeing as the empty parking lot was filled with seagulls. They sat there, mob-like, all twelve million of them, watching me and Olivia with beady black eyes as we stood on the kerb weighing up whether going inside the motel would likely end in our deaths.

'When you said you had somewhere we could go, I thought you meant, like, your estranged cousin's house, not some creepy murder motel.' Just as I said it, the blinds on a window across the parking lot flickered. I crouched my head into my shoulders and muttered, 'Fuck me, this is terrifying.'

'Would you relax? It is not. I know the owner.' Olivia nudged me with her shoulder. 'My family used to come here every summer when I was little.'

'And did you stop because you got bedbugs?'

'No,' Olivia said. 'Getting rid of bedbugs gets easier after the fourth time.' At my narrowed eyes Olivia folded her arms over her chest. 'I'm *kidding*,' she said.

'I really don't think you are.'

Inside, the motel was just as bad. The carpets were a dingy brown-orange and the walls were made out of wood panelling from a seventies horror movie. Behind the concierge counter and the thick glass wall that barricaded it sat a small man in a beige-and-yellow-striped polo shirt, his four remaining strands of hair carefully smoothed over his shiny brown head.

'Can I speak to the manager please?' Olivia propped her elbows up on the counter and dropped her head in her hands.

The man barely looked up from what sounded like a tiny TV stashed somewhere we couldn't see, clearly uninterested in the fact that the girl approaching the desk was wearing a shirt stained with blood.

'Me,' he said.

Olivia's back straightened. 'What happened to Raoul?' she said.

'Gone,' the man said.

'Gone?' Olivia repeated. 'Gone where? This place was his life.'

'Jail, back to Turkey, on vacation,' the man shrugged, but only barely, 'I don't remember.'

I paced away from the counter and did nervous laps around the lobby. A disc-shaped light was hanging above us, letting out a glow that crackled with bugs every few seconds. Olivia followed me into a corner near an obviously broken payphone, her hands tucked under her armpits.

'What're we going to do now?' I hissed. For some reason, I couldn't stop watching the guy behind the counter, even though I was pretty sure he'd already forgotten we were there. 'We can't leave the ice cream here.'

'Just let me talk to him.' She glanced over her shoulder. 'I think I can work something out.'

'How do you know he even has a freezer?' I said. 'This isn't the kind of place with a restaurant. At least not one that doesn't exclusively serve severed heads.'

'Jesus Christ, do you always go from zero to apocalypse?' Olivia said.

'Only when I'm in the Bates Motel!'

Olivia rolled her eyes. 'This is not the Bates Motel, OK? I spent a lot of good summers here.'

From behind the plexiglass, the guy at the front desk

cleared his throat harshly and spat somewhere I couldn't see.

'I just, I can't with this,' I said as I spun on my heels and charged out of the motel, the sunshine stinging my eyes.

Behind me, Olivia let out a sound of frustration before following me. We didn't stop until we reached the middle of the mostly empty parking lot, where I leant against the Killer truck and tried not to think about what my hair would look like when Ellen decapitated me and stuck my neck stump on a spike outside the Columbia Heights Metro Station.

'Everyone's gonna use my mouth as a gum trashcan,' I moaned into Charles Manson's dented forehead.

Olivia slammed her fist into the side of the van, startling me out of my panic. 'Why are you like this?' she demanded from beside me. Her anger was like a force field, crackling hot and electric against the pavement. 'I thought you were supposed to be cool, not some awkward freak that's afraid of his own shadow.'

I winced against the truck's metal door. 'I-I never said—' I stammered.

'I trusted you to get me to New York,' Olivia said. 'You were supposed to help me, not wuss out.' She scraped her feet into the blacktop and laughed darkly. 'And now look – another little bump in the road and Hugh runs away. You like to pretend you're so cool and different, with your grandpa music and your solo mystery dude vibes, but it's all just an act.' She edged closer to me and spun me around so my back slammed into the truck, her finger jabbing my chest. 'Everything about you, it's all fake. It's a cover-up to hide the fact that you're nothing but a scared. Little. Boy.'

Her face pushed in so close to mine, I could feel her breath on my cheeks. I opened my mouth to say something back, but the sound of screeching tyres cut me off. Olivia whirled around so fast, the tips of her hair whipped my face. Her mouth dropped open as a black van peeled into the Little Sandy Inn's parking lot. 'FBI' was detailed on the side in hard white letters, except there was a Y spray-painted over the I.

'Who—' Olivia started to say as the van roared in our direction.

We cowered against the side of the truck as the van sped toward us, stopping less than a foot away from the tips of our shoes. Before it could even fully stop, the van's side door slid open and three guys in black bomber jackets zipped up to their necks and matching aviator sunglasses jumped out.

'Move, move, move!' the fourth guy in the driver's seat shouted through his open window as the other three ran toward us.

The one in front slipped a brown scratchy bag over Olivia's head while the guy directly behind him grabbed her around the waist and yanked her toward the van. As he dragged her backwards, Olivia screamed, her arms pinned down to her sides and her legs kicking helplessly.

As I lunged after her, the final guy elbowed me so hard in the chest, I lost my breath. 'Sir, this doesn't concern you,' he said gruffly.

'What — what're you doing?' I wheezed. 'Where are you taking her?'

The other men didn't answer as they shoved Olivia into the van. As her feet disappeared around the door frame, all I could hear was her swearing loudly and threatening to cut everybody's pinkie fingers off with hedge clippers.

'Subject 348-65 has been apprehended,' the driver said into an oversized walkie-talkie. 'We're heading back to base now.' He waved to the guy holding me back. 'Johnson, let's go.'

As Johnson turned away, I grabbed his shoulder. 'Wait,' I said. 'How does the FBI know about her? Are you going to take her away to do secret tests?'

The man swivelled back toward me, his forehead creased. 'FBI?' he said slowly. 'We're not FBI. The van clearly says FBY.'

I frowned. 'You obviously just spray-painted a Y over the I.'

The guy forced a laugh. 'What? No we didn't.'

'Yes, you did.'

'Johnson, get in the van!' the driver barked.

The final not-FBI agent jogged back toward the van and dove inside. 'He knew we were FBI,' I heard him shout to another agent. 'I told you the van wouldn't fool anybody.'

As the van's door slid back into place I shouted, 'What the fuck is going on?' But before anyone could answer, the tyres squealed backwards, flooding the air with the smell of burnt rubber.

And then, just as quickly as it had arrived, the van disappeared down the street in a cloud of exhaust. In the silence it left behind, all I could hear was the faint rumbling of carnival rides from the boardwalk and a car backfiring down the street. Olivia was gone.

THE END

. . . 'This is not the Bates Motel, OK? I spent a lot of good summers here.'

Olivia picked at a piece of egg-coloured paint flaking off the walls.

'Granted, it didn't look like cancer on wheels back then, but still,' she said. 'A freezer's a freezer, right? As long as it's cold, we're good, and we can keep driving to New York. Just let me do my thing.' She began backing away toward the counter again, hands raised in surrender.

'I can't watch this,' I said, and stumbled outside, feeling like I was going to be sick.

The kerb was warm and grainy underneath my jeans, but I barely noticed it above the heaving feeling in my stomach. Eyes on the street bordering the motel, I half expected the spray-painted FBY van to come squealing around the corner.

A few minutes later Olivia emerged from the lobby and sat beside me on the kerb.

'Done and done,' she said. 'One freezer, at your service.'

My head snapped toward her. 'He's letting us use the freezer?' I said.

Olivia nodded. 'Yep. And in exchange, we've got the honeymoon suite booked for the night.'

'Excuse me?'

'It was the only way he'd agree to let us use the freezer. It was like a "this bathroom is for customers only" type of deal. But the freezer's in the kitchen, and I've been reassured by Emilio there are approximately zero severed heads inside.'

'Emilio?' I said.

'Raoul's body snatcher.'

'Oh.' I nodded. 'But what about New York?'

We really were less than two hours away, and yet somehow, we'd gotten off track again. It almost didn't seem possible.

'What about it? Just because we have the room booked doesn't mean we actually have to stay here. You said so yourself, we'll get the truck fixed and start moving again. We can grab the ice cream on the way back.'

Recorded audience laughter and a wah-wah sound rang out from the TV behind me. 'You really think Mr All-My-Friends-Are-Mannequins won't eat it while we're gone?' I said.

Olivia pursed her lips and pretended to consider this. 'That, I can't promise. But if your sister needs the ice cream so bad, she can just come up here and get it.'

'Yeah, that could work,' I said, 'except for the fact that she doesn't have a portable freezer.' I pressed my fists into my eyes. There was only one thing left to do. 'I'm gonna have to call Ellen and tell her what happened. There's no avoiding it.'

'Whoa, whoa, whoa, pump the brakes, Mr Apocalypse,' Olivia said. 'We'll just find a mechanic.'

'What, by looking up Ice Cream Truck Generator Mechanic in the phone book? Only Ellen will know who to call.'

'I was thinking Google, but we can go old school.'

'Yeah, Google with what phone?'

At this, Olivia sighed. 'OK, fair point,' she said. 'Fine. Then I'll leave that super-fun family phone call to you.'

Olivia placed her hands on her knees and pushed herself to her feet. When I looked up, her shape was almost totally blocking out the sun, her skinny shadow ringed with yellow. She bobbed from foot to foot, an electric current running up her legs.

'I am the Yes Man, Hugh! Or, the Yes Woman. I'm making things happen. Now I just need to book the room.' She held out her hand, palm up, and waggled her empty fingers toward me. 'Credit card, please.'

12

THE MATRIX

Posted in MOVIES by <u>Hugh.jpg</u> on December 11 at 1:12 a.m.

Oh good, Keanu Reeves can fly. The ending of what was basically one of the most epic, mind-blowing movies of the 1990s consists of the main character Superman-ing his way into the sky for absolutely no reason. Excellent.

I was pretty sure at least eight people had been murdered in our motel room. The blue carpet, so worn down it was almost as flat and solid as the concrete underneath it, was more covered with unidentified black stains than not, and the wallpaper, printed with little brown stars, was peeling in big, powdery strips. A long sliding glass door covered with a red velvet curtain led out to a balcony, while inside there was a desk, two nightstands and a random plastic chair that looked like it was stolen from the DMV. In the middle of it all was a huge heart-shaped bed attached to a coin machine.

'Aren't you gonna carry me through the door?' Olivia

asked, outstretching her arms. 'This *is* the honeymoon suite.'

'Pass.'

Olivia tossed her bag on the floor and took a running dive on to the bed's bright red comforter, starfishing out so her Converse-covered feet dangled over the edge. I pushed open a second door beside the front one and flicked on the orangish light to investigate. Bathroom.

'Do you think Emilio hides in the ceiling and watches the guests every night?' I asked, turning the light off again just as a fat fly crashed into the mirror above the sink.

'I would bet my life on it.'

Olivia dropped a few quarters into the coin machine and watched the squat metal pillar expectantly.

'What does that even do?' I said, sitting beside her.

Just as I finished the sentence, the wall behind us began to hum, and before I knew it, the whole bed was vibrating. I jumped off and spun around to look at Olivia, who was still sitting on the bed as it wobbled from side to side. A giant grin had spread across her face, her teeth rattling in her jaw.

'I think I can feel my spine disconnecting,' she said as she flopped back on the bed, her entire body shaking.

'I thought they only had vibrating beds in movies,' I shouted over the noise.

'Every year, me and Mom saved up quarters for these machines. One year we had so many, we didn't even have enough time to use them all. It was just one long back massage for the whole vacation. Dad *hated* it.'

Her eyes shut as the blissful smile returned to her face. After a few minutes, the bed went quiet again, and Olivia pushed herself upright.

'Well,' she said, a little out of breath. She nodded her chin toward the phone on the nightstand. 'It's now or never.'

She was right. It was time to tell my sister what'd happened, that the tubs were safe, but only just barely. Olivia and I had had to scrape what was left of the ice cream into plastic shrimp containers Emilio had stacked up in a corner beside a mop bucket and rat traps. We filled the containers to their tops so that, when the lids were sealed, ice cream oozed out from the sides. Only Banana Bundy had some left over, which Olivia promptly ate with her hands. Ellen wouldn't be happy, but it was better than letting it all melt.

I sank back down on to the bed and stared at the plastic salmon-pink phone and its circular dial sitting on the nightstand.

'Do you and the phone need to be alone?' Olivia said.

The sounds of ominous organs were swelling in my ears. 'No,' I said over them, 'I think I need support during this trying time.'

Olivia patted my back. 'Just remember, if your sister throws you out, you can always stay here.'

I ran my fingers across the digits on the phone, trying to muster up the strength to dial. Ellen would be mad. She would probably scream. Punch something. But other than that, what was the worst that could happen?

- Ellen, super pissed about, you know, the obvious, would let Dan move into our house just to spite me. Stoked to redecorate, he'd make it so every room was themed after a different island in the Caribbean, with his and Ellen's room as Margaritaville, a place Dan genuinely thought was real.
- She'd upload that video of me in second grade singing Britney Spears's 'Lucky' with my shirt knotted around my belly button to YouTube, pointing out the fact that it was definitely not ironic because I, at one point in my life, wrote a letter to Britney asking her to be my girlfriend.
- When I got home, nothing would be there. Not even just that my sister threw all my stuff out into a sad heap on the lawn, but my house would literally be gone. All that'd be left was a smoking pile of rubble after Ellen shot off fireworks in the kitchen and burnt the whole place down.

It was probably best I was breaking the news to her over the phone.

I dialled her number and waited, receiver vibrating against the side of my face. When Ellen answered, I sucked in a deep breath and tried to attempt a laugh but failed.

'So, remember when I said I was hanging out with Razz today?' I said. 'Turns out that was,' I bit my lip, 'well, basically a complete lie.'

After twenty minutes on the phone with my sister, I hung up and sat in silence with the receiver in my lap.

'Was she mad?'

Olivia was pushed up against the bed's headboard, knees pressed into her chest.

'She said "New York?" in the same way she would've said "Kanye West's sex dungeon?"'

Olivia grimaced. 'Yikes.'

When I called, Ellen sounded as though she'd been eating nothing but sandpaper all day. Her voice was scratchy and exhausted, words muffled into the phone.

'I don't even know how to deal with this,' she'd said. 'I mean, how does one deal with this?'

'The ice cream's safe—'

But Ellen wasn't listening to me. She was too wound up in her own panic.

'I'm gonna have to make all the ice cream from scratch. I mean, what other option do I have? I'm gonna have to call Jake, tell him I've got the measles or something and I can't work the double he's had me scheduled on for like the last three weeks, and then I'm going to have to hole myself up in the kitchen like Gollum and remake every goddamn ice cream flavour. I won't sleep. I just can't sleep.'

'Don't do that,' I insisted. 'We're driving back tonight.'

'Like fucking shit you're driving back tonight. That truck only made it like a hundred miles before it crapped out. I'm not letting you drive all the way up to New York and then back again. I'm finding you a mechanic and until then, you're staying in Jersey for the night and New York tomorrow. I'm calling Aunt Karen.'

Aunt Karen was my mom's sister. She lived in a tiny

144

apartment in Manhattan right next to Central Park, but I hadn't seen her in what felt like a million years.

'What? No, you don't need to call Aunt Karen. The truck's fine. It's the generator that's broken.'

'Nope. Absolutely not. I have even less faith in your driving abilities than I do in the truck. The guy who complains about driving in sunglasses going like five hundred miles in a day? Ha!'

'But then how will you get the ice cream back in time for your meeting if we stay in New York tomorrow?'

'My meeting's not until the afternoon. You leave before the sun comes up, and maybe I won't disown you.' Ellen gave a manic sort of laugh. 'And who is this *we* you're helping? You keep saying we. Who is we?'

Olivia had been watching me the whole time, her eyebrows raised in concern.

'It's this girl from school,' I said into the phone. 'I have to help her get her stuff back in New York. The rest of it – you wouldn't believe me even if I explained.'

'You know what, you're probably right. There's a lot about today I don't believe. Starting with the fact that my little brother is more of a sociopath than Jeffrey mofo-ing Dahmer.'

'That's sort of a stretch,' I said.

'Is it a stretch?' Ellen said. 'Is it actually? You stole my truck even after you knew about the biggest godforsaken meeting of my life.'

No matter how loud or dramatically I'd complained, begged and even threatened, Ellen wouldn't budge. She didn't care that it was the generator's fault the ice cream had been at risk. She wasn't taking any chances.

Ignoring her and leaving for New York with both middle fingers pointed at the rear-view mirror was still an option, but it was a thought so stupid, I didn't even bother acknowledging it. I was lucky Ellen was still talking to me in the first place.

'OK, so, slight setback.'

I swivelled around on the bed, but the look on Olivia's face told me she already knew what I was going to say. Which wasn't that surprising, since she'd been sitting behind me for the entire conversation.

Her eyes were bright and her jaw was clenched shut. 'I told you not to call her. We have to go now,' she said.

'Ellen wants us to stay here until she can find a mechanic.'

'And how long's that gonna take?'

'I don't know.' I glanced away from her, gaze landing on the square glass box that held the light bulb in the ceiling. It was dotted with little black smears that were almost definitely dead moths. 'She said she'd see what she could do, but we shouldn't hold our breaths. It's Saturday, so the mechanic probably won't come until later tonight, and by then, there won't be any point going to New York because Clark's show will already be over and we don't even know where he'll be.'

'Brooklyn,' Olivia insisted.

The comforter underneath us was scratchy and thick, like the material for a bathrobe. I kept my head down as I raked my fingernails against it, trying to mask how desperate I was not to argue.

'You want us to search all of Brooklyn for Clark Thomas?' I said.

'It's not that big.'

'Brooklyn is huge,' I said. 'There's no way we'll find him. Forget the haystack; that's like finding a needle in the ocean.'

'Then what do you suggest we do?'

As if in answer, a door slammed down the hallway and the radiator in our room began to hiss.

'We'll have to stay here tonight,' I said above the whistle of air. 'I mean, we already paid for the room.'

What else were emergency credit cards for if not to pay for motel rooms whose walls were almost certainly infested with ghosts?

'Here?' Olivia said, eyes bugging out of her head. 'You want to stay here? At the Bates Motel?'

'You were the one who said this place wasn't going to murder us,' I said.

I was almost petting the comforter by then, fingers picking at a hard, unidentified grey spot.

'Yeah, that was before I knew I had to actually sleep here.' Olivia's foot thumped against the bed so the springs squealed. 'Hugh, we don't have time for this. Clark's band is going on tonight.'

'Yeah, and tomorrow night. We'll get the crate back then.'

'But what if they're so terrible the venue doesn't want

them to come back for a second night? You've never heard them before. Clark's voice is awful.'

'That part, I don't doubt,' I said.

But there was nothing I could do, nothing I would do, to make my sister more upset than she already was, and Olivia knew it. If Ellen wanted us to stay here for the night, then I'd do it. I'd already betrayed my sister for Olivia that day. It was Olivia's turn to sit this one out.

Sensing defeat, Olivia flushed red. She brushed down her shorts so they covered her knees, leant over and grabbed her bag from the floor, then slung it over her shoulder.

'Where're you going?' I said as she made her way toward the door.

Olivia hissed out a breath. 'If we're not going anywhere tonight, I at least need to get out of this room. I feel like I'm being eaten alive.'

'But Ellen wants us to stay here.'

Olivia whirled around and retrieved her hat from her pocket.

'Correction,' she said as she smushed the hat down on her head. 'She wants *you* to stay here. She didn't say anything about me.'

The door slammed behind her as her footsteps faded down the hallway. 'I don't want to stay here either,' I shouted, but I knew she was already too far away to hear.

I threw my body back on to the bed and curled my hands into fists. Us staying in New Jersey wasn't just a wrench in Olivia's plans, or even for Ellen and the ice cream. It kicked up a whole new problem.

Because it didn't just mean we wouldn't get to Clark until tomorrow. It meant I wouldn't get to say goodbye to Razz.

'Where the eff have you been?' Razz said. 'How many times does a human being have to call you before you decide that yes, that human being is worthy of your acknowledgement?'

Razz's sarcasm at the sound of my tentative hello almost made things worse; sarcasm was the best I could hope for once he heard my news. The next logical step was rage.

'My phone kind of fell out a window,' I said.

But Razz wasn't really listening. 'If we don't start binging *The Hobbit* now, we're only gonna make it through movie two, and you know that's the worst one,' he said. 'I've already opened the Birthday Cake Oreos. They're the only thing that've been keeping me going after watching not one but two ladies from my grandma's hula-hooping class have a heart attack in their talent show this morning. And yes, if you're wondering, the show did go on. Literally.'

Still lying on the bed, I propped my knees up and gave an uneasy laugh.

'When are you coming over?' Razz asked.

I swallowed. It was do or die.

'I'm in Ocean City,' I said slowly.

'Maryland?' he said.

'New Jersey.'

With a deep breath, I word-barfed the Olivia saga into the phone, minus a few key points. Namely, the bone-stitching thing. Razz sat through it all quietly, his soft, rhythmic breathing the only indication he was even still there.

'The generator broke down and now I'm stuck here until tomorrow,' I said, heart beating fast. 'We can't even go to New York till then, but I'll be back in DC tomorrow night.'

I'd already resolved I wasn't staying with my aunt Karen in New York. There wasn't time. Despite what Ellen said, I was a perfectly acceptable driver. Plus, Olivia was right; the eighties did give us cell phones. The truck would be fine.

'Do I even need to say I won't be in DC tomorrow night, or did you get a brain injury and forget?' Razz said.

'Yeah, I know. I mean, no, you don't need to say that, because I know. I don't want to stay here, believe me, and Olivia *definitely* doesn't—'

'Oh, I'm so sure you're super psyched to end your alone time with Columbia Heights' very own manic pixie dream girl. This is the guy who has the world's biggest boner for it-girls.'

This comment, so out of nowhere, threw me off.

'What?' I said, trying to blink some sense into his words. 'I do not have a boner for it-girls.'

'Uh, yeah you do. First Becky Cayman and now Olivia. With Becky, you become this knuckle-dragging Neanderthal. At least she has enough sense to know she's just pretty. Olivia thinks she's some hipster enigma. I mean, changing your clothes every four weeks? What is this, a Taylor Swift music video? Olivia doesn't even have the audacity to be original, much less know how unoriginal she is.'

'Where the hell is this coming from?' I said. 'You don't know what you're talking about.' There were so many insults flying, I wasn't sure which was more annoying. 'That whole outfit thing was high school.'

'OK, first of all, high school was three months ago. And second of all—'

'Dude, you don't even know Olivia,' I said as I knocked my knees together. 'She's not like that.'

'Oh, she's not like that, she's misunderstood, boo-hoo.' Razz gave a hard, shallow laugh. 'God, you're so predictable. How did I not see this coming?'

I'd never heard him like this before, so mad and mean. It was unexpected and jarring, like a cat that suddenly talked or Michael Myers putting his knife down in the middle of *Halloween* and asking Jamie Lee Curtis if she wanted some Jell-O.

'Why are you being like this?' I said.

'Because we were supposed to spend my last night in DC together. You're supposed to be my best friend, and now you ditch me for some girl you saw scaling a house two days ago? Are you kidding me?'

'I'm sorry, am I hallucinating?' I said, blinking. 'What are you actually talking about? You're the one who's going to California. You don't need me.'

'Yeah, because that's logical,' Razz said. 'I'm moving to a state where I know zero actual people and I won't need you any more. My literal only friend. Why can't you just admit you're choosing Olivia Moon over me? And you'd choose Becky too, I can guarantee it.'

'I'm not choosing anyone,' I said. 'My sister wants me to stay here until the truck can get fixed.'

'Yeah, and if saying bye to me was important to you, you'd figure something out. You're a smart dude. You just like to pretend you're helpless and lame.'

'This has nothing to do with you,' I said, 'and even less to do with Becky Cayman. God, you're like, obsessed with her. You'll use any excuse to bring her into things when she's not even on the same planet as this conversation.'

'I am not obsessed with Becky Cayman,' Razz said, fury shaking in his voice.

I rubbed my knuckles against my legs, eager to push my weight into something.

'Then why are you always talking about her? You wanna know what I think? I think you're jealous she has a bunch of friends and you don't have anyone.'

There was a long, anger-filled pause as Razz breathed loudly into the phone. My tongue felt heavy in my mouth as my brain tripped over the words I'd just said. The words I couldn't take back.

'Except me, obviously,' I said. 'You have me.'

'If you knew, even for one second,' Razz said, every word eking out of his mouth slowly, 'what you're actually talking about, you would never say I'm jealous of Becky

Cayman ever again.'

'Razz, you're not even making sense,' I said. 'Look, I didn't do any of this to hurt you. Can you please just—'

'Whatever, dick.'

A surprised laugh bubbled up from my throat.

'Wow, good one,' I said as I sat up, shoulders rolled back. 'I was gonna say, if you could just stick around until tomorrow night I'll come over and say goodbye, but I think "Whatever, dick" probably sums it up.'

'Yeah, I think it does,' Razz said. 'Have a great time in what is literally the most disgusting place on earth.'

'Ditto,' I shouted back.

The silence of Razz ending our call reverberated in my head. Staring down at the receiver, lying limp and quiet in my hand, I couldn't help but think I was dreaming. Then the dial tone kicked in and everything came crashing down.

13

TAMMI TERRELL

Posted in PEOPLE by <u>Hugh.jpg</u> on June 17 at 10:57 p.m.

Tammi Terrell was only twenty-four when she died. By twenty, she was signed to Motown and was twenty-one when she recorded 'Ain't No Mountain High Enough' with Marvin Gaye. It didn't matter what she'd done, who she was, or what she was supposed to do. That she deserved more. A brain tumour killed her. Like they do.

By the time Olivia came back, the sun was setting over the 7-Eleven across the street, leaving in its place a fuzz of neon-white lights that glowed from beyond. Even though I'd never been to Ocean City before, I knew it was the boardwalk creating the haze. We'd passed it on our way in, its hot-dog stands, arcade games and carnival rides crammed with tourists who were eager to suck dry the remaining drops of summer.

With the clock on the nightstand broken, I didn't know what time it was any more. The only thing burning in my mind as I lay on the bed and stared at the water-stained ceiling was Razz.

When the door swung open, signalling Olivia's return, I lifted my head from the pillow. In her arms, she carried a bucket of fried chicken and a jumbo-sized Slurpie whose contents had turned her entire mouth blue.

'What're you wearing?' I said.

Olivia shoved my legs off the bed and sat in their empty place, forcing me to pull myself up into a sitting position as she plopped the bucket of chicken down between us. Her khaki shorts had been replaced by what looked like a pair of men's swimming trunks, their blue fabric printed with little surfers that caught waves up and down her thighs. On top, she was wearing one of those oversized T-shirts that were spray-painted with the cartoon bodies of someone else; in this case, it was a gorilla wearing a yellow polka-dot bikini.

'Here,' she said, ignoring me, 'I got us dinner.'

Her fingers, glistening with grease, shook the edge of the bucket so the pieces of chicken danced inside. I plucked up a leg and took a bite, sighing at the taste. I didn't have the strength to mention what'd happened with Razz. The strength or the dignity.

Within a minute, the chicken leg was reduced to bone in my hands. I dropped it on to the nightstand and grabbed another.

'Are you still mad?' I said as I took a bite.

Olivia tilted her head from shoulder to shoulder, top teeth gnawing her lip. 'Do I wish your sister wasn't holding us captive in New Jersey?' she said. 'Sure. Am I frustrated? Yeah, maybe. But do I want to talk about it? No, not really.'

The chicken lowered from my mouth as I tried to follow her train of thought.

'So . . .' I trailed off.

'It doesn't matter.' Olivia cleared the air with a wave of a fried chicken breast, little crusts of skin flaking off on to the bed. 'Look, I'm sorry I've been so pushy about getting to New York. I just need that stuff back. It's all I have left of my mom.'

With the sudden drop in Olivia's voice, she set the chicken down on her lap and glanced at her shirt, finger tracing a bikini strap.

'I know, and believe me, I want to get it back too,' I said. 'I don't know what I'd do if somebody took all my parents' stuff. Granted, most of it is actual junk, but I'd probably rather have their collection of taxidermy mice than not.'

Olivia laughed. 'If Clark took your parents' things, you'd go after them.' she said.

I leant back on the bed. 'I mean, I'd like to think I would,' I said. 'But part of me thinks it's better I'm helping someone else do it first. If I were doing it for myself, I'd probably just come up with eight million excuses as to why I'd be fine without it. This way, I don't want to let you down.'

'Aw,' Olivia said in a high-pitched voice. 'You like me. You really like me!'

'Don't get used to it,' I said. 'I mostly just love fried chicken.'

156

'That's because you're human.'

I wiped my hands on the bedspread. 'Where'd you go?' I read the side of the bucket. 'Besides Southern-Fried Chicken Bros and 7-Eleven?'

Olivia adjusted the straps of her hat, which were tied around her neck. 'Everywhere and nowhere,' she said. 'But let me tell you, that is not the New Jersey I remember.' She picked up a chicken leg and held it in front of her mouth. 'Is it weird that I'm kinda nervous about going to New York?'

I swallowed a mouthful of Slurpie and frowned. 'You're telling me this now?'

'I used to go to New York all the time. My grand-parents live there, so we'd visit them for Thanksgiving and the Fourth of July, and we'd go to all the stupid parades and firework shows over the Brooklyn Bridge. But when my mom died—'

A knock on the door cut Olivia off. We swapped glances, chicken dangling mid-air.

'Do you think that's the manager?' I said. My teeth were cold and my mouth was sour from the Slurpee.

'He wants even less to do with us than we want with him,' Olivia said quietly.

I focused my eyes on the door, but didn't stand. For some reason, my heart was pumping in my throat, hands clutched around my knees and fingernails leaving half-moon prints in my jeans.

'Maybe it's the mechanic,' Olivia said, a bare chicken bone caught between her fingers.

Swallowing, I stood. The knocking had resumed again, so loud it wasn't even a request any more; it was a command, just a never-ending stream of impatient pounding.

'OK, OK,' I said to the knocker, trying to muster some form of courage. 'Of course there's no peephole, because that would be way too convenient.'

I swung the door open but froze, the urge to slam it tingling in my fingers.

Taking in a deep, shaky breath, I stepped backwards. Standing on the other side of the threshold, his stupid leather jacket slung over his stupid shoulder, was Dan, Dan the Tax Lawyer Man.

Dan and I walked out to the parking lot in silence, a black, rectangular toolbox tucked under his arm. Dressed in bright-pink pants and a light denim shirt unbuttoned far enough down that it revealed a triangle of chest hair, Dan looked like he'd come straight from a frat party. He stopped short of the truck and waited as I climbed into the driver's seat and unlocked the hood. Once the hatch was open, he disappeared behind the hood without a word.

After a few seconds of listening to Dan's tools clink against the engine, I swallowed and said, 'What're you doing here? I thought Ellen was finding an ice cream truck mechanic.'

Dan didn't emerge from behind the hood as he gave his answer. 'Yeah, well, turns out that's not so easy on a Saturday,' he said.

'Do you even know what you're doing?' I said as I climbed out of the truck.

'More than you do.'

The urge to roll my eyes was overwhelming.

'I tried to tell Ellen there's nothing wrong with the truck. The generator just died.'

I slammed the door behind me and leant against it, still not ready to actually stand next to Dan. Something about his arrival in New Jersey felt like an intrusion, as if he were once again prying his way into somewhere he didn't belong.

Instead, I watched the street. Even though the air was warm, tempered by a salty breeze that swept over from the boardwalk a few blocks away, a chill crept up my arms, covering my skin in a thousand nervous little bumps. The streets bordering the motel were heavy with people, mostly crowds of dudes in tank tops and women in those confusing towel dresses, their sandals scuffing along the sidewalk where sand had somehow invaded far from the beach. The street lamps were on, the slow descent into night turning the sky the colour of a bruise. Through the haze, I could still see people's tan lines and the angry red sunburns edging around them.

'Ellen's not really in the mood for taking you at face value right now,' Dan said.

His voice had an edge to it I'd never heard before, miles and miles away from the puppy-dog tone he usually pulled with my sister.

'Is she really mad?'

Dan stood suddenly, his body pulled taut in one over-sized muscle. The movement sent a wrench clattering on to the pavement.

'What do you think, Hugh?' he said, arms out wide. 'Would you be pissed off if your brother stole your truck two days before the biggest meeting of your life?'

A sudden gust of steam rushed through my chest. 'If it's that big of a deal, just take the truck back,' I said, hoping desperately he wouldn't take me up on the offer.

'Believe me, I tried to convince Ellen she should,' he said. 'I wanted to come up here and drive the truck back without you, see how you like being totally stranded. But Ellen insisted you'd bring it back on time, even though she has absolutely no reason to trust you.'

This time, my eyes rolled on their own. 'Says the guy who showed up in our lives ten minutes ago,' I said.

Dan barked a laugh. 'I don't need to have been here for longer than ten minutes to see what you're doing. You just conveniently hijack your sister's truck after finding out she needs it for this huge, possibly life-changing meeting?' He pointed at me with a grease-covered finger. 'Poor Hugh doesn't want Ellen to sell the truck because he'd actually have to find something to do with himself.'

'You want to talk about hijacking?' The cold was offi-cially gone from my arms, replaced by a flood of warmth that made my skin itch. 'Ellen and I can't even say hi to each other without everything being about you. It's like, *Oh good morning Hugh, say something nice about Dan or he'll cry again.* You can't stand it when me and my sister talk about anything that doesn't involve you.'

'And that makes me such a shitty person,' he said. 'I'm sorry I want to actually know what we're talking about when I'm having a conversation.'

'Not everything has to be about the law and keg stands,' I said.

'I'm not asking you to stop talking about the things you guys like. I'm just asking you to explain it to me.' He waved his arms in half-circles, his usually perfect hair dishevelled and frizzy as it flopped around his face. 'Give me a little context.'

'We shouldn't have to explain everything to you,' I said. 'I've known Ellen my whole life. If we sat down and explained every single joke, our entire day would be one giant footnote.'

'But that's what people do, Hugh. When somebody new comes into your life, you adapt. I get you and Ellen have your own thing going, but I just want the three of us to have our own thing too.'

Behind us, a group of guys were singing Neil Diamond's 'Sweet Caroline', their voices one big roar that swallowed up the dusk.

'But why do you have to pout about it all the time? You're like a four-year-old who doesn't want to go to bed before *Buffy the Vampire Slayer*.'

Dan sighed, his arms dangling at his sides. He charged past me to climb into the back of the truck and I followed at his heels.

'OK, I don't always react well, because sometimes it's

really hard being on the outside of you two.' He crouched down on to his knees and began examining the side of the freezer where the wires were split. 'Like that reference, for example. What the hell does that mean?'

Arms folded across my chest, I leant against the door frame. 'When Ellen was little she used to cry if Mom and Dad made her go to bed before *Buffy* played.'

'See?' Dan was firing himself up again. 'You could have just said that.'

The fabric of my hat was suddenly leaving my head sweaty and hot. Raking my nails across the damp, itchy skin, I grumbled, 'I shouldn't have to bend my entire life around you.'

'Asking you to give a little context once in a while is hardly demanding you bend your entire life around me.' He paused to let a pair of boys not much older than me lumber through the motel parking lot, each carrying a six-pack of beer. When they passed, Dan lowered his eyes to the ground and cleared his throat. 'You and me, we both want the same thing for Ellen.'

'You to go away?'

Dan laughed a nasty little sound and rubbed a hand down his face so it scratched against his unusually stubbly cheeks. 'You're unbelievable. Do you know what your sister was like when she called me today? When she found out the truck broke just like you knew it would, she tried getting hold of a mechanic, but none of the garages up here were answering. She was completely panicked because she promised you the mechanic would get here tonight, but she refused to bother me at my barbecue until she was on the verge of a nervous breakdown.'

'I knew it!' I exclaimed. 'I knew you were frat-broing it up today.'

Dan drummed his fingers against the side of the freezer, the motel's outdoor lights pouring in through the dashboard and highlighting his messy hair. 'She's been crying all day,' he said, ignoring me. 'Did you know she won't even think about this meeting on Monday because she's so worried you're face-first in the centre-divider on the Turnpike?'

I lifted my arms out in a wobbly T. 'I'm fine,' I said, suddenly feeling not very fine. 'I told her I could've come back tonight if she just let me keep driving. There's no reason she shouldn't be thinking about the meeting.'

'God, you think everything's about me? Everything's about you!' Dan threw his arms above his head, wrists slapping the ceiling. I flinched, for a second convinced he might actually dive out of the truck and try to hit me. 'Why is everything always about you? Ellen needs her truck this weekend, but you need it more. I apparently get in the way of you and your sister, so I gotta go.' Since we'd started our conversation, more than one person walking by the motel had stopped to eavesdrop, but Dan didn't seem to care. 'Regardless of whether or not you like me, I'm not going anywhere. I know you think fraternities are lame and Coldplay sucks, but I have a good job, I'm not addicted to gambling or porn or crack, and I just want to take care of your sister. I want her to be happy and finally have the chance to pursue her dreams. The same ones she's put on hold for the last two years so she could take care of you.'

I stared at Dan, unable to speak.

He cleared his throat. 'In order for that to happen,' he continued, 'you and I have to get along. But first things first, you need to grow up.'

With this, a renewed sense of outrage rushed through my chest. 'Me?' I said, jaw dropping. 'Says the guy who wouldn't talk to my sister for an entire day after she asked to borrow your jacket.'

That was true. That had actually happened.

Dan dropped one of his tools and swore under his breath. 'That's because I told her, like, fourteen times to bring her own,' he said. 'Whatever, Hugh. You got me. I'm not perfect. I am seventy million miles in the wrong direction from perfect, but I'm trying really hard to be the person your sister needs me to be. And you know what? I might pout sometimes, and I might like Mariah Carey more than you do—'

'More than literally anyone does,' I interrupted.

'—but I will spend the rest of my life making sure I don't hurt Ellen the way you did today.' With that, he leapt out of the truck and scooped up his toolbox. 'The generator's fixed. Some wires just came loose,' he said. His voice was clipped by the motorcycle helmet he crammed down over his head. 'Truck's fine too.'

Dan's motorcycle was parked at the foot of the parking lot near the motel's blinking sign, far beyond the shadow of the ice cream truck's boxy frame. I waited as he strapped the toolbox just behind his seat and swung the kickstand up.

'You don't have to be an asshole,' I shouted after him, but Dan didn't turn back. Besides, the insult felt weak, and I almost wanted to apologize.

Without a wave or another word, Dan was gone in seconds, leaving me feeling the most alone I'd felt all day.

After Dan left, I waited on the kerb outside the motel's lobby, watching the night darken and the air change from salty breeze to cool and sharp. Over the sound of carnival rides in the distance, all I could hear was Dan's voice, accusing me of cartwheeling all over my sister's dreams. Up until today, I would've just dismissed it as a classic Dan pout fest, all everybody-look-at-me, without any truth. But now, I wasn't so sure. Was I standing in the way of Ellen's dreams? Had I done it all – stolen her truck, downplayed her meeting – on purpose?

'Was that the idiot boyfriend?'

Olivia dropped beside me with a thud, hands braced against her knees. I nodded silently, but for once, it felt wrong calling Dan an idiot. He'd been the one to rush up to New Jersey to defend Ellen, to be pissed off on her behalf. And, ultimately, to bail me out.

The rest of me felt dull, numbed by the combination of shame and sheer exhaustion. If I was being honest, I was glad we'd missed Clark's show. I was too tired to navigate the streets of New York.

Dropping my head down to the top of my thighs, I glanced at Olivia. 'The generator's fixed,' I said. 'We can put the ice cream back in the freezer when we pick it up tomorrow on our way to DC.'

'Emilio will be grateful,' Olivia said. She was watching the street, where crowds of people still flocked toward the boardwalk, moths attracted to neon lights and the smell of cotton candy. 'After we load everything back up, how about we get out of here and drive?' At the look of wide-eyed panic filling my face, Olivia smirked. 'Not to New York, Señor Risk Taker,' she said. 'There's a lot of Ocean City yet to be seen.'

I looked down at my wrist, where there wasn't a watch. 'Isn't it kind of late to go out into Jägerbomb Central?' I said. It had to have been close to ten o'clock. 'If we want to make sure we actually drive to New York tomorrow, we should probably get an early start and not go to bed at two in the morning.'

But Olivia was already shaking her head, silencing me with flicks of her white-blonde hair. 'No, no, no,' she said. 'When you need cheering up, time doesn't exist. And you, kid,' she patted the side of my face, the rough leather of her wrist cuffs scratching my jaw, 'need some serious cheering up.' She was watching me closely, one arm wrapped around her legs and feet tapping into the gravel. 'I heard what the idiot said about your sister selling the truck. If these are your last few days in it, we should probably make them count.'

'Were you eavesdropping?' I asked.

Bouncing to her feet, Olivia extended a hand in my direction. Even in the dark, I could see her eyes were glowing.

'Enough to know I'm right.'

14

WHITNEY HOUSTON

Posted in PEOPLE by <u>Hugh.jpg</u> on February 2 at 3:56 p.m.

Anyone who says Whitney Houston's voice wasn't one of the best of all time isn't your friend. It was the sound of liquid gold. She died in a bathtub, and I can't help but think about how cold she must've been, knocked out, unable to call for help. Most deaths are quiet, but hers was painfully so.

Ocean City was an elephant herd of noise and colour, the boardwalk blurring into a crayon melt of reds, pinks, blues and blinding yellows. Music blared from restaurants and bars, swelling so loudly that the crashing waves were just an afterthought in the distance. The carnival rides rose up into the skyline, their sharp metal angles leaving slash marks in the night. Every ride was in motion, the Ferris wheel turning, a roller coaster catapulting down a drop, sending kids screeching with a mixture of terror and glee.

Everything about it, the smell of fried food, the dinging

carnival games, felt familiar, even though I'd never been to New Jersey before. It was the feeling of being a kid, of pure, fearless fun. The rides were mesmerizing even though they could and probably would kill me or at least rip out a good chunk of my hair.

Beside me, Olivia was bobbing in her seat, electrified by the energy outside. The streets were clogged for what felt like miles, leaving us to snail-trail behind a long line of minivans and sports cars. Still, the air between us was thick and alive. We drove the ten blocks between the motel and the boardwalk in silence, Olivia preoccupied with the scenes outside and me having too much fun watching her hilariously ridiculous reactions to literally everything.

'Do you know where we're going?' I said finally after passing the fourth Mexican restaurant offering two-for-one margaritas.

'More or less,' Olivia said. 'You're gonna want to turn here, by this dancing taco.'

She pointed to the corner ahead where, sure enough, someone in a taco costume and a huge foam sombrero was dancing and passing out fliers for what I was 99.9 per cent sure had something to do with two-for-one margaritas.

I followed Olivia's directions until we landed in an abandoned lot, its four corners filled with stained couches, thirty million empty Gatorade bottles and a refrigerator with the words 'KIM K IS JESUS' spray-painted on the side. There weren't any street lamps, so the lot was almost completely pitch-black except for the rainbow glow of the Ferris wheel raining down from a few blocks away.

'Now what?' I said, turning the engine off.

Olivia swivelled toward me in her seat. 'I'm gonna make you a deal,' she said.

'A deal?' I repeated.

'A deal.' She tucked her hair behind her ears. 'So. You're an ending-obsessed dork, yes?'

'I feel like "dork" is a little strong.'

'Fine. An ending-obsessed strange person. Better?'

'Barely. But I also wouldn't say I'm obsessed. My thing with endings can be best described as an interest at most. Would you say Leonardo DiCaprio is obsessed with acting?' I gave her a pointed look. 'No, it's just what he does.'

Olivia shook her head. 'Wow, so much to unpack there,' she said. 'First, are you comparing yourself to Leo DiCaprio?'

'Well, no.'

'Second, acting is his job. He gets paid for it. Do you get paid to be so scared of leaving Washington, DC that you basically hyperventilate your way through Baltimore?'

'I'm not scared, I just—'

'No, you don't. So, now that I think about it, what I'm proposing isn't actually a deal. It's more of a challenge. I want you,' she pointed at me, as though there was a crowd around us and she needed to specify who she was talking to, 'to go in there. With me.' Olivia gestured behind her.

'What—?'

I turned. On the other side of the lot's fence was a giant domed building beaming Batman-style searchlights into the sky. An old-school sign framed in bright purple lights announced it as, MR MONKEY'S WORLD-FAMOUS CLUB & CASINO.

I looked back and forth between Olivia and the Vegas-wannabe casino. 'No,' I said. 'No, no, no, no, no. I cannot go into,' I swallowed, not even sure my brain would let me say it, 'Mr Monkey's World-Famous Club and Casino.' To my surprise, saying it aloud actually gave me a little relief, as if getting the words out of my head meant my body had expelled some kind of poison.

Olivia folded her arms across her chest. 'Not with that attitude you can't.'

Cars were coursing past us and into the Mr Monkey's parking lot, horns honking and lights flashing like it was Woodstock for the clinically depressed.

'I thought this was supposed to cheer me up,' I grumbled.

'It will in the long run. Look, I just think you need to get over this whole ending thing. Just because you take a risk sometimes doesn't mean you're going to die. If you were to bite it right now, all they'd write on your tombstone is, "He Was Aiming for Predictability".'

'Don't talk about dying,' I said, clutching my shirt. 'It gives me heartburn.'

'I mean, think about it. Everything around you is changing anyway, even with you sitting still. Sometimes things happen and you just have to go with it.'

I bit my lip. I knew this. Didn't she know I knew this? All I'd ever done over the last two years was deal every stupid day with how much my life had changed and there was nothing I could do about it. Didn't she get that by just being alive, I was going with it? Who cared if I had to mitigate stuff a little bit in order for the whole thing to be digestible?

'What do you have against Mr Monkey's?' Olivia continued. 'Have you ever *been* to Mr Monkey's?'

'No, but I don't need to. I'm pretty sure I know what I'm gonna find.'

From the looks of it, everybody in there was at least fifty and so sunburnt, their skin resembled beef jerky. Whenever the automatic doors to Mr Monkey's swooshed open, a swell of Journey's 'Don't Stop Believin'' and guys in Hawaiian shirts poured out.

'Plus, it has a mascot,' I said. A monkey in a yellow suit jacket and purple pants was dancing on top of the casino, waving around a microphone in one hand and a beer in the other. 'No reputable establishment has a mascot.'

'Disneyland,' Olivia said, counting on her fingers. 'KFC. McDonald's. Chuck E. Cheese.'

'Those are terrible places,' I said.

This time Olivia turned her entire body in her seat, legs tucked underneath her, so I could see the full flood of horror on her face. 'How *dare* you,' she said.

'Even if I wanted to go into Mr Monkey's, which I don't,' I said, 'we can't. I'm not eighteen until November.'

'I'll sneak us in,' Olivia said. 'There's a secret door around the back that the cooks keep propped open so they can go outside and smoke.'

I rubbed a hand down my face. 'I'm not gonna bother asking how you know that,' I said.

'OK, fine. I had a feeling this was going to happen.' Olivia smoothed down the front of her T-shirt and rolled her shoulders backwards. 'Here's the other half of the deal.'

'I thought you said it wasn't a deal.'

'If you won't go into Mr Monkey's,' she said, 'you can go for plan B.' She tapped the windshield. 'You hit me with your truck.'

'Excuse me?' I said.

She shrugged. 'Both are a vacation from Hugh's Magical Land of Boringness. One just involves more blood.' She raised her eyebrows. 'I'll let you decide which one.'

'I'm not hitting you with the truck. We only just got the generator fixed.'

'Hugh, I'm sorry, but this is your only other option. You can't just live the rest of your life being scared shitless of endings. It's this, or watch me dislocate my shoulder. Take your pick.'

'Why are those my only two options?'

'Because I said so. I mean honestly, what's the worst that can happen in Mr Monkey's? We go in, they've got a terrible cover band, there are loads of people who smell like cigarette smoke and Jack Daniel's, we get kicked out. The end.'

'Or we go in and accidentally stumble into the Ocean City mob's headquarters and they don't like my shirt or something and they give me cement-block shoes and drop me off the side of some expensive yacht into the Atlantic.'

I drummed my feet nervously against the pedals. 'If I die, my sister will be totally alone. Do you want that on your conscience?'

Olivia squinted at me. 'Do you even hear the stupid shit that comes out of your mouth sometimes?' she said. 'Cement-block shoes? Where do you think we are? This is a tacky seaside casino, not *The Godfather*.'

My teeth skimmed along my lower lip as I watched a bachelorette party in matching pink tiaras stumble on sky-high heels through the front door of the casino. Seeing them, I couldn't help but think Olivia might be at least a little right. Cement-block shoes? What did I think this was, a Scorsese movie?

Olivia was watching me, her lips flattened into a line. 'One hour,' she said. 'Give it one hour, and if you hate it, we'll leave. I'll go back to the motel and we can talk about how much you hate the ending to *Shutter Island*.'

I squinted. 'How did you know I hated—'

'Wild guess.'

It was only an hour of my life. After everything that'd happened that day with Ellen and Razz and Dan, it felt nice to have things with Olivia on a relatively steady path. Did I want to risk breaking it by insisting we go back to the motel and eat barbecue chips out of the vending machine? We'd come this far, out of DC, out into New Jersey. I wasn't dead yet.

Olivia, sensing my determination crumbling, buckled her seat belt. 'You're bigger than this, Copper,' she said. She smiled at me, sending a bolt of warmth up my neck that caught me by surprise. 'Now park your stupid truck and let's do this.'

Olivia was right. Nobody cared about two teenagers sneaking into Mr Monkey's World-Famous Club & Casino. In fact, I wasn't even sure anybody registered our presence, much less our age.

'What if there's puke everywhere?' I hissed to Olivia as we entered through the door to the kitchen, which was literally wide open. I was already having second thoughts. 'Or all the cover band plays are Barbra Streisand and Maroon 5 songs?'

Olivia ignored me as she walked calmly down the busy lanes past chefs and waitresses and waiters who were mostly too preoccupied with cramming cold French fries into their faces to care we were there.

The swinging door to the kitchen emptied us out on to the main casino floor, which immediately assaulted us with neon lights, dinging bells, loud drunken laughter and playing cards hissing between hands. Reflected in Olivia's eyes were pools of rainbows, transforming them into twin disco balls. It was sensory overload, so loud that any worried thoughts I might've had were instantly drowned out by a steamroller of noise.

'See,' Olivia said. She pointed toward the stage in the far-right corner of the room, where five guys with matching hair down to their butts were pogo-stick jumping to a screechy guitar. 'They're a Guns N' Roses cover band, not Barbra Streisand or Maroon 5.'

Sure enough, the sounds of 'Welcome to the Jungle' – the song Dan played on his phone every time he won at Pictionary – were starting to play, swirling up and reaching the casino's ceiling, where there was a recreation of Michelangelo's *Creation of Adam* painting, except Adam was Bon Jovi and God was Bruce Springsteen.

Olivia slung her arm around my shoulder. 'Is it everything you dreamt of?' she asked.

I swallowed, the lump in my throat hard and golf-ball sized. 'And more.'

'Two hours,' Olivia said, holding up two fingers as she began moving toward the maze of slot machines. 'Maybe two and a half.' She held up both hands, palms out. 'Three hours max.'

'You said one hour,' I shouted, chasing after her.

Sprawling out on either side of us were endless rows of slot machines. They were eventually cut off for card tables whose fuzzy green surfaces made them look like lily pads against the casino's ocean-blue carpet. The place was crammed, packed with guys in tank tops slapping down cards and one, sometimes two or even three people hovering over the same slot machine. All the while waiters and waitresses dressed in matching suits with little black bow ties weaved in, out and around them, balancing trays of cocktails and chicken wings on their shoulders. It was a struggle not to knock them over as I darted through the crowd, following the airbrushed edges of Olivia's shirt as it billowed behind her.

She finally slowed down at the rim of the dance floor,

waiting for me to catch up before grabbing me by the wrist and tugging me into the tangle of people.

Once we made it to the middle of the floor, I shouted, 'What're we doing here?'

I tucked my arms against my body, avoiding stray elbows that flew inches from my face. What I meant by 'here', I wasn't exactly sure: here as in the dance floor, here as in Mr Monkey's, or just here as in two basically parentless teenagers wandering around New Jersey?

'We're dancing!' she screamed back.

I wasn't sure you could call what Olivia was doing dancing. She was jumping in the air from the balls of her feet, arms fastened to her sides. She looked more like a salmon trying to swim upstream than someone that was aware of the heavy hair-metal beat, or the way not-Axl Rose was rolling on the floor with his red bandana tangled around his neck. But when Olivia latched on to my wrists again and waved them back and forth so they noodled above me like a pair of snakes, I wasn't even half as humiliated as I expected to be. In fact, something inside me unlocked.

Suddenly everyone around us was gone, leaving just me and Olivia both bouncing on our feet, rubbery arms waving over our heads. For once, all the possible ways this could go wrong weren't at the front of my brain. They weren't there at all.

In the middle of the crowd, it didn't matter that we were teenagers and definitely didn't belong there, that we didn't have parents and how everyone we knew currently wished we were dead. It just mattered that we were there, her and me.

As it turned out, casinos were actually kind of fun. They were basically a sweatier version of Disney World but for adults and with way worse music. I couldn't help but think Razz would've found it all hilarious, but who knew if I'd ever find out.

So far, not a single person had threatened to give me cement shoes. Olivia and I alternated between dancing, stealing chicken wings off people's plates as they cranked the levers on the chiming slot machines, and people-watching. We stuck close to the dance floor so that if security came by, we could dart back into the crowd of people before anyone realized we didn't belong. Most of the time I was so out of breath from laughing, I didn't even remember that our mere existence there meant we were technically breaking the law, or that I was completely surrounded by swarms of drunk people. Until I found the bar.

It appeared in front of me like a sticky mirage, its dark wood surface, red bar stools and neon-bright 'Funky Barrel' sign materializing in a cloud of tequila-scented smoke. I fought off a gag, remembering the only time I'd ever had tequila. It was in Becky's basement – because duh – and involved me doing the YMCA, stuffing toilet paper down my shirt, and a whole lot of barf, in that order.

Olivia caught me staring at the Funky Barrel and nudged me with her shoulder.

'G and T, anyone?'

Tucked into her chest was a tall glass filled with a clear, bubbly liquid and two lemon wedges bobbing on top.

'Yeah, hard pass,' I said. 'Where'd you even get that?'

'Swiped it. People really have no idea what's going on around them when they're sitting in front of a slot machine,' she said.

'I thought gin and tonics were supposed to have limes in them.'

'Yeah, well, apparently not in this classy establishment. And like I always say, when life gives you lemons, fuck shit up.' Olivia waved the glass under my nose but I swatted it away. She shrugged, then bit down on the plastic straw and sucked in. 'Suit yourself,' she said, the straw still between her teeth. 'You don't know what you're missing.'

'Actually, I do,' I said, glancing away.

'Oh really?' Olivia said. 'So, it's not that you never drank, you just don't any more. Let me guess, was the last time you did two years ago?'

I bit my lip and felt my throat tighten. Couldn't we just go back to making fun of the cover band? For once, everything was starting to feel normal again. Why did Olivia have to ruin it?

'Maybe.'

Playing with the ends of my shirt, I watched as a group of women in prom-fancy dresses gathered around the bar, arms stretching up to clink shot glasses. They were part of the bachelorette party I'd seen outside. Around them were families, couples and even the odd solo dude, the ones that watched everyone a little too closely and just made you feel kind of sad. Deep down I knew these people were all just having fun. Their night of vodka and beer and whatever else didn't have to end in someone having a big fat ker-splat against a highway divider. But then most nights never really looked like they were heading in that direction, at least not at this stage. Maybe not at any stage. Maybe everything only ended in ker-splat when it was too late.

'You know that if you drink you're not gonna end up like the guy that killed your parents,' Olivia said suddenly.

It felt like she'd punched me in the stomach.

'Maybe it's not him I'm worried about becoming,' I said.

Olivia shot me a look. 'What, so you're afraid of becoming your parents? How does that make any sense?'

I sucked in a deep breath and shook my head. 'Never mind.'

'Look, Hugh, everybody has their own ending,' she said. 'If anyone should know that by now, it's you.'

'Yeah, well, I'm not like you. My actions actually have consequences,' I said.

'Only if you let them.'

There was something in her tone, the way she made it all sound so clean and easy, that made me clasp my hands so tight, my fists turned white.

'I know that drinking gin isn't necessarily going to make me drive my car off a bridge or into the side of a school or whatever, but if it means I can avoid one more way of dying before I'm fifty or doing something that inadvertently hurts someone like me, then I'll do what it takes.'

Olivia looked at me, startled.

'Look, I just,' I said, choosing my words carefully, 'sometimes I worry that if I did drink again, I wouldn't – I don't know, that I wouldn't be able to stop.'

'So what?' Olivia said. 'So we leave the truck in the parking lot and get it in the morning. I'm not saying you should get hammered and go for a joyride.'

'That's not what I meant,' I said. 'It's just – I don't really drink any more, OK?'

At this, Olivia tilted her head, eyes squinted. I didn't like the way she was looking at me, as though I were a math problem on a whiteboard she was trying to figure out.

She ran her tongue across her top teeth. 'Not even for Becky Cayman?'

It was such a bizarre thing to say, I had to blink it into focus. My eyes scanned Olivia from head to toe, trying to decipher what exactly she knew. But that would be impossible. Nobody knew about me and Becky, especially not Olivia Moon.

'Not you too,' I groaned, unable to avoid thinking about my argument with Razz. 'Why does everybody keep saying things like that?'

'So, then it's because you're afraid.'

My nose wrinkled. 'If you're saying I'm afraid of smashing my body up against somebody's dashboard, then yeah, you got me,' I said. 'But I'm not that stupid.'

'It wasn't your parents' fault that guy made a mistake.'

'A mistake?' I said. 'A mistake is when you order pizza from Papa John's instead of Domino's.'

'OK fine, mistake is the wrong word. But you know what I mean. What were they supposed to do differently? It was their wedding anniversary; they were allowed to go outside and not be afraid of dying.'

At this, something inside me snapped. I turned on Olivia so fast, she flinched.

'I get that you think you know everything,' I said, 'but did it ever occur to you that you don't actually have any idea what you're talking about?'

Now it was Olivia's turn to erupt, eyes fogging over with anger. 'And did it ever occur to you that you're the one making yourself feel like this? All you do is wallow in your own self-pity. What happened to your parents sucked, but it was a freak accident. It doesn't mean the next time you have a sip of shitty beer, you're going to become the other guy.'

The fabric of my shirt was bunched up in my hands, revealing a sliver of stomach that was struck by the casino's overwhelming air conditioning. Even though it was a near-Arctic breeze, I felt suffocated. My head was swimming and the colours from the ceiling lights were blurring together.

Releasing the fabric from my hands, I sucked in a deep breath. I don't know what made me say the next part: anger, sadness or just the need to wipe that smug look off Olivia's face.

'There was no other guy, OK?' I said to Olivia's stony expression. The words were heavy in my mouth, their permanence weighing me down. 'I lied. My parents were the drunk ones.'

15

THE HUNGER GAMES: MOCKINGJAY

Posted in BOOKS by <u>Hugh.jpg</u> on April 8 at 11:27 p.m.

The whole HG saga ends in a pretty satisfying way, but what's really disappointing is how Katniss's story closes. She basically marries Peeta and has a kid with him because she doesn't have anything better to do. She's like, well he loves me, right? Isn't this what people do? Gee Kat, I don't know. Maybe if they're sociopaths?

After my parents died, there was one memory of my dad I always came back to. No matter how many times I shoved it deep down into the shadows of my brain, it still crept in whenever I least expected it, hitting me so hard I felt sick.

It was usually Ellen that went to baseball games with my dad down at the stadium in Navy Yard. They were both huge Nationals fans, whereas I was more of a Tarantino devotee, but Ellen had to work that day, so I agreed to take her seat at the game.

Dad was dressed in red from head to toe, broken only

by his pink skin and thick, bushy beard. I wore an old Nationals T-shirt that was so small it clung like a fungus to my body's every crack and crevice.

We had cheap seats just over the left side of the stadium, central enough so we had a decent view of the field, but right in the sun so the light beat down over our chairs and radiated back at us in an eye-watering white. Dad was happy to be there with me, even if he had to explain every pitch, hit and goal, or whatever. I knew this because he kept repeating it every time the Nationals swapped places with the Phillies, both teams scattering like red ants across the grass.

'Why don't you come to more baseball games with me?' he said for the seventh time.

'Because you never ask me,' I said.

Plus, I usually spent my Saturdays and Sundays at Becky's house or down on U Street buying candy from CVS.

'Well I'm gonna ask you more,' Dad said, nodding. He dug his hand into the cup of peanuts wedged between his thighs. 'This is fun! Are we having fun? I feel like we're having fun.'

I told him I'd believe it when I saw it but he kept slapping me on the back and pulling me into a bear hug that left me squashed into his side, his beard scratching my forehead and shoving my hat backwards.

There were two guys with matching buzz cuts sitting in the row in front of us and slightly to the right, empty beer cans crushed at their feet. They were so loud, almost yelling as they talked to each other, and whenever the Nats did something even remotely correct, they leapt to their feet and twice almost crashed into the girls sitting in the row below them. Every time they spilt something on the group of girls they tried to start a conversation, but most of the time the girls just ignored them or smiled politely before turning back to the game.

Then, maybe six innings in, one of the Buzz Cuts dipped his fingers into the pool of cheese on his plastic nacho container and flicked it on to one of the girls' hair, spraying an orange-yellow goo all over her ponytail. I was mid-sip on my soda, and felt it surge up my nose as I choked in surprise.

'Oh shit,' Buzz Cut #2 said loudly, but his words were so muddled together it sounded more like 'Ooohhhshhiiiii,' and ended in a burp. The girl with the cheese hair whirled around, her glare a mixture of shock and disgust. 'I'm so sorry honey, he's such a douchebag,' the guy said, then took a swing at Buzz Cut #1 and sniggered.

The girl combed her fingers through her brown pony-tail before angrily turning back around to a handful of napkins from her friend. I couldn't tell if my dad was watching this interaction. His eyes were fixed on the game, his jaw working slowly over a peanut.

'Hey, wait a second,' Buzz Cut #1 said as he set a hand on the girl's shoulder, his fingers newly licked clean. 'Let me say sorry and buy you a drink or something.'

'No, it's fine,' the girl snapped. 'I'm just trying to watch the game.'

'Come on, let him buy you a drink,' Buzz Cut #2 said. 'He's good for it, I swear.'

But the girl had already turned away again. She and her friends were whispering to each other while simultaneously trying to make it look like they couldn't care less about the morons behind them. The Buzz Cut twins, however, weren't prepared to give up so easily.

'Hey, I'm just trying to be nice to you,' Buzz Cut #1 said.

This time he wrapped his greasy fingers around her ponytail and yanked down so hard, the girl tipped backwards with a yelp.

'Don't touch me,' she shrieked, wrangling her hair away.

Buzz Cut #2 was laughing awkwardly but Buzz Cut #1's face had hardened into a half-smile, half-scowl.

'Take it easy sweetheart,' he said, his voice edging between cool and mocking. 'Why don't you give us a smile? Every woman's prettier when she smiles.'

There was a murmur of outrage from the girls, but I was more focused on my dad as he shot to his feet. His hand clamped on to Buzz Cut #1's shoulder and gripped the pale green fabric of his T-shirt so hard, there was a loud rip as the neck gave way.

'She doesn't owe you anything,' my dad said, pulling Buzz Cut #1 back into his chair. 'Now sit the hell back and watch the game.'

Buzz Cut #2 swallowed and eyed my dad through droopy lids. 'Mind your own business, Sasquatch,' he slurred.

But Dad wasn't distracted by the lame insult. 'It's my business when you're wasting perfectly good nacho cheese to commit harassment,' he said down to the Buzz Cuts.

A blush swallowed my face and I froze, hands clenched in my lap. 'Dad, don't—' I said, but he spun around and gave me such a withering look, I couldn't get the rest of the sentence out.

'Hugh, when people are idiots, you do something,' he said.

When he turned back around, both Buzz Cuts were staring up at him with hard, red-faced expressions.

'I don't want to have to kick the shit out of you in front of your kid,' Buzz Cut #1 said, nodding his jaw at me as he flexed his fingers.

I shrank behind my dad, both ashamed by my wimpiness and thankful for my father's bulk. The only time I'd even sort of been in a fight was when, hyped-up on Red Bull and Reese's Pieces, I'd challenged a guy at CVS to a dance-off, which ended abruptly when he shoved me into a rack of Corn Nuts. These guys were almost definitely ex-cage fighters. My dad was only an English professor. His height made it look like he might be able to give you a black eye but really, he'd just quote Hemingway at you until you died of boredom.

'There won't be any shit-kicking today,' my dad said calmly. He freed Buzz Cut #1's shoulder and sat back down, hands folded over his thighs. 'But you will leave these women and any others that do or do not smile at you alone.' He tilted his head to the side and assumed his professor voice: sing-songy, slightly high and dripping with sarcasm. 'You see, it's funny, smiling. You do it when you're happy or excited. Sometimes even when you're so elated that you cry. But you don't smile when some jerk throws nacho cheese in your hair.'

The Buzz Cuts looked at each other and laughed again, mumbling something about my dad wearing women's underwear as they turned back around, but everyone in our immediate vicinity knew who'd won. After the sixth inning, the Buzz Cut twins disappeared and Dad and I watched the rest of the game in a contented silence. I'd never been so proud of him in my whole life. I glowed with it for the rest of the game, so much so that I forgot who the Nationals had played that day until I looked it up on the internet later.

I kept that memory of my dad filed away in the back of my head for a long time, lurking just under the surface of my thoughts and ready to be plucked up for whenever I needed a good story. It was proof that my dad was a good person. That he wasn't afraid to stand up for what he thought was right, even though he was outnumbered and to just watch quietly would've been way easier. I had so many stories like this about him and my mom too, like the time she drove a guy on crutches forty-five minutes to Alexandria after she found out he didn't have enough money on his Metro card to get home.

They would do anything for anyone. That's just how they were.

So then why did they leave me?

Olivia and I left the casino as quietly and unnoticed as when we'd arrived. The wall between us was back up again, taller and even more barbed-wire-covered than before. Only this time, Olivia actually seemed to care. Stopped at stoplights back in the truck, I'd catch her glancing at me out of the corner of her eye, hands twisting the cuffs on her wrists.

The night my parents died, they weren't so drunk that they were falling over on the sidewalk, or jumping up on their dinner table singing ABBA songs into their forks. Their waiter said they'd only had most of a bottle of champagne between them, but that was because someone from an adjacent table had bought it for them when he heard it was their anniversary, and they were too polite to refuse. Their car was halfway across the bridge when a school bus changed lanes right into my parents, whose car had been in the driver's blind spot. The police said my dad probably would've had time to get out of the way, but the alcohol had dulled his senses and he reacted so slowly that the impact of the bus scraping into the side of our car forced him off the bridge and arcing gently into the Potomac River.

'The police said when they pulled them out of the water, my mom didn't have her seat belt on,' I said. The inside of the truck was so quiet, I could hear my toes shifting around in my shoes. I tried to focus on the crack-ing sound, at the way my muscles twinged when I curled my feet too tightly. 'But they could tell by her injuries that she'd had it on when they crashed, which meant she was able to get it off on her own, but they think she stayed in the car to try and help my dad and couldn't do it in time.'

Imagining them holding hands as the icy water closed in around them, knowing this was the end but at least they had each other, brought a feeling to my chest that was something like warmth. I braved a glance at Olivia, who was watching me with such soft eyes, I had to look away again. Her sadness almost made it worse.

Outside, the streets were even more heaving than before, coughing people out on to the sidewalk. There was the occasional family dragging sleepy kids back to their hotels, but mostly it was groups of drunken adults, their voices loud and slurry in the night.

'I'm sorry I lied about my parents,' I said barely above a whisper. 'It was just – when you hear that somebody died because they were drunk, it's like it stops being a tragedy. It starts feeling like it was just inevitable.' I turned back to look at Olivia again, who was watching me with owl eyes, her gaze not even flinching as a group of guys in dinosaur costumes thundered past us singing the *Jurassic Park* theme song. 'But it wasn't my parents' fault. It wasn't,' I insisted.

I don't know what made me tell her about my parents: Olivia's smugness, her confidence in her ability to read me, or maybe even just the sourness of the lie.

'They were good people,' I said, thinking of the baseball game and the Buzz Cut twins. 'I didn't want you to think they were these villains.'

'I would never think that,' Olivia said. She hadn't

spoken for so long, the sound of her voice made me jump. 'They can be good people who died when they were drunk. What happened doesn't completely erase everything else they did in life. They still loved you. They were still your parents. Why does everything have to be so cut and dried with you? Hot, cold. Right, wrong. Black, white. Ever heard of a little thing called grey?'

I sighed. 'I guess,' I said. 'But it felt good to give them a different ending, almost like I'm giving them a second chance.'

'I get that.' Olivia nodded. 'But maybe it's going to take more than that. Maybe it's your whole attitude about the thing that needs to change. Like the way you are with alcohol. I'm not saying you should go out and get hammered every day, or even drink at all. That's not the point. This is not a peer-pressure PSA. But you can't let fear over your parents' endings affect everything you do. Because the only way to guarantee a truly shitty ending is by living a truly shitty life.' She paused, staring at me with her face screwed up, as if there was something huge and gooey dangling from my nose. Instinctively, I swiped at my face, but after a few seconds, Olivia sputtered a laugh and said, 'God, I am such a fortune cookie.'

As we pulled up to a red light, I chewed my lip and watched her through the darkness as she stared out the window. Deep in my stomach, I could feel the hollow pit where the lie was still curled into a tight ball. It felt warm and familiar, and I knew I shouldn't like it but I couldn't help myself.

'You don't have to lie about them, not to me,' Olivia said into the glass. 'I know what it's like to love people that disappoint you.'

'I know,' I started to say, swallowing. 'And I'm sorry—'

Olivia turned around in her seat quickly, her face transformed by a half-smile. It was almost as if I'd imagined her voice in the quiet darkness of the truck.

'What would you say if I said there's one more thing we have to do tonight?' she said breathlessly.

I frowned. 'I'd say you're insane.'

'I promise it'll be worth it. Just pull over right up here.' She tapped her finger against the windshield. 'It'll take like, two seconds.'

Her eyes were glinting. Everything about her was electric, leaving the air in the truck heavy and filled with static. I sighed. I couldn't help it. Because if I knew myself even a fraction of how much I thought I did, I knew I'd do whatever she wanted.

16

BLOCKBUSTER
Posted in MISC. by <u>Hugh.jpg</u> on July 29 at 5:42 p.m.

For this entry, an acrostic poem:
Borrowing movies will never be the same.
Largely because it's not a thing any more.
Oh, Blockbuster, why did you go out of business?
Could it be because renting movies is stupid and pointless?
Kleptomaniacs brought your sales down, didn't they?
Buying movies. Psh. As if.
Under no circumstances will I buy a movie.
So that was a lie, but you get me #heyNSA
Take me back to simpler days.
Et *tu*, Netflix?
Rest in peace, sweet prince.

We parked on the sidewalk in front of a CVS, where a group of guys in backwards hats were skateboarding up and down the curb. Olivia hopped out and ran inside, disappearing into the CVS's brown-grey light.

194

After a few minutes, she returned with an envelope and a pair of scissors with squiggly edges. She tore off the scissors' plastic wrapping and pulled a picture out of the envelope. When she turned the picture toward the street lamp outside, I realized it was of me.

'Where'd you get that?' I said, reaching for the photo.

It was a picture of me from freshman year, when my family drove Ellen to college. We detoured into Salem and went to one of the witch trial museums, where Ellen made me pose endlessly in front of the life-size Puritan statues with floppy white hats and big buckle shoes. In the photo, I had my arm around a toothless woman who was chopping off a chicken's head.

Olivia started to cut my shape out with the squiggly scissors. 'Facebook,' she said, then waved her hand. 'Take me back to the motel, driver.'

The Little Sandy Inn looked like even more of a ghost town when we got back. Most of the windows were dark, except for a few with a creepy orange glow behind shut curtains and the lobby, where the front door gently swayed in the breeze. I followed Olivia around the back of the building toward a small concrete courtyard with a broken volleyball net, a few plastic lawn chairs and a lima-bean-shaped pool that was surrounded by a chain-link fence. On the other side was the street, mostly empty and quiet.

'I didn't know this place had a pool,' I said as Olivia and I sat down near the steps.

I nudged a few broken beer bottle shards that were

scattered along the pool's edge with the toe of my shoe.

Olivia wrenched off her shoes and socks and dipped her feet in the water. 'Yeah, well, it's not exactly Instagram-worthy,' she said, shivering.

Around the rim of the pool was a layer of green scum, mossy and thin. Floating on the surface was half a pink foam noodle and an empty Sprite can, while an old pair of sunglasses sat at the bottom of the deep end on the opposite side.

'So, remind me why we're here when I could be sleeping?' I said, tucking my legs underneath me and rubbing my face. It felt like I'd scrubbed my eyes with a sponge.

'We, my good sir, are gathered here today for your funeral.'

I dropped my hands and frowned. 'My funeral?'

'Yep. We're giving you a Viking burial.' She set my picture down on the concrete next to her and began folding the envelope into small triangles. 'Well, the old you. It's time to move on.'

'What's a Viking burial?'

'Back in the day, whenever a big Norse dude died, they'd put them on a ship with a bunch of food and gold and whatever, then light it on fire and push it out to sea.'

'You're giving me a ceremonial burial?'

Olivia swatted my arm. 'Don't trivialize it,' she said. 'I'm serious. The only way you're going to stop obsessing over endings is by having one. Tonight, we say goodbye to the old Hugh and hello to the new one. The one that hijacks ice cream trucks and steals chicken wings from unsuspecting gamblers.'

'So, the version of me that's a thief?'

'Basically.'

In Olivia's hands, the envelope transformed into a tiny sailboat she tucked my picture into. She produced a lighter from her back pocket and set the sailboat on the surface of the water before flicking the lighter to life and lowering the open flame to the paper boat's lone sail. The flame was slow to catch, at first just letting out a little orange glow on the paper triangle, but it spread quickly until eventually the whole sail caught fire.

After a few seconds of silence, Olivia said, 'I feel like you should say something.'

'Like what?'

'I don't know. Something profound.'

'Uh,' I said, spreading my fingers over my knees, 'I'll try not to think about dying so much any more.'

'No, god.' Olivia let out an exasperated sound. 'I mean, like, something that shows you've changed. This might be a ceremonial burial but you need to believe in it in order for it to work. Otherwise we're just arsonists.'

The breath that came in through my nose reached every corner of my skull, leaving my head feeling weightless and clean. As lame as the whole burial thing was, Olivia was right. I *had* changed, at least a little. I still might've thought way too much about ending the same way my parents did, or at least as abruptly, but the old me would never have left DC, much less stolen my sister's truck. Maybe it was time to acknowledge it formally, watching a picture of myself throwing a thumbs up at a papier mâché mannequin getting slowly engulfed by flames.

I cleared my throat. 'OK. So. That thing about *Buffy* from earlier.' Olivia's forehead wrinkled, her mouth opening to cut me off, but I held up a hand to stop her. This was something I was only just starting to really wrap my head around. Something I hadn't been able to admit to myself yet. 'Just hear me out. What you said about the *Buffy* ending being perfect for *Buffy* – you're right. It *is* perfect for that show. It's dumb and it's jokey but also vaguely heartfelt, and yet . . . I still completely hate it.' I shook my head. This wasn't coming out right. The thoughts were still too new, only half formed. 'What I'm trying to say is, maybe it's not just bad endings I hate. Maybe it's something more and I'm just, I don't know, like, projecting. Or whatever.'

Olivia sniffled and wiped an imaginary tear from her eye. 'I think I might cry,' she said, before turning back to the sailboat. It'd almost completely crumpled in on itself, the soggy paper sinking quickly. 'RIP Predictable Hugh.'

We sat in silence for a few seconds, watching the pulpy ash disappear, until the quiet was cut in half by the sound of Olivia hissing through her teeth. She pulled her hand up to her face so the only thing I could see was blood dripping down her arm and on to her thighs.

'What happened?' I said, grabbing her hand.

'I cut my hand on that stupid beer bottle,' she said. 'Who throws glass?'

A tiny sliver of glass was embedded in her skin, just barely sticking out of the cut. I nudged it with my fingernail, wiggling it free so it dropped somewhere on the concrete.

'Do you need a Band-Aid or some—' I started to say, but just as I did, the cut began to disappear, its edges slipping backwards as if to creep away from my touch.

'Not necessary,' Olivia whispered.

Too stunned to speak, I watched as the cut slowly shrank. My fingers, still hovering in the air, twitched.

'Can I . . .' I trailed off, not even sure what it was I wanted.

But Olivia nodded at the unsaid question. My fingers landed on the cut itself, lightly touching its wet, squishy surface as her skin tightened and stretched back into place. Neither of us moved as it stitched itself together again, even when the skin circled my fingers, carefully healing around me. The only sound beside the pool was of Olivia's and my breathing, until finally her hand was fully back together again, the trace of any cut erased.

After a few more seconds of silence, I said, 'What's it like living without consequences?'

'The same as living with consequences,' Olivia said without looking at me, 'except I don't care about them.'

'Yeah, but it's gotta be weird, not having to worry about dying all the time.'

She shrugged, healed hand dropping back into her lap. 'I wouldn't know what that felt like,' she said. 'Plus, you don't have to worry about dying all the time any more. That's so Old Hugh.'

'But what's New Hugh going to worry about?'

Olivia laughed and sat back, tipping her head up so she stared at the starless sky. 'What're you going to do in college when everybody's running around in their underwear and painting each other with highlighters? Please tell me you won't be the guy that's complaining about hygiene and curfews.'

'I'm one step ahead of you,' I said, waving my finger in the air for whatever reason. 'I'm not going to college.'

Olivia squinted at me. 'I did not see that one coming,' she said. 'I'll admit, I'm actually kind of disappointed in myself for getting that wrong about you.'

'Nah, don't be,' I said. 'I surprised everyone with that. I mean, I'm pretty sure I could've gone somewhere, but I felt like living in my childhood bedroom with my older sister just made me cooler somehow.' I didn't like the way Olivia was looking at me, her eyes squinted. 'What about you?' I said, averting my gaze to the fence, where the empty shoreline was only a few blocks away. Out there, waves were crashing in one giant sweep, the sound blurred together so the roaring was a constant undercurrent of noise. 'Where are you going to college?'

The laugh that erupted out of Olivia was the loudest and most genuine one I'd ever heard from her. She wrapped her arms around her stomach to keep from shaking, her face screwed up in an uncontrollable grin.

'College?' she finally managed between gasps of laughter. 'Me? With what money? My college fund is currently on a poker table in Atlantic City.'

'But you could get scholarships or something,' I said. 'I

mean, I don't know what your grades look like, but—'

'Hugh, no.' Olivia shook her head, silencing me. Her smile was sad and faraway. 'That whole college dream died with my mom.'

'Same,' I said.

The boat was gone now, just a few scraps of black-looking paper floating in the pool. I watched as one drifted toward the pool filter and eventually disappeared into the small square cave.

'My mom killed herself,' Olivia said.

She was staring down at her knees, not blinking.

'What?' I said eventually. 'But how—'

'Exactly,' Olivia said. 'I've spent a lot of time thinking about what's worse: the fact that she managed to do it, or that she had to have tried a bunch of different ways before she figured out what worked.' The lighter at her feet was small and made of bright green plastic. Olivia flicked the flame on and then off, as though her thoughts were a trillion miles away. 'She was there in the morning before I went to school, and then when I got back from soccer practice, I found her in the bathroom.'

'Olivia,' I said lamely, 'I'm really sorry.'

She blinked at the tiny orange flame. 'It's OK. I don't think about it a lot any more.'

Olivia's eyelashes fluttered in a slurry of blinks. It took me a few seconds to realize she was trying not to cry. Sensing me watching her, she ran the back of her hand along her eyes and turned her face away so I couldn't see the tears snaking down her nose. I watched as the muscle along her jaw tightened and the breathing through her nose got louder. Without thinking, I reached my hand over and laced my fingers in hers, her touch sending waves of warmth throughout the rest of my body.

'Why did you pick me?' I asked suddenly. 'To come here, I mean. To help you.'

The question had been on my mind since that first phone call yesterday.

Eyes trained on a line of palm trees sitting on the corner of the street, Olivia said, 'Because we're the same, you and me. Just mirror images flipped upside down.'

It was a classic, cryptic Olivia answer, but it somehow made sense.

Olivia finally turned toward me, her cheeks slick with tears. She opened her mouth as if to say something, but stopped. There was a tension humming between us, a need to reach up and wipe the tears off her cheeks coursing through me.

I curled my free hand into a fist. 'Even though I've basically been an anxiety tornado this whole time, I'm really glad you did,' I said quietly.

She laughed through her tears. 'Me too.'

Two days ago, being here, in New Jersey, with Olivia, would've felt impossible. Part of it still did. As if to prove it was really real, Olivia squeezed my hand. I glanced up at her, eyes darting down to her lips and back up again. Olivia nodded silently, so small it almost wasn't there. I started to lean in, the seconds moving agonizingly slowly, but just as my mouth reached hers, the ground rumbled from somewhere deep underneath us.

Olivia jerked backwards and gasped as the earth began to shake, the whole world tilting from side to side. The motel and buildings across the street shuddered violently, but miraculously none of the windows shattered. Even the palm trees swung back and forth in time with the buildings, as though they were all duct-taped to the same pendulum.

Olivia's grip on my hand tightened. 'What's happening?' she shouted over the noise.

Just then, a cotton ball of white landed on top of her head and melted into her hairline. We both looked up at the sky as more cotton balls fell, landing on our shoulders and at our feet. I swiped my fingers at a flake that landed on Olivia's cheek and frowned; it was cold and wet.

'Is it snowing?' I said.

But Olivia wasn't looking at me. Her eyes were back on the sky, her shoulders suddenly shaking. 'What is that?' she whispered.

I followed her gaze up past the buildings and into the dark night sky, where a large peach smudge had appeared. As I blinked, the smudge came into focus, transforming into what looked like two eyes and a nose, staring down at us.

'Is that . . .' I trailed off.

'A face,' Olivia said.

'But how?'

Just as I spoke, something happened; it was as though I escaped from my own body, like my soul was stepping out on its own, like a camera panning out. Suddenly I was looking down at me and Olivia, as though I was floating, seeing us both holding hands beside the pool and staring up into the sky. Then, I was actually in the sky, farther away, looking down on the motel as the ground continued to quake. Another second passed and I was even higher up, this time looking down on all of Ocean City, at the boardwalk and Mr Monkey's, at the beach and the too-blue tide rolling in. And then, finally, I wasn't looking at Ocean City any more at all, at least not how I knew it. The me that wasn't actually me was in what looked like one of the tacky gift shops peppered up and down the Ocean City coast, with bright-pink trucker hats and ugly T-shirts hanging from the awning that stretched out over the boardwalk.

A little girl in a wetsuit the colour of blue cotton candy was standing in front of the gift shop's snow globe display, shaking a little glass dome as flakes of white swirled around the water inside. From over her shoulder, I could see the scene trembling under her grip. The boardwalk, the buildings, the palm trees, the motel, the two little pinprick figures standing next to the ant-sized pool. I knew instantly it was me and Olivia, watching her, watching us. We were still completely oblivious to the fact that we weren't real and never had been.

THE END

. . . Olivia finally turned toward me, her cheeks slick with tears. Not snow. She opened her mouth as if to say something, but stopped. There was a tension humming between us, a need to reach up and wipe the tears off her cheeks coursing through me.

'Hugh?'

The voice, jabbing through the air from a few feet away, made the hair on my arms stand straight. Without turning to face it, Olivia's hand dropped from mine, leaving a cold blankness in its place. She, like me, didn't need to see the person to know who it was. We'd both know that voice anywhere.

But it didn't make sense. How were they here? Now? At this exact moment?

Standing on the sidewalk on the other side of the fence with her arms folded across her chest, long hair whipping around her shoulders, was Becky Cayman.

17

THE SPICE GIRLS
Posted in MISC. by <u>Hugh.jpg</u> on November 27 at 3:12 p.m.

Geri Halliwell is a traitor and that's all I have to say about that.

What was she doing here?

'What're you doing here?' I asked.

Somehow, I wasn't imagining this part. This was real.

Becky frowned. 'What're *you* doing here?'

My brain was firing in two different directions, desperate to grab Olivia's hand back but nervous about Becky's reaction. Plus, I wasn't even sure Olivia would take my hand back in the first place. There was something about Becky Cayman that made other girls jittery, even if those other girls were as out-there as Olivia Moon.

I glanced at Olivia, not sure how much of our road-trip story she wanted me to tell. But she was scrambling to her feet, pretending to look interested in something at the bottom of the pool.

'We're going to New York. It's a long story,' I mumbled,

climbing to my feet. 'But seriously, what are you doing here?'

As Becky neared the fence, I walked toward her, swallowing hard. A look of concern and delight mingled on her face.

'Ellen called my mom this morning,' she said, grasping the rungs of the fence so her car keys jingled against the metal. 'She said the truck was missing and asked if I knew where you were. Then when Mom called her again tonight for an update, Ellen said you were here, with some girl.' Becky's hair spilt over her shoulders and chest, covering the straps of a short pink dress. She flicked her eyes toward Olivia. 'Rutgers isn't that far away.'

I swallowed again. 'Where's your family?' I asked, craning my neck to see down either side of the empty street.

'They're staying at a hotel near school,' Becky said. 'I didn't have time to tell them I was leaving. Are you OK? What's going on?'

I followed Becky's gaze to Olivia, who was still standing next to the pool and pretending to disappear. 'I'm fine,' I said quietly.

Becky rocked on the heels of her feet, arms crossed over her chest. 'What're you even doing in New Jersey?' she said. Her voice lowered. 'And why is Olivia Moon here?'

'I—' I started. 'It's a whole big thing. Look, I'm really, *really* sorry you drove down here. But it's super late—'

'You're not actually going to leave right now, are you?' Becky said, her eyebrows shooting up. 'After I drove an hour to get here?'

'I didn't know Ellen called you,' I said.

'I was worried about you,' Becky said. She bit her lip and gave a half-smile, saying just loud enough for her voice to travel, 'And I know this sounds stupid because I just saw you yesterday, but I kinda missed you already.'

Underneath my hair, my ears burnt. I shifted uncomfortably from foot to foot, hoping Olivia had suddenly gone deaf.

'I – that's—' I said, but Becky cut me off.

'Can you at least come for a walk with me?' she said. She shoved herself backwards into the middle of the sidewalk. 'I'm gonna go out on a limb and say it's the least you could do after I missed my first college party to be here.'

'Just go,' Olivia said as she pushed the hair off her face. I could've sworn her voice was shaking.

'But—' I stammered.

'You'll be back in like, twenty minutes,' Becky said. 'We're not going for a marathon, just to the beach. It's literally like, two blocks away. I can smell it.'

'I-I—'

I don't want to.

That was all I wanted to say. *I don't want to go for a walk.* I just wanted to go back to the room, to the vibrating bed, and fall asleep. With Olivia.

But nothing came out.

The scuffing of shoes slipping back on to Olivia's feet sounded from somewhere over my left shoulder before she appeared just a few steps behind me.

'Seriously Hugh, just go,' Olivia said. Her eyes were still wet with tears. As if she knew exactly what I was seeing, she dabbed at them with her fingertips. 'I've got my own room key.'

She crossed through the gate leading back to the parking lot. 'But what about tomorrow?' I said.

Olivia spun around. 'I just want to be alone right now,' she said.

Her voice, so suddenly breathless with anger, made me freeze. I watched as Olivia walked down the hallway toward our room, not turning back, and I had the very distinct feeling I was on my own.

The stretch of beach Becky and I found was eerily silent, an almost purple-grey line illuminated by the moonlight. In the distance, the sea was just a block of black that occasionally moved, the waves rising up and caving in on themselves before they could take a solid shape. Combined with the sky, it looked like one of those paintings from my Art History class sophomore year, the ones with the coloured rectangles that were supposed to represent who the hell knew what.

For the entire two blocks, Becky walked with her shoulder rubbing against mine as she detailed the drive up with her family and I nodded along, not really listening. I was supposed to be with Olivia, pogo-stick dancing to bad Guns N' Roses covers, holding her hand beside the pool and telling her about my stupid snow-globe ending.

'But how could you be in the snow globe *and* watching

the girl in the gift shop?' she would say. 'That's like Plot Hole 101.'

We'd laugh and laugh and she'd remind me that all that was so *Old Hugh*. New Hugh wasn't supposed to care about that stuff any more.

But Olivia had basically shoved me toward Becky like she couldn't get away from me fast enough, like I'd meant nothing to her. Like everything that'd happened between us meant nothing.

Had I said something to piss her off? I rewound my memories in my head but found nothing. Nothing except me basically pouring out my lame, boring past, everything about my parents and my sister, all over the Jersey Shore, on which Olivia essentially did a really energetic tap dance while flipping me off.

Becky shed her flip-flops and looped them through her fingers as we trudged across the sand, past crushed plastic water bottles and forgotten beach toys. We walked a few more steps before she tossed her shoes and purse on to the shore and gestured for me to sit down.

'Is this the part where you murder me?' I asked. The sand was cold underneath my hands as I eased myself on to my butt beside her flip-flops. 'Because you could've just done that in DC.'

With her back to the waves, Becky swooped down so her legs straddled either side of me, face just millimetres from mine. Her entire expression was a smile, perfectly straight teeth erasing her eyes into slits.

'Nope,' she said, before leaning in to kiss me.

My mind went fuzzy the way it always did when Becky and I kissed. Instinctively, I wound my hands around her waist, working them up her back until they landed at the edges of her hair. But my brain took over when I felt Becky manoeuvre her hands down to my belt and start to peel apart the buckle.

'Whoa, hold on,' I said, pulling away. My breathing was ragged, like I'd just run a hundred miles. 'What're you doing?'

'What does it look like I'm doing?'

'It looks like you're trying to take my pants off on a public beach.'

Becky giggled and bent down to kiss me again. 'Exactly,' she whispered against my mouth.

Her hands, working fast, had already managed to unbuckle my belt. They were now slipping down around the waistband of my boxers, catapulting my heart into my mouth.

'We can't do this here,' I said, whipping my head around. There weren't any shapes in the dark besides the sky and the sea, but that didn't mean other things weren't lurking out there. 'There could be creepy pervs watching us, or the Loch Ness Monster.'

Or Olivia.

Olivia.

My anger from a few minutes before dissipated into confusion again, sending my hands flying away from Becky and down to my sides, where I dug up fistfuls of sand. Just ten minutes ago, I was holding hands with

Olivia, feeling closer to her than I ever had before. Now I was on a beach with Becky Cayman in my lap. Each scenario was like the ending to two very different choose-your-own-adventure stories.

Because it felt wrong, sitting there with Becky. Different. I'd always wondered if what I was doing with her was supposed to be more, since we kept coming back to each other week after week, but now I knew why it'd never turned into anything else; because I was missing a feeling. The way I felt with Olivia.

'The Loch Ness Monster lives in Scotland,' Becky said, snorting. 'You clearly haven't read *Outlander*.'

When she dipped in to kiss me again, I leant backwards.

Her arms dropped to her sides. 'What's the matter with you?' she said.

I swallowed. 'I just feel weird about this.'

Becky sighed. 'This should help.'

Rifling through her purse, she pulled out a small metal flask. She screwed off the top and held the open flask to my face, where a tangy metallic smell met my nose.

'What is that?' I said, struggling not to lean back any farther.

'Whisky,' she said. 'It was a going-away present from Sam.' Becky held the flask up to her nose before passing it back to me. 'I was supposed to save it for Rutgers, but I had a feeling you'd need it.'

'Don't you have to drive back tonight?' I said.

'It's not for me, it's for you.'

I turned the flask over in my hands, feeling the grooves

of the sparkly little diamond things that ran along the sides. I recognized the flask; it was the one Becky and I used to sneak sips out of on school trips to the Smithsonians, or on weekends in the park. Something about the mention of Sam and this flask, even just what was inside, made me twitch.

'So, what, are you and Sam like a thing now?'

Even in the dark, I could sense Becky's satisfaction with this question. Equally, I wondered if she could tell how pathetic I felt. How confused. I didn't even like Becky like that, not really. So why did the thought of her with Sam make my stomach twist?

'Um, hardly,' Becky said, snatching the flask back. She set it and the little lid down next to her. 'And even if we were, what do you care?'

'I don't,' I said, rubbing the side of my head and doing a terrible job of sounding nonchalant. 'I was just asking.'

Becky leant back and planted her hands in the sand. 'So, Sam can't steal me whisky but you can mysteriously drive to New York with Olivia Moon?'

'That's completely different,' I said. 'I'm doing her a favour. Sam just wants to get you drunk.'

I knew Sam. Sam was the guy that told every girl at a party she was the prettiest one in the room until finally someone believed him and followed him into a closet. He was one of my best friends for a while, but even I knew he was creepy.

'Maybe Sam's doing me a favour too. And why the hell

are you driving Olivia to New York? Since when are you friends?'

'We weren't until a few days ago,' I said. Maybe we still weren't, not any more. 'Clark Thomas stole something from her and I promised I'd help get it back. He's in New York now, playing a show or something.'

Becky was watching me through narrowed eyes. 'Yeah, but she's crazy,' she said, 'like actually crazy.'

'No, she's not,' I said.

'Have you even seen those things on her wrists? It's like morbid central, always reminding herself of her mom. Who does that?'

At the mention of Olivia's mom, I lurched myself up straight, zeroing in on Becky's face to see if she was joking. She wasn't.

'What're you talking about?' I asked, my voice suddenly electric.

Becky circled her thumb and pointer finger around her wrist as she groped for an explanation. 'The summer before high school started, Olivia's mom slit her wrists. And then her dad just like, abandoned her. He came up to New Jersey or something after finding out his wife had just offed herself and left Olivia there alone.'

I sat there, frozen, letting the news sink in.

Her mom slit her wrists.

Olivia's mom slit her wrists.

That was why Olivia wore those leather cuffs, because she was protecting herself. Her wrists were her only weakness.

214

'How do you know all this?' I whispered.

Now that I'd put the pieces together, this information felt precious. I wanted to cup it in my hands and tuck it away somewhere small and safe.

'I don't know, my mom told me. Cheer moms are like cultists. They know everything about each other.'

'But what happened to Olivia's dad?'

He was in Atlantic City a lot, but from the way Olivia talked about him, it seemed like he came home at least occasionally. She wasn't alone all the time. Right?

'Apparently the child protection people or whoever told him if he didn't come home, then they'd put her in foster care and charge him with child neglect, or like, whatever.' Becky's arms fell into her lap, tugging down her dress so it covered the goosebumps on her thighs. 'So, he came back.'

The thought dropped in my stomach like a stone. Olivia's dad didn't come back because he wanted to. He came back because he was forced to, and Olivia knew it.

'Look, it's really sad and it's really hard, but that was like, almost five years ago,' Becky said, seeing the expression on my face. 'Olivia hasn't done herself any favours. Me and Lily tried to be friends with her and help her after everything with her mom, but she didn't want anything to do with us. She pushed everyone away.'

'Can you blame her?' I said. 'Everybody she ever cared about left.'

It was no wonder Olivia was always acting like she

didn't need anybody else. The fact that she'd asked me to drive her to New York was practically a miracle.

Becky's shoulders sagged as she sighed. Her fingers made their way back to my belt, but this time, they were just absent-mindedly playing with the holes etched in the leather.

'I know, I know, you're right,' she said. 'But it hurt, the way she just turned her back on me. We were friends and then she was gone. But like, still there, you know?' The metal flask, standing upright and forgotten in the sand, caught the light as a cloud finished crossing the moon. Becky plucked it up and clinked her fingers against the metal sides. 'She used to sleep over at my house every Friday, and we always dressed up together for Twin Day with Lily at school. She even came to Thanksgiving at my house once, when her parents went to New York to visit her grandma.' Becky shook her head so her hair fell in her face. 'I don't know, it's stupid. I felt like, when Olivia pushed us all away, it was because we weren't good enough for her. I know she was like, grieving or whatever, but still. All I wanted to do was help her, but she had this way of making you feel so stupid and unimportant.'

That was at least something I could relate to. I thought of the way she'd turned back toward the motel without a second thought, after everything that'd happened.

I brushed away a line of sand that was caught on Becky's arm. Her eyes were turned down toward her lap, her lower lids wet with undropped tears.

'I don't want her to do that to you.' Becky tipped her face up and met my eyes. 'You have to be careful, Hugh. She'll make you think you're helping her and you guys are good friends, and then a second later she moves on to the next best thing. I've seen her do it a million times, and you don't deserve that.'

'Yeah, I don't think that's gonna happen,' I said, hands making their way up to Becky's waist again. She was shivering. 'For starters, we're not good friends.'

Anger was slowly making its way back into my veins. Olivia wasn't even here. Everything between us already felt insignificant, like I'd just imagined it. Just because I felt something didn't mean she had. In fact, I was almost positive holding her hand meant more to me than it did to her, because why else would she insist I go with Becky? She was the one that wanted to be alone, that wanted me gone. Becky was the one who wanted me. After all, she'd driven all the way here because she was concerned about me.

Before Becky could screw the tiny lid back on to the flask, she tilted it back in my direction, a question mark dug into her face. I thought for a long minute. Of Olivia. Of my parents and the Viking burial. Of New Hugh. The beginning after the ending.

'Fuck it,' I said, taking the flask from Becky's hands.

I tipped my head back and let the whisky drain down my throat. Thick and spicy, it burnt the back of my mouth and swam in my chest, leaving my eyes pricked with tears. As the drink emptied into my stomach, the tang in my throat faded from fire to something else. Something satisfying.

For the first time in years, I felt warm. Happily, un-believably, indescribably warm.

18

LA LA LAND

Posted in MOVIES by <u>Hugh.jpg</u> on August 25 at 4:25 p.m.

I get Ryan Gosling and Emma Stone can't be together at the end of *La La Land* because they have to prioritize their dreams over each other, but they could've at least made the tipping point of their break-up believable. They can't be together because they don't want to do long distance? Emma Stone's going for like three months. Big deal. Just say your dreams are more important and get on with the show. You're still breaking our hearts.

'Sex on the beach' is like a cool cocktail name or dumb, romanticized one-liner in a movie or song, but nobody ever romanticizes the ungodly amount of sand that, when you do it, finds its way into your butt crack.

Back in our motel room, Olivia was asleep with her back facing the door, body squished up against the heart-shaped bed's right edge as if she were trying to take up as little room as humanly possible. Her legs were curled up into her stomach and her head was barely on the pillow, her body just a little lump under the covers. Even though I usually slept in just my boxers, taking off my pants to sleep next to Olivia felt wrong. Plus, there was a good chance a whole hourglass's worth of sand would come tumbling out, making what Becky and I did at the beach pretty obvious. Not that it really mattered. Clearly Olivia didn't care. But still. I didn't want to subject myself to hours and hours of teasing. I knew how cliché I was, but Olivia didn't need to.

Ellen and I had shared a bed before, when we went on family vacations to the Outer Banks, and there were a couple of times Becky and I had accidentally napped together when we went to each other's houses, so I knew the rules about sleeping with girls: she needed all the covers, I wasn't allowed to touch her, even accidentally – not that I ever would or could – and all the pillows were hers to claim. I climbed into bed beside Olivia and, taking her lead, confined myself to the left edge of the heart, leaving a football field of space between us.

The bed was riddled with road bumps that bulged into my neck, back and legs. Just as I settled in under the heavy covers, Olivia whipped her body around so she lay on her back, hands clenched in fists at her sides.

'Are you drunk?' she hissed.

'Um, no,' I said, snorting a laugh. It was a cross between an actual laugh and a nervous one, but I hoped Olivia couldn't tell the difference. 'Approximately seven sips of whisky do not make me drunk. I'm a boy.'

'Well, you're something.' Olivia crossed her arms over her chest and kept her face pointed defiantly toward the ceiling. 'I thought you said you wouldn't drink for Becky Cayman.'

'I never said that,' I said as I rolled on to my side. A bulge in the mattress jutted up like Mount Everest into my ribs. 'I said that was a weird thing to say, because it was.'

'Same difference,' Olivia said.

She let out a long, angry breath through her nose. Weak light from the parking lot streamed in through the curtains, cutting a line around her clenched jaw.

'Are you mad at me?' I said lamely.

Because of course she was mad at me. Even through the darkness and blur of whisky, I could tell that much. But why she was mad at me was another mystery altogether. I'd done exactly what she wanted. I gave her space.

Unless. *Unless.*

Unless it was all one of those stupid girl tests, in which no meant yes and yes was so obvious, it was usually accompanied by an eye-roll.

Had this been a stupid girl test I'd completely and totally failed? Did, 'Go hang out with Becky' actually mean, 'You better stay with me right now *or else,*' and I'd missed the signs, mostly because I wasn't even looking for them?

Hands slapped against my face, I rolled on to my back and breathed into my clammy palms. '*Shit,*' I groaned. 'I'm so stupid.'

Obviously, this was a test. My one chance. And I'd totally blown it.

'Becky Cayman is one of the worst people I know,' Olivia said under her breath. 'She made me think we were best friends, but really I was just one of her minions she changed like underwear. One second, she'd say nobody got her like I did, not even Lily, and the next she wouldn't talk to me. She'd do that to you, make you so confused about where you stood so you became obsessed with trying to figure it out. That's why everybody pretends to love her, so she won't turn her flamethrower on them. She acts like she's got more friends than Taylor Swift, but really, everybody's just afraid of her. She's the loneliest person I've ever met. Also like Taylor Swift.'

This was all feeling way too familiar.

'She's really not that bad,' I insisted. 'And can we leave Taylor Swift out of this?'

Maybe I *was* drunk.

'You would think that,' Olivia said, not taking the bait. 'Becky's like, obsessed with you.'

'What?' I said.

At this, Olivia's eyes flicked over and finally met mine. It took everything in me not to scoff. I was so sick of having this conversation, with her, with Razz. Why did everyone think Becky Cayman was the centre of my universe? The gravity to my every move? This was the twenty-first century. You could have sex with someone on a public beach and not have it mean anything.

'You don't know what you're talking about,' I said.

Olivia nodded so her whole body rocked back and forth. 'Oh, believe me, she's obsessed with you. You've been off limits to everybody since the first grade, by Becky's orders. If anybody so much as complimented your

T-shirt, Becky made sure they knew what a big mistake they'd made.'

'That's not true,' I insisted. 'Becky and I aren't even really friends.'

We were something else. But what, I still wasn't sure.

'You don't need to be friends with someone to have a claim on them. That's not how teenage girls work,' she said. 'I would know, I used to be one of her enforcers. And I'm still a teenage girl.'

At this, I laughed. 'Becky Cayman is not Cersei Lannister,' I said. 'She doesn't have enforcers.'

'Are you sure about that?'

'God, why is everyone always saying shit like this?' I said. 'First Razz and now you—'

'Razz Nadine, an excellent example. He liked you in tenth grade.'

'—you're both always acting like all roads with me lead back to Becky. She's my neighbour, not my best friend.' Then, Olivia's words finally clicked in my head. 'Wait, what?' I said suddenly. 'No, he didn't.'

Razz. Razz? My Razz? Liked me?

'Oh, yes he did,' Olivia retorted. 'Apparently he told Becky he had a crush on you sophomore year. I wasn't even hanging out with them any more, but I heard the story. Everybody did.'

For some reason this thought hurt, settling into my chest like a nail.

'Apparently, Becky pretended to be cool with it, so Razz wouldn't suspect what was coming. Then the next day, Becky told everyone they weren't allowed to talk to him any more. It was like, instant shut-out.' Olivia didn't sound so smug any more. Her voice dropped to something resembling a murmur, hands nervously picking at the strings that dangled from the comforter. 'I remember he showed up for lunch and I kid you not, all the girls stood up at the exact same time and left him sitting there by himself. It was like a movie. One day he had everything and the next, nobody.'

'I don't remember that,' I said.

'Yeah, well, you weren't surrounded by it like I was. Becky's world is its own universe. Nobody would even be Razz's partner in any of his classes. Someone told me he got kicked out of group chats, people deleted him on everything. It was like he didn't exist.'

'What, and I'm like, magically the only person who didn't get the memo?' I said.

'Obviously Becky wasn't gonna tell you not to talk to him,' Olivia said. 'That would mean she'd have to admit she's a controlling psycho.' Olivia let out a long sigh and swiped a hand across the top of her hair. 'I wasn't even friends with her any more and I still went along with it. That's the effect Becky has on people. Her wrath is like cigarette smoke. You can cover it with gum or perfume, but that smell is always there deep down. You're always afraid of her, no matter how far away you get.'

With this, it was as if Olivia had vacuum-sealed the entire room. I couldn't breathe any more. When Razz and I first started hanging out just the two of us, I knew he didn't really have friends but I thought he'd made that choice on his own. He'd left Becky and that group because of whatever weird Razzy reason and was instead forging his own dark, moody path. The thought that he'd been forced out never occurred to me.

'That doesn't make sense,' I said, eyes trained on the ceiling. 'Why wouldn't Razz tell me? He always made it sound like he was just jealous of Becky, not that he didn't like her because of – well, that.'

'He probably was jealous of her,' Olivia said. 'I know I was. Nobody's more confident than Becky. I mean, she's the most insecure person I've ever met in my life, but she'd rather die than let you see it. Razz fed off her confidence. We all did. Becky's the kind of invincible that makes you feel safe from other girls. But she had you quarantined, Hugh, and everybody knew it.' She rolled on to her side so she could face me again, comforter tucked up high under her chin. 'Why do you think none of the girls at Mount Luther would come near you? You've got indie band hair and a cool truck. *Hello.*'

'But Razz is my best friend,' I said. I couldn't even attempt to touch her last statement without feeling light-headed. 'I'm forty million times closer to him than I'll ever be to Becky.'

Razz, my best friend, whose bedroom I'd been in more times than I could count, whose mom always set a fourth place at the dinner table for me even if she didn't know I was coming over. Razz, who tried to tell me about Becky. Razz, who I was ditching on his last night in DC.

Razz, who I ignored.

Olivia yanked the comforter down and kneaded her fists into the sheets. 'It's not the same. Even if he doesn't like you like that any more, it still sucks, knowing you aren't allowed.'

'But if Becky liked me back then, why didn't she say anything?'

'Because that's not what it's about. For Becky, it's not about being with somebody, but knowing everybody else can't.' Olivia's eyes scanned me from across the bed. 'You're funny and you're smart and you like cool music, and nobody can have you except her. Why do you think she came here tonight? Do you really think she was worried about you? No, she was claiming her property.'

'It's just—' I stammered. The taste of metal swirled around my mouth so my tongue felt heavy and thick. 'I can't – that can't be true. I would've seen that. I would've known.'

But – and this was the part I couldn't wrap my head around yet – maybe I should have known. Even still.

Becky Cayman is *an evil dictator.* Those were Razz's words. Right there, all along. Maybe I would've known if I'd actually listened.

'Oh, Hugh,' Olivia tutted, reading my mind. Even with the light slipping in from outside, her face, turned toward me, was now covered in shadows. The only thing I could make out were the whites of her eyes, wide, almost glowing with accusation. 'You think you see everything, but your eyes are practically on the back of your head.'

226

19

DEXTER (SERIES)
Posted in TV by <u>Hugh.jpg</u> on June 1 at 5:54 p.m.

Dexter is a serial killer that kills other serial killers, and by the end of the show, everyone he 'cares' about dies. After he's ruined basically everything (EVERYTHING), it looks like he'll finally get some closure (/a very deserved death) when he guides his boat into a storm, but nope. He faked his death! Surprise! He's now living a new life as a dirty lumberjack while the lives of everyone he ever knew are completely and totally in a shambles. Good work, D!

As the sun rose, the light flooding the hotel room turned the walls a dingy shade of dishwater brown. I hadn't realized before how many stains were splotched up and down the peeling wallpaper. Most just looked oblong and kind of like beige jelly beans, but others were a faded brown-red, maybe from blood, maybe from puke. I was afraid to think about it for too long.

Instead of sleeping, my eyes were more or less glued open all night no matter how hard or loudly my brain begged to shut down. Thoughts of Razz rushed through my head, the strange stains on the walls morphing into his face, the water rings his beanie and manga hair.

Before Olivia could wake up, I tiptoed alone across the motel room and into the hallway, quietly making my way into the parking lot, which was silent except for the buzz of nearby cars. Above me, the sky was a weak grey streaked with clouds, leaving the air cold and clear. Only when I got on to the highway did I realize I didn't actually know where I was going. The map Olivia bought could take me to New Brunswick, but I'd have to rely on signs to get to Rutgers. The night before, Becky had mentioned living in something called Langston Towers, or maybe Lynton Towers, but I figured I could ask someone once I got on campus.

Because with Olivia's new information, I couldn't wait until Thanksgiving to talk to Becky face to face and see if what Olivia said was true. I had to go now.

The Rutgers campus was actually gargantuan, all red brick and tree-lined walkways leading toward elaborate fountains and immaculately trimmed bushes. I had to ask a few people about Becky's dorm – which was called Lynton Towers, and apparently there were two of them, because that makes sense – and then beg the person sitting at the front desk to call Becky's cell and tell her I was downstairs in the lobby.

A dull headache pounded just behind my left eyebrow, the universe's attempt at reminding me of yet another reason why I stopped drinking. I kneaded my knuckles into my forehead as I leant against the front desk and waited for Becky to emerge.

The elevator doors across the lobby slid open a few minutes later, revealing Becky in a white T-shirt and pair of pink pyjama shorts printed with smiley-face emojis. She rubbed her eyes and tightened the loose ponytail draped across her shoulder.

'Hugh, what're you doing here?' she said as she trudged toward me, her body still slow with sleep. When she leant in for a hug, everything about me tensed. Becky pulled away and frowned. 'What's wrong?'

'Could we sit somewhere and talk?' I said.

'Yeah, sure.' Becky pointed down a hallway. 'There's a coffee shop over there.'

'You have a coffee shop in your dorm?'

Becky rolled her eyes. 'This is New Jersey. The bigger the better.'

The coffee shop was basically dead, which wasn't that surprising seeing as it was seven in the morning on a Sunday in a college dorm. There were a few tall tables and chairs scattered around the empty room, the far end of which had a cinderblock wall painted an eye-watering red. As I sat at a tall table in the corner of the room, Becky returned from the counter with two cups of water and slid one toward me. I gulped it down all at once, the coolness bringing a little relief to my head.

'So, what are you doing here?' Becky said. Her eyes were panda-smudged with make-up. 'I thought the whole beach thing was a pretty decent goodbye.'

Though she wasn't smiling, I could hear the smugness in her voice.

I glanced down at my hands, fingers tracing the indents in the little plastic cup. 'Did you ice Razz out in tenth grade?' I said quietly.

No fanfare, no build-up.

From the way Becky's arm, resting on the table, went stiff, I could tell this wasn't what she was expecting. But then, Becky probably never expected anyone to confront her, especially not me. Not about anything she deemed meaningful. I was just another one of her impressionable minions.

'What're you talking about?' she said.

'In tenth grade, did you or did you not, tell everyone not to talk to Razz?'

Her attitude went from prickly to incredulous with a husky laugh. 'No, I didn't tell everyone not to be friends with him.' Becky combed her fingers through her pony-tail. She glanced around the room to make sure nobody could hear us. Then, she lowered her voice. 'Why are you doing this right now?'

'Because,' I said, hearing my dad's voice in my head; for once, the memory didn't make me want to die, 'when people are idiots, you do something.'

Becky's eyebrows shot up as though she might challenge me, but after a few seconds her face went neutral again. 'I didn't ice him out, OK?' she said. Then, she rolled her eyes and waved a hand through the air. 'God, that sounds so juvenile. What am I, the freaking mafia? That was like, two years ago. I got mad about something stupid and then told Lily I didn't want to talk to him and *she* told everyone else not to be friends with him.'

'That's not what I heard,' I said.

She leant back in her chair and folded her arms across her chest. 'Who're you getting your information from, Olivia Moon?'

When I didn't answer, she scoffed.

'So, what, now you're boning Olivia and everything she says is the word of God?'

'I'm not doing anything with Olivia—' I started to say, but didn't want to take the bait. 'Stop trying to make this about anything other than the fact that you took away everyone my best friend had. Do you have any idea how messed up that is?'

'I didn't take anyone away from him.' Becky held up air quotes around the word 'take'. 'If I told people not to talk to him like Olivia says I did, that was on them. I didn't like, hold a gun to anyone's head.'

'You had power over everyone and you knew it,' I said.

Becky's jaw stiffened, her eyes settling on the tabletop, its glossy wooden surface carved with pencil marks. Her teeth worked quietly over her tongue before she finally swallowed and said, 'I didn't think it was going to get that bad. I was just – I was mad, and once it'd started, I could hardly take it back. Not without looking like a total idiot.'

I drummed my fingers against the table's slick surface and said quietly, 'So you took away everyone my best friend had and couldn't make it right because you'd *look bad*?'

'It's not that easy—' Becky started to say.

'What, to be a decent human being?' I said. 'Yeah, apparently not.'

She stared down at her fingers, the veins underneath her skin stretching as she clenched and unclenched her hands. After a few seconds, she glanced up, her voice dropping.

'Look, I knew he was trans before anyone else did,' she said. 'He told me, that summer before tenth grade. I was the only one who knew his parents were going to help him start transitioning. If I wanted to hurt him, I could've told people, but I didn't. I didn't really want—'

A jolt of disgust ran through me. 'You knew he was trans?' I said, leaning back. So many thoughts were buzzing around in my head, it felt like bees had invaded my skull. 'You knew what he was going through and made it so he had nobody to talk to? That's your big fucking favour?'

'I didn't – that's not what I meant,' Becky said quickly. 'I didn't understand what I was doing.'

'Wake up Becky,' I said. 'That's not an excuse.'

Becky breathed loudly through her nose as her gaze darted around the floor. 'OK,' she said suddenly, 'if I'm so shitty, where were you?' Her eyes glittered with tears. 'You just want to blame someone, but you weren't exactly helpful, were you? He's your best friend. Then why was he so alone?'

I blinked, wanting to respond but knowing I couldn't. Instead, I swiped my hands against my jeans before wedging my fingers between my thighs.

'What I did was stupid and mean. I get it.' A tear slipped down her cheek. 'But don't yell at me when you're really mad at yourself.'

Her words hit me straight in the jaw, so hard it was as though I could already feel a bruise starting to form. But I couldn't show her the way my brain was spinning, not now. I shook my head, hair falling in my eyes. 'Whatever, Becky,' I said. I hated how lame I sounded. How petty and spiteful and cornered and defeated.

With one loud push that sent the legs of my chair scraping across the shiny linoleum floor, I pulled myself to my feet and started to walk back toward the doors to the parking lot. Becky stood and reached out a hand that didn't even come close to touching me.

'Where are you going?' she said to my back.

If I didn't know any better, I'd think she was starting to sound panicked.

'I can't be here any more,' I said.

'Wait, Hugh, come on.'

I turned as I reached the double doors. Becky was hugging her arms around her stomach. She was almost a different person, unrecognizable from the cool, unshakeable Becky that cocooned herself in my sheets back home. Bleary and wet with tears, her red eyes focused on her feet.

'Just stop, OK? Please don't go.' Her voice shook. 'Look, I'm sorry. I would never do anything like that now, you know I wouldn't.'

'How would I know that?' I said. 'I don't even know you.'

'How can you say that? You're literally the only person who knows me. Nobody else knows how much I like Jane Austen, or that I wrote a book in seventh grade.' She forced a laugh. 'Lily thinks I was writing love letters to Harry Styles.'

'Big freaking deal,' I said. 'That stuff doesn't matter. It's how you treat everyone else,' I held a hand to my chest, 'how you treated my best friend, that matters to me.'

'Look, you're mad right now. I get it.' She blinked down at her hands. 'I deserve it. But can we just talk about this at Thanksgiving? Once this all dies down a little bit?'

An overwhelming sadness rushed through me, washing down my arms and all the way to my toes. There was no way to look at Becky without feeling it. The whole last year, everything between us. It all just made me feel so sad.

'I don't think so,' I said, my voice heavy.

Becky shut her eyes and swiped at the tears that leaked out. 'Hugh, please,' she said. I'd never heard her so shaky before, everything about her unstable. 'This happened two years ago. You know I'm not like that any more.'

I shook my head, suddenly feeling more exhausted than I'd ever felt in my whole life.

'Honestly Becky? No, I don't,' I said. 'I thought I did, but I really don't.'

Because Olivia was right. Up until then, I didn't see anything or know anyone. Not really. Not Razz, not Dan, not Becky and definitely not Olivia. I never had.

234

20

TRUE DETECTIVE (SEASON TWO)
Posted in TV by <u>Hugh.jpg</u> on October 23 at 10:13 p.m.

I'm going to let my sister's thoughts on this one speak for themselves: WHY BOTHER MAKING RACHEL MCADAMS THIS BADASS COP IF YOU'RE JUST GONNA SHIP HER TO VENEZUELA? SHE DID NOT WORK HER BUTT OFF ON THIS CASE JUST TO GET PREGNANT AND SENT TO SAFETY WITH THE ONLY OTHER FEMALE CHARACTER SO THE MEN COULD 'SACRIFICE THEMSELVES' IN THE NAME OF MACHO BULLSHIT.

We drove the rest of the way to New York in silence, Olivia watching the line of trees flashing by us grow thinner until they became housing estates and then mini-malls. All the while, I was thinking up the million ways I could tell Razz I was sorry:

- Hire a small plane and write in the sky: *Rzz ima dck.* (The smaller the sentence, the less nauseated I'd feel with all the flipping. He would understand.)
- Sing him that goodbye song from *The Sound of Music.*

Because I wasn't bad at/afraid of saying goodbye. I'd say goodbye in forty languages. Any language he wanted. Swahili? *Kwaheri*. Sign language? Wave. Elvish? *Namárië*.

- Send him a Morrissey-gram that was hand-delivered by Morrissey circa 1986 and consisted of a naked Morrissey circa 1986.
- Promise to never compare him to a satanic potato ever again.
- Drive him to California and let him pick the music the whole way.
- Memorize every word from his favourite movie (*Men in Black III*) and convert it into a stage performance starring Lin-Manuel Miranda, with a special guest appearance by Will Smith playing an alien Will Smith.
- Just say over and over and over again until my voice was gone: I'm sorry I'm sorry I'm sorry, you were right you were right you were right.

When we made it to New York, I left the ice cream truck in what I hoped was a free parking zone not far from my aunt Karen's apartment. It was somewhere near Central Park, behind a squat dumpster and a Chinese takeout place with plastic cats that waved at us from the front window. I could trace my steps back to Karen's building without asking for directions. Each block brought back a new memory, or technically an old one: a pretzel Ellen bought from a cart that was no longer there; Mom's favourite bagel place, now a Starbucks. We turned right at the stop light with the green handprints circling its base, walked two blocks until we found the little bodega with a colourful quilt instead of a door, and then, seventeen steps later, reached my aunt's building. Number 215.

The doorman, Sunny, let us up. Short, round and full of the kind of energy that made your eyes water, he remembered me from all those years ago and pretended Olivia was my sister, only shrunken. And blonde.

I faked a laugh, smiling as he walked us to the elevator, but there was a hole in my stomach the size of a Frisbee. The last time I saw Aunt Karen was at my parents' funeral, when she was fully prepared to take me back to New York as her orphaned-nephew-slash-ward. When Ellen told her I wanted to stay in DC, she wasn't hurt or anything; at least she didn't act like it. Deep down, she was probably relieved.

Aunt Karen had never gotten married, didn't have kids and worked as an editor at a big publishing company in Manhattan. Her and my mom were best friends, so I knew she'd have taken me in without question, no matter how much I would've screwed up her life. She was always close to me and Ellen, too. My sister and I only had one uncle – my dad's brother – and he lived in Wisconsin on a farm. We used to visit Aunt Karen every summer, but once my parents died, things changed.

As the elevator crawled higher and higher toward the fifteenth floor, all these thoughts spiralled through my head in a nervous hurricane. Outside of Aunt Karen calling us every Christmas with a yearly recap that mostly consisted of her telling Ellen things and then Ellen relaying them to me with missing details and a lot of sound effects, we'd barely spoken since my parents' deaths. The strings connecting us between New York and DC were brittle and old and unused. Because what was there to say? And what would we say now? Maybe there wasn't anything for us to talk about, and that was the part I dreaded the most: the radio silence, a gap the exact shape and size of my parents sprawling open between us.

Olivia wasn't much help in talking me down from my anxiety funnel. She just squished herself into a corner of the elevator and kept her eyes on her feet. We were both very strategically avoiding any and all topics that involved Razz or Becky or basically anything else. We hadn't actually spoken since I picked her up at the motel. If she wondered where I'd been that morning, she didn't ask.

When the elevator doors yawned open, door number eight sat at the end of the hallway. Aunt Karen's apartment. I walked slowly towards it, then knocked and waited. And waited. And waited.

'She's probably in the bathroom,' I mumbled.

Olivia was behind me, back leaning against the closed elevator doors as she did her best job of pretending she couldn't hear me. Faint traces of music trickled in from under my aunt's front door, so I knocked again, harder this time.

'Come in, it's open!' someone shouted from the other side.

Glancing back at Olivia, I shrugged and turned the doorknob. We were met instantly with the smell of flowers coming from a red candle the size of my fist. Inside, only a few lamps were lit, casting a foggy orange glow across the small living room. As my eyes adjusted, I took in more of the apartment; it was tight, compact and incredibly warm. Fleetwood Mac played softly from a record player in the corner and a window was open halfway, letting in a light breeze and the sounds of cars honking from below. The room was filled with furniture – a bookcase that stretched from floor to ceiling, a worn mustard-coloured couch, and my grandma's old loveseat printed with big antique roses – but it wasn't busy like my house. Mom always joked that while she and Aunt Karen both rebelled against Grandma Jean's military organization with the same chaotic approach, Karen's actually had some style.

The entire apartment was half the size of my house's downstairs, but it was cosy. It consisted of a living room, two bedrooms, a bathroom so small it could only fit one of those tall hotel showers, and a skinny kitchen that felt crowded if more than one person was in it. Originally the apartment came with one bedroom, but Aunt Karen halved the kitchen and made a closet-sized second bedroom with bunkbeds for guests.

Running my fingertips along the dinner table's glass surface, I wandered into the living room, my footsteps echoing on the hardwood floors. An empty plate except for one long spaghetti noodle sat on the coffee table, which was really just an oversized emerald-green cushion with a tray on top.

'Hughie!'

A voice broke through the sugary sounds of Fleetwood Mac, followed by bare feet slapping against the floor.

I turned and saw my aunt Karen sliding toward me, practically naked from the waist up. She was wearing a straight black skirt that reached her knees and a black bra, nothing else. As her arms wrapped around my shoulders, I glanced back at Olivia, horrified.

My aunt pulled away quickly, totally oblivious. 'God, I was supposed to be in the Village fifteen minutes ago.' All at once, she was a ball of movement again, darting back down the hallway and into her bedroom. 'This guy I'm meeting is a girl from work's cousin. He's from France, and he barely speaks English. Don't get me wrong, I don't mind if he doesn't speak English, but when we were texting he asked if I wanted to eat him tonight. Not with him. Eat *him*.'

I tried apologizing to Olivia with my eyes, but she was already sitting in the loveseat and spinning it on its wheels so she faced the windows overlooking New York City.

'To be honest, I've gotten worse invitations, but it caught me off guard for a first date.' Karen emerged from her bedroom wearing a red shirt with little gold buttons she slipped into place one by one. 'I'm fairly positive it's going to be a boring night, but if I get a few martinis out of it, then no harm, no foul. Oh, Christ.' Her arms slapped down to her sides as she stared at her shirt. It was one button off so the crinkly fabric hung at a weird angle. She shrugged and pulled the shirt up over her head. 'I didn't want to wear this anyway,' she said, and disappeared again.

A few minutes later, Aunt Karen returned wearing a dark green skirt and a sweater the same yellow as her couch. She tucked her short dark hair behind her ears.

'Do I look like a French schoolgirl?' she said, gesturing to her clothes. 'That probably wouldn't be the worst thing in this scenario, but I feel like I should at least attempt to dress like an adult.'

I shook my head.

Satisfied, Karen sidestepped into the kitchen and retrieved a glass of red wine. At the sight of it, my heart sank just a little. I couldn't help it. As she sipped, she watched me over the rim of the glass and smiled.

'I'm sorry but I just can't get over how grown-up you look. It's blowing my mind.'

The glass landed on the table with a light thud and I flinched, expecting wine to go flying. But it stayed in its glass, just like it was supposed to.

Aunt Karen flung her arms around me again, and this time she lingered, head digging into my shoulder.

'I'm just so glad you're here. Tell me everything. How are you? What're you doing in New York? Ellen said you were driving up here to meet a friend and the truck broke?'

She craned her neck around me to see Olivia.

'Yeah,' I said slowly. 'One of our friends is playing a show in Brooklyn tonight so we're going to surprise him.' The lie of calling Clark Thomas my friend tasted like old fish. Swivelling, I held a hand toward Olivia. 'This is Olivia.'

Olivia barely turned from the window. She just lifted her hand from the chair's arm in a half-wave.

Aunt Karen smiled. 'You guys must be exhausted. Where are your bags?'

'We didn't think we'd be staying tonight, but you know Ellen. She's convinced I'll kill us if I drive back down in the dark.'

Karen swiped my arm lightly. 'Give her a break, this is her everything we're talking about. I mean the truck, of course.'

'Of course,' I said.

'Are you hungry? I had spaghetti for a late lunch but obviously I made enough for ten people, because even though I'll be fifty in three and a half years, I still can't measure pasta for one.' Her wine glass was in her hand again, the thick red liquid sloshing in circles. 'It's nothing fancy, just plain spaghetti, but it's food.'

'I thought you said you were going on a date,' I said.

'Well, yeah, but to an oyster bar in Greenwich Village. And at five o'clock. If this Frenchman really was on the menu I might consider fasting, but otherwise I never eat seafood this far south.'

Everything about her reminded me of my mom: her thick black hair, the sharp curve of her jaw, her jerky movements and the way her hands flailed as she talked. But for some reason, this realization didn't hurt as much as I thought it would. It just was.

'And get this,' Aunt Karen said. Her fingers flared in every direction. 'His name is Marius.' When she said this, her eyes popped, waiting for my reaction. 'Marius,' she repeated when I didn't answer. 'Like from *Les Misérables*.'

'Oh right,' I said. 'Razz has made me watch that movie like eighty times. Marius is the only one that doesn't die.'

Aunt Karen's hands shot up to cover her ears. 'Oh my god, spoiler alert!' she shouted, the whites of her eyes expanding. 'I've never actually watched the movie all the way through. I can't make it past Anne Hathaway getting her teeth pulled out by all those terrifying women.'

'You've never seen *Les Mis*?' I said. 'You're like the worst New Yorker ever.'

A sly smile spread across my aunt's face. 'Oh sweetheart, you don't even know the half of it.'

As my aunt Karen hurried between the living room and her bedroom, the bathroom and the hall closet, looking for everything she'd ever owned – her purse, her lipstick, her hairbrush, her strappy red sandals with the 'fat heel' – I slumped into the couch and sat as an unfamiliar feeling slowly enveloped me. It wasn't nerves or even awkwardness. It was warm, comfortable and unexpectedly easy.

But as my eyes pulled up to the wall across from me, the feeling evaporated. Because on the other side of the room was a picture wall. With pictures of my parents. And me.

The pictures were stacked up and over the front door, creating an archway made of a hundred tiny black eyes. Without realizing it until I was actually there, my feet carried me over to the other side of the room, not stopping until my nose was practically pressed to the thin panels of glass. Not all the pictures were of me or Ellen or my parents; some were of Aunt Karen and her friends, my grandparents and their little Jack Russell, Booby. But the ones with my parents stuck out to me as though they were framed in neon.

Me and Dad at the National Zoo, waving at the red panda that was asleep on a tree branch. Dad's beard was so small then, just a puff of brown hair he let me cling on to with my peach-pit fist.

Mom and Aunt Karen as little kids, each wearing matching pink triangle earrings, the tips scraping their big, padded shoulders.

Mom and Dad on their wedding day, Mom wearing what Ellen called her 'glorified burlap sack' dress.

Mom, Aunt Karen and my grandparents at the lake house they rented in Michigan for a few summers. Everyone looked exhausted and red, two army-green canoes tipped over at their feet.

Mom and Dad when Ellen was born. Red-faced, crying, happy. All three of them. Mom, for it to be over. Dad, to take my sister home. Ellen, to be on dry land.

Dad leaning down to show six-year-old Ellen this shrieking, raisin-shrivelled lump. Me, just born, hair already a black mop on my head. Ellen's bangs were jagged and toothpick-stiff after she'd cut them with nail clippers.

All four of us at Ellen's high school graduation. Proud. Overheated. Hungry.

Me and Ellen at mine. Alone.

I dragged my fingers along the pictures, feeling the cold glass instead of my parents' faces. We hadn't stared at each other like this since the real deal. On the day of their funeral I could barely look at the paper programmes Ellen had printed out. The cover was stamped with my parents' wedding photo, and every time I looked at it I felt sick, picturing them in that car, their faces cold and lifeless. But I wasn't thinking about that as I stood in Aunt Karen's living room. For the first time, I wasn't thinking about my parents' ending at all. I was thinking about how much I missed them.

'OK, I'm probably not going to be out late but if you two make it back before I do, Sunny knows to let you up. Here are the keys.' There was a clink as Aunt Karen dropped the key ring on to the dinner table. 'I put the spaghetti in the fridge in case you get hungry.' She swept her arms down from her chest to her waist. 'Do you see me? Do you see what I'm doing here, kids? This is called being responsible. Check me out.'

'It's really impressive,' I said. After gazing up at the pictures, I sat back on the couch, legs tucked underneath me. In spite of everything else, I felt light-headed and giddy. 'I almost didn't recognize you.'

Aunt Karen narrowed her eyes playfully. 'Smart ass,' she said. Then, with her purse slung over her shoulder, 'There are towels in the bathroom, one for each of you, but if you get crazy there're more in the drawers under the sink. Don't judge my organization methods, I am very limited on space in this apartment. I used to keep the towels on the top shelf of the bookcase, but pulling them down naked after you've taken a shower is a one-way ticket to perverts on your fire escape.' Her arms hung limply at her sides, lower lip pushed out. 'I feel really bad leaving you here,' she said. 'I haven't seen you in a million years and now I'm running off to join the French Revolution. I should just cancel – I can politely refuse oysters next weekend.'

'No, don't,' I said quickly. 'I mean, seriously, it's OK. We've got to go to this show soon anyway. I'll come back another weekend.'

If Ellen didn't murder me first. Ellen or Clark or Olivia or Razz.

Karen glanced down at her watch, the one with the worn leather strap she'd had for ever. 'All right, if you're sure,' she said, sighing. 'What time are you planning to leave tomorrow morning? They moved your mom's favourite bagel place to the other side of the park but if we get up before noon, they should still have enough blueberry bagels for us to get two each.'

Olivia was still staring out the window, fingers tapping listlessly against her thighs. She didn't notice the uneasy look I pointed in her direction, or the way I swallowed so hard I felt it in my ribs.

'Ellen needs the truck tomorrow, so she wants us to leave at six,' I said. That part at least wasn't a lie.

'Oh, OK.' My aunt nodded, then waved her hand. 'Yeah, sure, whatever you have to do. If I see you, I see you.' She beckoned me up and into a hug, pulling me in so tightly I could smell her fruity shampoo. 'You know you can always come up here and stay with me anytime you want,' she said into my shoulder. 'You don't even need to call, you can just show up. There might be a strange Frenchman here, but you've seen worse.' She pulled away and laughed. 'Oh god, who am I kidding? You're more likely to find me eating KFC and watching *The Real Housewives of Orange County* than with a man, which I'm totally comfortable with, by the way.'

As she moved toward the front door, fumbling with her keys, I crossed into the kitchen for a glass of water. A voice in the back of my head reminded me of the empty glass of wine on the dinner table, of the speed at which my aunt talked, as though at any second she might collapse and flop around on the floor like a dying fish.

I pulled open the cabinet under the kitchen sink and peered into the trashcan. There were no bottles on top, just an empty plastic tube for the dry pasta, a jar for tomato sauce, some paper towels and broccoli trees fuzzed over with grey mould. Only when I looked up again did I notice the bottle of wine sitting perfectly still and obvious on the counter. It was more than half full, missing a glass, maybe a glass and a half.

'Would you cork that for me?' my aunt asked, seeing me. She hovered in the doorway to her apartment, a flustered look on her face. 'I got that for Christmas last year from one of my authors. A three-dollar bottle from Trader Joe's after seventeen rounds of edits. Can you believe that?'

21

With my aunt gone, the living room was suddenly silent. Olivia hadn't torn her eyes away from the window since we got there, her arms, legs and face so still, she looked like a creepily lifelike mannequin.

'It's almost five o'clock,' I said to Olivia, faking my best nonchalant voice while nervously rocking back and forth. 'We could go find dinner before heading over to Brooklyn, or we could just eat the leftover spaghetti my aunt made.'

The timeline of our oncoming night sprawled out in my mind with colourful board game squares. Talking about our agenda was something I could do. It was practical and had nothing to do with how badly I'd failed my best friend or the girl I maybe, probably, definitely liked.

'If we drive, we'll probably have to find parking, so we should try to leave soon,' I said. 'I don't know what traffic's like on Sundays, but I'll be shocked if it's anything short of obnoxiously terrible.'

The plan from this point was simple. We'd had to make it at least look like we were staying with my aunt Karen so Ellen wouldn't get tipped off we were going to drive home that night. Now that we'd made an appearance, we'd go to the Cabinet in Brooklyn, where Clark was playing, grab Olivia's stuff, then head back down to DC, picking up the ice cream and dropping my aunt a phone call from a payphone somewhere so she'd know we weren't dead. By then, Ellen would find out our plan but it wouldn't matter because we'd already be halfway through New Jersey. I'd drop Olivia off at her house, then coast up to Razz's place, arms filled with gas station candy, a life-size cardboard cut-out of Johnny Depp as Captain Jack Sparrow – Razz's first real crush – and a mouthful of apologies, if he was even still there. Then, I'd get the ice cream to Ellen.

But first, I had to get through the North–South Korean border that was Olivia Moon.

As I spoke, nothing about her suggested she'd heard my plan. It was as if I was talking to myself, a crazy person on the street she was actively trying to ignore.

'Olivia?' I said as I waved my arms in front of her face. 'Hello? Ground Control to Major Olivia?'

She blinked and tucked her hair away, revealing a very

pink ear. 'Hmmm?' she mumbled.

'Do you want to get dinner before going to Brooklyn?'

'I don't know,' she said.

'Well, how hungry are you on a scale of one to cannibalism?'

We'd only had lunch a few hours ago from a drive-through corndog stand just outside Ocean City. Most of mine had ended up under my seat, after the squishy breaded coating flopped off the stick and fell between my legs.

Olivia shrugged and said, 'No.'

'That wasn't a yes or no question,' I said. 'Can you wait to eat until after we pick up your mom's stuff? Blink once for yes, twice for no.'

Another shrug.

'Olivia,' I said, reaching out and touching her arm.

She didn't even flinch. Her eyes were dull and glazed, fixed on some distant point I couldn't pick out. She looked small and shrunken, somehow, like she was disappearing one slow, half-dead blink at a time.

My knees cracked as I crouched down beside her. From this angle, I could stare up at her waxy expression, but her eyes didn't follow me, didn't even register my presence.

'Look, I'm really sorry about the whole Becky thing. I shouldn't have left. I genuinely don't know what I was thinking.' I shook my head, hair falling across my forehead. 'I mean, like, you were right. I thought I knew her better than anybody else. Razz tried to tell me and I actually defended her to him. I am the universe's worst friend and brother all mixed up into one really terrible human sandwich.'

'What?' Olivia whispered, her eyes just a glassy wall.

I realized then that she wasn't actually looking at me. There was no point to focus on, distant or up close. She was just looking.

A twinge of panic flickered through me.

'Olivia, we have to go,' I said gently. 'I know you're mad at me and I totally get it, but we still have to get your mom's stuff back before Clark dicks off to Canada.'

We watched *One Flew Over the Cuckoo's Nest* in English senior year, and it creeped me out how much Olivia resembled Jack Nicholson after they fried his head. It was like someone'd pulled her brain out through her ear with a pair of tweezers, leaving behind an Olivia-shaped shell.

From the street, there was a sudden blast of a song I didn't recognize, a really angry rap backed by what sounded like someone running a car into a drum kit. The sunlight caught the windows surrounding my aunt's building, sending little shards of rainbow scattering across the wall.

The song's sudden assault on my senses reminded me of something. A foolproof, snap-you-back-to-reality trick that, until yesterday, had never failed. Considering how often it'd been used in the Copper household before, its chances of success were still high. And I was running out of options. At that point, I was willing to try anything.

Stevie Nicks' voice had died out on my aunt's speakers just as she was leaving, so I walked over to her record collection and thumbed through the albums one by one until I found what I was looking for. I wasn't sure how I knew it would be there. I just did.

Then, with my back to Olivia, I replaced Fleetwood Mac's record with the new one and watched as it went around and around, very aware this was probably my last chance to make things right.

Was I really going to do this? It was the only thought bouncing around in my head as the bass rumbling of a piano swirled up to fill every corner of the living room. Olivia's head twitched slightly at the new invasion of sound, but otherwise she stayed still in the chair, body facing the window.

Shutting my eyes tight, I tried to coax some movement into my shoulders, bobbing them up and down in a half stretch, half pep talk. Just singing the song in this case wasn't good enough. For one, I didn't know if Olivia knew the words. And for two, I had to go big.

In a single weekend, I'd somehow managed to enrage and alienate myself from the only two people I'd consistently spoken to for the last two years. I'd gone from being boring and predictable to Columbia Heights' Public Enemy #1. And that wasn't even considering Olivia. Before yesterday we barely knew each other, but now, she was already disappointed in me. And could I blame her?

But I wasn't going to let her down. Not after everything she'd been through with her mom and her dad and Clark. It seemed like the people in Olivia's life either wanted something from her or didn't care enough about her to want something in the first place. They were two very different sides to the same Olivia-shaped coin, and I was determined not to be one of them.

As Levi Stubbs' voice reached up into a high croon, I swivelled Olivia around in the chair so she faced me. Her eyes widened in surprise as they met mine. Then, I started to lip-sync.

'*Sugar pie, honey bunch,*
You know that I love you . . .'

As I mouthed the words, I shimmied above her, wiggling my hips and shoulders in a way I hoped looked intentional. After the first two lines, Olivia dropped the dazed look on her face and swapped it for one of dread. She cowered into the chair, clearly hoping I would stop if she didn't engage, or afraid that whatever I had was contagious. Her jaw dropped as I bounced from side to side, pointing to her every time Levi Stubbs said 'you' just in case she was unsure who it was I was trying to drag face-first into my humiliation spiral.

'*I can't help myself,*
I love you and nobody else.'

My hips moved to the rhythm of the tambourine, and when I reached my hand out to her, Olivia sank even farther into the chair as if she wished it were a portal to another dimension. Without warning, I grabbed the hand that was resting on her knee and pulled her to her feet, causing her to yelp in surprise.

'*In and out my life,*
You come and you go.
Leaving just your picture behind,

And I kissed it a thousand times.'

I pulled her into my chest and swayed to the beat. The song was oddly applicable to Olivia's and my situation – minus the picture-kissing – but that wasn't why I chose it. Ellen and I called the Four Tops' 'I Can't Help Myself (Sugar Pie, Honey Bunch)' our Oldies Distraction trump card. We only used it in really dire situations, when the light at the end of our argument tunnel looked like it was somewhere out on Pluto.

As Olivia squirmed underneath my clammy hands, I hoped it would work on her too.

'When you snap your fingers, or wink your eye,

I come running to you . . .'

Olivia whirled out in a spin, her hair unfurling. In that second, it felt like all eyes in the universe were on us, and while I wished it was a moment in which I wasn't sweating so much, I was actually starting to not care. Even Olivia, red-faced and flustered, was fighting off a smile.

'I'm tied to your apron strings,

And there's nothing that I can do.'

Then, without meaning to, Olivia laughed. It was more of a bark, an eruption that caught her off guard. She covered her mouth to stifle any other unwanted sounds. Pulling her back in my arms, I rocked her around the room just like my dad used to do with my mom as the saxophone solo thrummed. I could feel Olivia staring up at me, her breath heavy.

This time, I sang along with the words, probably much louder than I meant to.

'Can't help myself,
No, I can't help myself.
'Cause, sugar pie honey bunch,
I'm weaker than a man should be.
I can't help myself,
I'm a fool in love you see . . .'

The line stopped Olivia cold, her hand becoming limp spaghetti in mine. As the song continued to whirl around us, her face was only a few inches from mine, her heart hammering into my chest. The breath in my throat slowed, catching behind my teeth. I knew what we'd been through to get to that moment. I knew what I'd done with Becky and Razz and everyone else was wrong. But the way Olivia looked, the way she felt; for once, something was right.

'Can I . . .' I said slowly, looking at her mouth.

Olivia nodded.

That's when I leant down and kissed her, the song still swirling around us. As Olivia's mouth moved with mine, my head swam. Everything about me buzzed, the feeling of her sending electricity running through my veins. When she sank back on to her heels, I moved my head down to follow her, hands pulling her closer into my chest.

After a few seconds, we both came up for air, our faces red.

Olivia swallowed. 'What was that?' she said.

I wasn't entirely sure how to answer. 'Uh, a kiss, I guess?' I said. 'Was that OK? I mean, not OK like, can you give me a Yelp rating, but—'

'No, obviously not that.' Olivia laughed. 'The dance thing. What were you doing?'

'Oh,' I said, feeling relieved. Everything before kissing Olivia was blurry. 'My sister and I call it the Oldies Distraction.' I couldn't help but stammer, my brain tripping over the words. Why was I such a dork? 'Usually it involves singing the song to each other instead of dancing, but I wasn't sure you liked the Four Tops enough to know the words.'

Olivia reached back and lifted my hand, thumb tracing along my palm. I bit my lip, watching her.

'Did it work?' I asked, barely above a whisper.

Olivia looked up at me, a microscopic smile inching across her face. She leant in and kissed me again.

'Yeah,' she said against my lips. 'I think so.'

22

AVENGERS: INFINITY WAR

Posted in MOVIES by <u>Hugh.jpg</u> on September 23 at 9:09 p.m.

Dear Marvel,

Am I really supposed to believe you've just killed off half your characters, the same ones that are going to make you approximately $4.6 bazillion in box office sales in upcoming franchises? I get that you wanted to trigger some sort of emotional reaction in me by axing basically the best characters in your universe and believe me, you did. I am really, really pissed off.

Sincerely,

Literally Everyone

From the outside, the Cabinet looked more like an after-school club for tortured art kids than anywhere that could fit an entire concert. Olivia and I sat in the dark a few cars down from the venue, the tub of spaghetti my aunt Karen left behind sitting open on the dashboard.

Outside, the city buzzed. It was like a living thing, breathing, shouting, laughing. I'd forgotten how huge

New York City actually was, making DC look suffocating in comparison. Even though the streets were narrower here, it felt oddly free, with people darting across the pavement and in between taxi cabs, food carts lined up and down the sidewalk and people pouring out of subway tunnels. As we drove through Brooklyn, a lot of the store-fronts had signs from businesses past. Bagel places, pet stores, record stores, takeout food. It was a city of layers, where its history was as meaningful as its present.

Since we'd left my aunt's apartment, things between me and Olivia had fallen back into place, as if the whole morning hadn't even happened. At every stop light, we narrated the conversations of groups crossing in front of the truck, and sang way too loudly to 'Ain't No Mountain High Enough' with me as Tammi Terrell and her as Marvin Gaye. More than once, we'd glance nervously at each other and smile, then look away quickly, pretending we hadn't. Everything about it was awkward and embarrassing and kind of perfect.

No matter how hard I was trying not to think about the past any more, I couldn't help but wonder what things would've been like if I hadn't stopped talking to Olivia. If, after that night two years ago, I'd kept messaging her, confronted her at school, done something. Anything. Would we still have ended up in the same place? Would anything with Becky have ever happened? Would endings have been even half as much on my radar? There were so many different options, it made my brain hurt. It was weird to think Olivia had been so close to me all along. I was only just now realizing what I'd actually missed.

'OK,' Olivia said, wiping spaghetti sauce from her mouth with the back of her hand. She pivoted toward me in her seat, face shrouded in a bluish shadow now that the sun had fallen behind the buildings. 'The crate is probably in the van. I'm going to go in the club, sneak into wherever Clark's hiding his stuff and find his keys. Then I'll call you over to park the truck next to his van, we break in, get the crate, drop the keys down a sewer grate, and then we bounce. Sound good?'

The Cabinet stretched up for three layers of windows, its front-facing wall painted with a seafoam-green mural of two ladies with big lips and flowing red hair. Their bodies were crossed with the wiry black legs of a fire escape that led down to the left side of the building, where a garage door was propped open. Occasionally groups of people dressed like Olivia – parachute pants and billowy black T-shirts – floated in, usually smoking. They all seemed to suck in their cigarettes as one, releasing into the night a cloud of sour steam, as if they were all the heads of the same, monochromatic dragon.

Olivia's plan sounded reasonable, except for one thing.

'You can't go in there alone,' I said. 'It'll go faster with two people.'

'You don't even know what you're looking for,' she said.

'They're just keys,' I said. 'Let me guess. Little metal ring, four keys, a Disneyland keychain and a lanyard that says "I'm the worst" all the way around it.'

Olivia pressed her shoulders into the chair and tried not to laugh.

I wound more spaghetti around my fork and shovelled it into my mouth. The noodles were ice cold and needed cheese, but they were better than a mangled corndog that'd been rolling around under my chair all day.

'Please let me come with you,' I said. 'What if these hipsters try to buy ice cream off me?'

'Ignore them like they claim their parents do,' she said as she unclicked her seat belt, hands lunging for the door. 'If Clark sees you with me, it'll be eighty times worse. Trust me.'

Olivia stepped out on to the sidewalk and stopped to look at me, one arm propping open the door. She blended in with the people walking behind her, with their black leather backpacks strapped to their shoulders, pink and blue and green hair, nose rings and mushroom headphones twice the size of their ears.

She was probably right, though. I would stick out. Me, in my old T-shirt ripe with sweat, dark blue jeans and too-white Vans.

'When you get back, can we get hot dogs in Times Square?' I said finally. 'There's something about the pollution in the air that just makes them taste more authentic.'

Olivia rolled her eyes. 'I thought we were in a mega hurry to get home.'

'We are. But we can't not celebrate once you get the crate. That'd be like, a waste of a triumph.'

'Yeah, OK,' Olivia said, her smile not quite reaching her eyes. 'Maybe.'

But before she shut the door, she scrambled back inside and across the seat and grabbed both sides of my face. When she kissed me, her entire body sank into mine, sending all the thoughts in my head straight to white. All the noise from the street disappeared, all the cars and the people and the everything. The only things in New York City were me and Olivia.

'Thanks,' she said, her face inches from mine, 'for all this.'

I blinked, my head still light. 'Uh, duh,' I said. 'What else was I gonna do this weekend?'

Olivia lifted her eyebrows. 'Eat ice cream, stalk me, cry yourself to sleep . . .'

'Yeah, *except* that.'

Suddenly, screaming erupted from beyond the garage doors leading to the Cabinet, and just like that, Brooklyn reappeared around us. Olivia and I turned to watch as a guy in a sparkly red jumpsuit carrying a guitar case fast-walked out to a van parked just outside the venue and a guy with a purple Mohawk charged after him. There was a blur of sequins as Jumpsuit Guy flung open the back doors of the olive-green van and tossed the guitar case inside as Mohawk Guy screamed over his shoulder.

'We sold four tickets. Four!' he shouted, just inches from Jumpsuit Guy's face. 'Tell me, genius, how am I supposed to run a business when the bands I book suddenly have a "change in direction"' – he held up sarcastic air quotes – 'overnight. Who wants to hear disco Billy Joel covers? I'll tell you who: nobody!'

There was something eerily familiar about Jumpsuit Guy. The way his blonde hair fireworked out from his long face, the clunky way he walked, like he was secretly a gorilla wearing a human suit. He sat down hard on the van's back bumper so the whole thing shook, and buried his face in his hands.

'Oh my god,' Olivia whispered, just as Jumpsuit Guy's identity finally dawned on me.

'Is that Clark?' I said.

Olivia nodded wordlessly.

'Is he wearing sequins?'

She nodded again.

Also in matching sequined jumpsuits were two guys and a girl I didn't recognize who appeared behind Mohawk Guy, hovering awkwardly against the garage door entrance with their instrument cases pressed against their chests.

'Who brings their own baby grand piano on tour with them?' Mohawk Guy was yelling. 'Do you have any idea how much it's gonna cost me to get this stupid thing airlifted out of my space?'

He threw an arm toward the Cabinet, where a black piano floated thirty feet up from the sidewalk. Ropes twisted around its shiny body, which were being lowered by a crane I hadn't noticed before.

Olivia patted my shoulder frantically. 'There's my mom's stuff!' she said, pointing toward the van and tapping the windshield with her free hand.

'Where?' I said, squinting.

'There, that crate.'

I leant even farther over the dashboard until I zeroed in on the flash of weathered wood in the van, just over Clark's shoulder.

Reaching for the door handle, I exclaimed, 'We have to go get it!'

'No,' Olivia said as her fingers tightened around my shoulder. 'I just told you, it'll only make things worse. I have to do this for myself.' She turned back toward the windshield and bit her lip. 'What do I even say?'

I swallowed. There was so much I wanted to say to Clark, but most of it involved shoving and swearing. Olivia was right though; she had to do this on her own.

'You just go up to him and you say, "Give me my mom's shit back you evil freak, or I'll rip your nips off." And then, if you punch him a little bit, that's cool too.'

Olivia exploded in laughter. 'That's actually kind of perfect.'

I shrugged.

'OK,' she said, nodding to herself. 'I'm gonna do this.' She wiggled her shoulders and took a deep breath.

'You can do this,' I said.

'I can do this,' she repeated. Before opening her door, she leant across the truck again and kissed me quickly. 'I'll be right back,' she said, then slipped out on to the sidewalk and shut the door behind her.

My chest felt heavy as I watched her inch toward the

van and stop just a few feet away from me and the truck. The crane outside the Cabinet was beeping now, the piano swaying gently as it edged closer to the sidewalk. I clenched my fists tight in my lap as Olivia glanced over her shoulder at me before clearing her throat and shouting, 'Clark!'

Mohawk Guy stopped yelling and Clark looked up, his face twisted in confusion. 'Olivia?' he said. 'What're you doing here?'

She looked back at me again and bit her lip. 'I-I'm,' she stammered. 'I'm here for – I want – give me back my – shit. My mom's – shit. Nips. Fuck!' She stomped over to the van and swung her fist back as if to strike. 'I want my mom's shit back,' she said, her arm hovering. '*Now.*'

Clark's face hardened as he took Olivia in, her wiry body contorted, ready to attack. He slowly rose to his feet; at full height, he was almost a head taller than her. Olivia's fist lowered as Clark took a step toward her, his mouth snaking into a terrifying smile. Even Mohawk Guy shot a nervous glance at the rest of Clark's band and stepped backwards.

'Look,' Olivia said calmly, 'I shouldn't have beaten up your car. I'm sorry. But you know that crate is all I have left of my mom. Can you just search deep inside yourself for your last, teeny-tiny shred of humanity and give it back?'

Even from far away, I could see Clark's tongue as it swiped across his teeth. He looked like a tiger licking its lips at the sight of a limping gazelle as he continued edging toward Olivia until her upturned face was only inches from his, where his eyes swept from her head to her toes.

Then, he sighed heavily and said, "K."

Olivia's head jerked back. 'Wait, what?' she said. 'Just like that?'

Clark shrugged. 'Yeah. I mean, to be honest, it's been kind of a burden.' He climbed into the back of the van and slid the crate toward him. 'It was stupid to take it in the first place, but I think I was just in a bad place with us breaking up and all. You know how shitty I am with transitions.' He held the crate out to Olivia and gave a tight smile. 'I'm sorry about everything with Casey. I just — my anxiety has been insane recently with school ending and Yale starting soon, and the band is taking a new creative direction, and that's been really stressful. I get so inside my head and then I shut off emotionally.' He threw a hand toward the girl in the matching jumpsuit standing a few feet away. 'Casey was there.'

Olivia sighed. 'Yeah,' she said, 'I get that.'

'I'm also sorry you had to come all this way to get your mom's stuff back. You know I'd never do anything to it. I should've driven it back to you myself, but I was just — I wasn't thinking straight.' He frowned. 'How'd you get up here anyway?'

Olivia hooked her thumb over her shoulder at me before turning around again. Clark followed her gaze and waved.

'Hey Hugh,' he called out.

I opened my door and stepped on to the street. It was so much cooler out now, and everything smelt like hot sugar and cinnamon from a nearby churro cart.

'Hey,' I said back.

'Well, I guess I should go,' Olivia said. 'Thanks for this. I hope you and Casey are happy. And I'm not like, saying that in a sarcastic way. I really mean it.'

Clark smiled. 'Thanks. I'll see you around?'

'Yeah.'

Olivia's arms locked straight as she struggled to carry the crate back to the truck. I jogged up to her and heaved it into my arms.

'Did you hear that?' she hissed excitedly. 'He just gave it back to me. I didn't have to rip anyone's nips off.'

'When he admitted to having human emotions, I thought I was having a stroke,' I whispered back. I shoved the crate into the back of the Killer truck and slammed the doors, clapping non-existent dust off my hands. 'That was like, way too easy. Now I have all this pent-up nervous energy I was supposed to use to punch in somebody's face.' I shook out my wrists and hopped from foot to foot.

Olivia's mouth quirked up in a smile as she nudged me up against the truck and kissed me deeply, her whole body easing into mine.

'We still have at least an hour before we need to go back to DC,' she said quietly. 'We could go to your aunt's apartment.'

Goosebumps blossomed across my arms. 'Yeah, OK – uh, sure, yeah,' I stammered like an absolute asshole. My thoughts were too blurry to pull out a coherent sentence. 'Sure. Yeah.'

Olivia laughed and shoved away from me so she stood in the middle of the sidewalk. Something about her looked brighter all of a sudden, as though getting the crate back gave her a little more life. Her eyes were shining as she smiled at me, her hair blowing in the churro-scented breeze, and I swore I'd never seen anything more beautiful in my entire life.

Then, a loud crack tore through the air, echoed by a low, rumbling groan. Somebody screamed, the sound of pure, primal fear, and as I looked up, I saw the piano jerk through the air, its ropes splintering. Before I could even open my mouth to scream, the final rope snapped and set the piano free so that it plummeted straight down on to the sidewalk and landed perfectly on Olivia.

Time moved slowly then, the seconds grinding by until everything eventually just stopped. My breathing slowed, nothing about me moved. I just stared.

And then, without warning, time snapped back into focus so that Clark was suddenly at my side, shrieking. Everybody nearby was screaming. But to me, standing motionless on the sidewalk and looking down at the piano, its smashed wood and rectangular keys scattered at my feet, it all sounded so far away, like they were talking through empty toilet paper tubes. For what felt like for ever, all I could do was blink.

'Oh my god!' Clark shouted as he lowered to his knees. His voice was trembling. 'Somebody call an ambulance!'

'She'll be OK,' I finally whispered. 'She'll be fine. She'll just stitch it back up.'

Clark turned toward me slowly, his jaw dropped in horror. 'What?' he said.

'Her – her wrists,' I said. 'It's only her wrists that can't get hurt.'

'Dude,' Clark said, 'a piano fell on her. I'm pretty sure her wrists are fucked too.'

I stumbled backwards until my body crashed into the cold metal of the truck. Where just a few seconds ago, Olivia had kissed me. Where everything had felt completely, totally, absolutely perfect. And – and now, it was over. Olivia was dead.

THE END

. . . Olivia lifted her eyebrows. 'Eat ice cream, stalk me, cry yourself to sleep . . .'

She slid back into her seat and on to the sidewalk, leaning over the dashboard one last time to scoop up another forkful of spaghetti. I crouched down to look for the piano hanging outside the Cabinet and sighed when I saw it was gone. That it had never been there in the first place. Not noticing my visible relief, Olivia dangled the noodles over her mouth before dropping them in.

'If I'm not back in an hour, wait another hour,' she said as she wiped her lips with the back of her hand.

I opened my mouth to tell her to be careful, to watch out for falling pianos, but she slammed the door shut before I could get the words out. Settling back into my seat, I shut my eyes tight, willing the image of Olivia crushed under the weight of the piano out of my head. I wasn't supposed to do that any more. No more endings, no more scaring myself.

Half an hour had gone by when the street lights came on. They cast mushy orange pools up and down the sidewalk as the sun behind the buildings grew dimmer and dimmer. While I rearranged my legs underneath me in as many different ways as I could − criss-crossed, on the dashboard, right leg on top, left leg on top, both legs propped up on the passenger seat − there was still no sign of Olivia.

By the time the first hour closed in, the mixtape Razz had made me called 'What Would Michael Jackson Do? Hint: It's Weird (and Friends!)' finished, so I slid in Marvin

Gaye's *What's Going On*. The inside of the truck echoed with the buzz of voices as the title track poured out of the speakers, followed by a silky saxophone. The voice that came out of Marvin Gaye on this song was my favourite one: understated and yet completely filled with soul. I loved growly Marvin, the one that hit these outrageous notes so hard his voice broke, but nothing compared to Marvin Gaye on 'What's Going On'. The way his voice swelled as the violins crashed behind him, lamenting all the mothers that lost their sons to stupid wars, pleading with the world to figure out what the hell it was doing. It was a song that always made me want to lean back and close my eyes, let it wash over me.

But as I sat there, feeling the same warmth that this album always gave me, I could almost hear Olivia's voice in my head pointing out the gaps in the logic I'd relied on so heavily over the last two years. *How can you still love Marvin Gaye's music if he had such a shitty ending?* Because I did. Behind my parents, he had what I considered the worst ending of all time, and yet his music was one of the few things that could keep me calm after my mom and dad died. This hole in my logic, it was something I'd started to consider when sitting with Olivia next to the pool in New Jersey, but now it was taking on a solid shape in my head. It was starting to make sense, revealing itself one note at a time as 'What's Going On' bled into the next song. As Marvin's voice crawled higher and higher, I sat up straight in my chair, the realization jolting through me like electricity. Olivia was right; it wasn't just endings I hated.

My whole fear around them; it was a fear of something else, what the endings represented. I was scared of losing the people I cared about. People like Olivia.

I ripped the keys out of the truck's ignition, cutting Marvin Gaye off mid-line.

'Sorry dude,' I said to the sky before clamouring out of the truck. Now that everything finally made sense, this couldn't wait.

The garage door entrance to the Cabinet was empty and, I realized as I walked through it, not actually a garage door at all. It was more of a tall metal gate, like the one that kept Dorothy and her posse out of Oz, except covered in band stickers. Just past the gate was a rectangular court-yard that was lined with cinderblock walls and paved with pebbles, where the kind of trailer you attach to the back of a truck sat forgotten in the middle along with a few picnic tables crowded with people. Clouds of smoke hung in the air above them as they talked, totally unaware of or maybe just uninterested in the loud clash of music filtering out from somewhere behind them.

At the end of the courtyard was a doorway lined with dark wooden planks. Even though it was a foot taller than me, I ducked inside and found a man sitting in a barber's chair, half his head shaved by the woman standing over him with an electric hair clipper in her hand. Angry Mohawk Guy was nowhere to be found, probably because he wasn't actually real.

'Where's the music?' I said stupidly.

The woman, bald herself except for blonde peach fuzz

that dusted her scalp, nodded her chin toward a doorway that led down a white tunnel lit with soft purple lights.

Walking through the tunnel, walls covered in drawings, paintings and a corner filled with balloons, I felt like I'd fallen into a dream. I'd been to shows before in DC, at Black Cat and the 9:30 Club with Razz, but nothing like this. Sometimes Razz would drag me along to shows out in Maryland to see bands I'd never heard of, where the venues were actually people's real houses. One show we went to had an elderly woman that chain-smoked in the corner of the kitchen and barked at anyone that forgot to take their shoes off at the front door. But this was weirder somehow. My brain swelled with the possibilities of where Olivia could be in a place like this. Maybe Clark had caught her rifling through his stuff and was holding her hostage in some back room packed with old carnival games. Or she'd gotten lost in the white tunnel and was burrowed up in a corner somewhere, where she could barely remember her own name.

I picked up my pace, winding down the tunnel until it emptied into a large concrete room. Every inch of the walls was painted with colourful patterns, then plastered over with posters and pictures. The band – three girls, all in long dresses and black lipstick – was at the back of the room, standing on top of a small stage raised a foot from the ground as they played to an audience of about forty or so people. Along the left-hand wall was a bar, then a small plastic table where a girl with two braids and a nose ring looped between her nostrils stared up at me.

'Tickets are seven dollars,' she said.

All that was on the table was a can of Diet Coke and a small metal cash box. She opened the box's top and made room for my incoming money.

'I'm not really here to see the show,' I said, craning my neck to get a better look at the room. The crowd was big enough so that picking apart each person took a little concentration. 'I'm looking for someone. Have you seen a girl with really blonde hair in a gorilla bikini T-shirt and swim trunks?'

'Gorilla bikini?' The girl frowned. 'Do you mean Bikini Kill?'

'What?' I said. 'No, her shirt has like a – never mind. Can I just see if she's here? I promise I'm not trying to sneak in.'

The girl rolled her eyes but nodded toward the crowd before beckoning the two girls who'd come in behind me forward.

If Clark wasn't onstage or outside, that either meant he wasn't here yet, or he was in the audience. After the band finished its song – it mostly consisted of wailing and the words 'die' and 'drown' and 'you will die and drown' – everybody clapped and nodded as if the girls had just made a speech about why air was important. Gaps between the crowd started to form as people shifted, getting ready for the next song, and that was when I saw it. Sitting on top of a fold-out chair, as if it had been waiting for me all along.

The crate.

Harps played.

Choirs sang.

The fold-out chair practically glowed.

Before anyone could beat me to it, I charged toward the crate and jammed my fingers between the wooden slats. It was heavier than I expected, a small row of records, some books, a red-and-pink scarf and a metal tin for chocolate-chip cookies clanking around inside.

There was no sign of Olivia anywhere. I hesitated at the back of the room again, crate getting heavier in my arms as I watched each speck of movement in the crowd. Then it occurred to me Olivia could be waiting for me by the truck. She might've spotted the crate, and when Clark spotted her, he probably chased her out of the Cabinet. She would be standing there, beside the truck, face wet with tears. *The crate was so close*, she would wail. Right under her nose. And then, just when she thought all hope of ever getting it back was lost, I would appear, sweaty and slightly out of breath, crate in hand.

I broke into as much of a sprint as I could, arms wrapped around the crate and holding it tightly against my chest. The white tunnel was green now, its lights rotating on a rainbow timer so that none of it looked familiar any more. My feet skidded to a halt as I swivelled my head around, trying to remember which direction I'd come from. But the sight of two people leaning against each other by the wall near the entrance stopped me cold.

It was Olivia.

And Clark.

Their faces were only inches apart, her head tilted back to look up at him, his hand clenching the back of her hair. His other hand was wrapped around her waist, easing her into his stomach. Clark's dirty-blonde hair was unbrushed and stuck up in chunks around his head, which was more just a brainless meatball on a stick than an actual body part. He was wearing a red T-shirt and black leather vest with cowboy tassels that Olivia looped around her fingers.

'Olivia?'

The two of them turned toward me as one, eyes meeting mine. At first, they looked confused. Clark even looked annoyed. But as clarity slid down Olivia's face, she pushed away from him in one quick movement.

'Hugh,' she started to say.

'Is this why you wanted to come in here alone?' I said.

A gulp travelled down her throat and into her chest. The two of them were still holding hands, thumbs linked together in a loose knot. It was like they'd been away from each other for so long that to disconnect now would mean sudden death.

I blinked, waiting for the vision to go away. To figure out that this was all just another stupid ending I'd invented. But this time, it was all real.

'What's this douchebag doing here?' Clark said.

Olivia turned back to answer him, her face a sudden curtain of calm. She was actually going to give him an excuse, like he deserved one. *Oh, this douchebag is here because,* I half expected her to say. Like appeasing Clark was the most important thing, after everything we'd done to get there.

I watched Olivia as she did this, as she placed two hands on Clark's chest and spoke to him with the kind of low murmur someone would use on a crying baby. A lump was forming in my stomach and my throat burnt.

'I'm gonna go,' I said.

But neither of them turned around as I took off running.

23

GREASE

Posted in MOVIES by <u>Hugh.jpg</u> on April 4 at 8:58 p.m.

This is what I imagine the discussion about *Grease*'s final scene looked like. 'Picture this: Danny and Sandy finish the song, get into their car, and then the car FLIES AWAY. No, not metaphorically. Actually. We are going to blow people's MINDS.' The whole thing was more like, a wop bop a loo bop, a wop bam

please

god

no.

By the time I reached the truck again, my breathing was coming in old–man huffs and my shoulders were screaming with pain. I scrambled inside and heaved the crate on to the passenger seat, the door slamming behind me just in time for Olivia to reach the kerb. She yanked on the passenger door handle but was too slow. I'd already locked it.

'Hugh, open the door,' she said, surprisingly calm. But

her hands, working frantically over the handle, gave her panic away. 'Just let me explain what happened.'

'What happened?' I said. 'I know exactly what happened.'

Me, waiting in the truck like an absolute dick-for-brains, not realizing what was going on inside. Finding her with Clark in the tunnel. Her, chasing me out on to the street. It was like a movie, down to the script. A movie with predictable lines and a terrible ending I should've seen coming all along.

'I'm such an idiot,' I moaned.

Pushing my head back into the headrest, I dug the heels of my hands into my eyes and let out a long sound of exasperation into my sweaty palms.

'You're not an idiot,' Olivia said. 'Well, you're acting like an idiot right now, but just unlock the door and let me in.'

A sudden burst of anger surged through me. 'I'm acting like an idiot?' I said, snapping my hands down into my lap. 'I thought we all agreed Clark Thomas was a bad idea.'

Olivia's eyes fell to the ground. 'It's not that easy—' she started to say.

'Not that easy to not make out with someone that steals your most important thing in the world just to torture you? That's the easiest thing ever. I literally cannot think of anything easier.'

I was just babbling then, unable to control the flood of pissed-off words dropping out of my mouth. If I could just say something to make her understand how much the shock and shame were stacking themselves up inside of me like a brick wall, maybe I wouldn't feel so stupid. Maybe she could be the one to wear a little pain like a fucking top hat for once and I could have a turn at being invincible.

'We weren't making out,' Olivia insisted.

'Yeah, not right then.'

'No, not ever.'

She cupped her hands over her eyes and pressed her face to the glass, even though I was pretty sure she could see me.

'Hugh, just open the door so we can talk about this.'

My eyes expanded in my head. 'What's there to talk about? You used me for a ride to New York,' I said. 'You made me think I was doing you some big favour, and then you – you and me, just an hour ago, we – I thought you liked me, but all you wanted was attention.' Everything was dawning on me, a slow curtain of comprehension closing in over my head. 'That's all you ever wanted. From everybody. You pretend not to care about anyone but you can't stand it when people aren't watching you. This whole time you made sure I focused on you, and then now that this is all coming to an end, you go right back to Clark.'

Olivia threw her arms up. 'I knew it,' she exclaimed, her cool expression finally cracking. 'Endings again. And again and again and again. You haven't changed at all. And you – you were always gonna give up and go.'

'Yeah, go with *you*,' I exclaimed. 'I came here for you. I did all this for you, because I care about you.'

Olivia's face flushed red as she flattened her hands against the glass. 'Yeah, that's why you went off and banged Satan's child bride in New Jersey, right? Don't think I didn't see all the sand on the bathroom floor. I'm not a fucking idiot.'

I shut my eyes and rested my head on the steering wheel. 'I didn't – look, I'm sorry about Becky. That was really, really stupid. I thought you wanted me to—'

'How would that make any sense?' Olivia said.

'It doesn't, I know.' I swiped a hand down my face. 'I'm sorry. But I did all that before you and me. You literally waited four seconds after kissing me to go hook up with Clark. Do you have any idea how much I feel like an absolute dick right now?' My clenched fists shook in my lap. 'Fuck, I screwed my sister over so badly. I ditched Razz. I messed everything up, for this?'

'What, so the only way any of this is worth it is if we hook up at the end?' Olivia said.

I shook my head and laughed darkly. 'You know that's not what I meant.'

I turned the engine on and buckled my seat belt. Cars and taxis were clogging the street, their bright brake lights forming a solid line of red. I had to get out of Brooklyn and away from the Cabinet. Away from Olivia.

'Hugh, please don't go,' she said. The steadiness inside her voice was gone now, replaced by a raw panic. 'Please. Please don't go. Just talk to me.' She was almost whining, hands stroking the glass. 'Don't feel like a dick. Please.'

At the sound of her pleading, I could feel my anger

dissolving into a sugary paste. Maybe I did deserve this after what I did with Becky. Maybe it was just a misunderstanding. But then the image of Olivia collapsing into Clark, his hands tangled in her hair, came rushing back so fast, it crushed the wind out of my lungs. Olivia saw it too, the resolve hardening back into my face.

'At least give me my mom's stuff back,' she shouted.

She knocked her knuckles against the window as if I'd forgotten she was there. As I stared straight ahead, quickly trying to map out my next move, the knocking got louder and louder until suddenly it was a pounding. I turned just in time to see Olivia crank her arm back and punch her fist into the window so hard, the glass splintered into a thousand tiny triangles.

When Olivia pulled her hand away, she gaped openmouthed at her knuckles, pulpy and torn, little shards of glass jutting out from her skin like sharpened scales. She flexed her fingers, and as she did, the glass fell and the skin was already starting to reform over her knuckles, creeping like ice over the bones until finally, there was no trace of any damage. The only thing left was the shattered window with a brown-red smudge in its centre and Olivia's expression, harder and more determined than ever.

Before she could rear back her fist for round two, I slid the gear into drive and sent the truck forward. Olivia jumped backwards, as if stung. With the truck on again, Marvin Gaye boomed in my ears, renewing the urgency that'd flowed through me as I ran down the street a few seconds ago.

'Are you really ditching me here?' Olivia shouted over the engine. 'How am I supposed to get back to DC?'

I shrugged, but could tell it looked as shaky as I felt. It didn't matter to me any more how she got home. It really didn't matter. None of it mattered because none of it had been real in the first place.

It mattered so little that I said with as much coolness as I could muster, 'Find your own ride home,' and sped away.

I spent the next three hours driving around New York City in misshapen circles. Aimless and numb, I criss-crossed Manhattan, sighing into red lights and resting my head against the steering wheel, the broken passenger window spiderwebbing out in the corner of my eye. It was just another thing on my long list of stuff for which I owed Ellen an apology.

Part of me wanted to call Razz and part of me wanted to drive straight back down to DC. Then there was the part of me I didn't want to acknowledge, the part that wanted to drive back to Brooklyn, the air in the truck silent and dark and peanut-butter heavy, until I found Olivia and we both went home. Together. But every time that part of me surfaced for even a second, it brought with it a fresh sense of shame that burnt like lava, hot in my veins.

I was so stupid. So so so so so stupid.

It wasn't just that I felt completely and totally rejected. Forget the fact that I'd danced with Olivia to my parents' wedding song or that we'd kissed like, a bunch of times, so much so that for a second, I let myself think she might actually like me back. The worst part was that after everything, she still had a place for Clark somewhere in her brain.

Was I really that bad? And did she really hate herself that much?

Then there was the crate.

From the passenger seat, it watched me with a disapproving quiet, lurching every time I took a corner too fast. Whenever I stopped in traffic, I reached over to rifle through the crate's contents, but something always stopped me just as my hand hovered above it in the dark. There was an invisible force field warning me about getting too close, and it wasn't just shame this time. I was embarrassed.

'I know I shouldn't have stolen you,' I said to the crate.

What made me better than Clark in this situation? At the first chance I got, I took away the one thing I knew would hurt Olivia the most. When faced with the opportunity to punish her, I didn't even hesitate.

'God, I am Clark,' I wailed.

No wonder she'd picked him. I was just some stupid, boring kid who made up stories about his parents and hooked up with the kind of people that ruined lives, who had no future and no college and nothing to offer except an extensive, useless knowledge of bad endings. I didn't even have a shitty leather vest.

24

SHUTTER ISLAND

Posted in MOVIES by Hugh.jpg on September 27 at 10:24 p.m.

This is not just a boring bash-fest for 'it was all just a dream' endings. I seriously don't mind them. But if I've just had to watch Leonardo DiCaprio run around an island playing detective for two hours, this better not all be a freaking dream.

An hour later, I ended up back at my aunt's apartment. I was still holding out hope that Razz hadn't left for California yet, which meant I could only stick around Aunt Karen's place for an hour; that would give me just enough time for a birdbath shower and maybe a twenty-minute nap before I had to get back on the road to DC.

Too tired to respond to Sunny the doorman's chirpy hello, I trudged to the elevator in silence. As I made my way to the fifteenth floor, I wondered where Olivia would stay that night. With Clark, in his van? Or were they already on their way to Canada, the idea of leaving me behind keeping them driving through the night?

When I finally reached my aunt's front door, exhaustion weighing me down, I sucked in a deep breath, prepared to wave away Karen's questions of how my night went. I patted my pockets for Karen's keys, but felt only empty fabric. Had I dropped them when running from the Cabinet? Maybe they'd fallen out in the truck. But when I tried the doorknob, the door swung open.

Though the overhead light in the apartment was on, the living room was empty.

'Aunt Karen?' I called out as I dropped the crate on to the dinner table with a thud.

The hall light was on too, leading to my aunt's darkened bedroom, but the bathroom door was closed. Underneath was a thin strip of light that broke apart with shadows as my aunt moved around inside. With Karen being home, I knew this now meant I'd either need to lie about why I was going out again or wait until she went to bed before leaving for DC, but I didn't have the energy to worry about it.

I rubbed my eyes with the heels of my hands, willing enough strength into my legs to drag myself into the kitchen to make coffee. Littered across the countertop was a half-eaten sleeve of Chips Ahoy cookies and a block of cheddar cheese next to some stale crackers.

'Guess the date sucked,' I mumbled to myself as I rifled through the kitchen cabinets. Hidden behind eight squares of chicken-flavoured Top Ramen and a bag of jellybeans so old they'd all mashed together in one solid rainbow block was a bag of ground coffee beans that looked like it hadn't been opened since the 1990s. 'Jesus Christ, she's worse than me,' I said, grabbing it.

'Karen, do you want some coffee?' I shouted. 'I'm making a pot.' I dumped the remains of the coffee dust into the small coffee machine next to the toaster and added quietly, 'As long as it's not radioactive.' The faucet burbled as I filled up the pot and poured the water over the greyish grounds. I flicked the pot on and called again, 'Karen?' From somewhere inside the coffee machine, something grumbled.

Underneath the bathroom door was the same smudgy yellow light. I knocked lightly. 'Aunt Karen, do you want any coffee?' I said. 'I get that like, this probably means you'd be awake until four in the morning but like, YOLO, I guess.'

A shadow flickered underneath the door, but still, my aunt didn't answer.

I frowned. 'Karen?'

Unease crept across my neck as I glanced down the hallway again at my aunt's bedroom, her rumpled bed just a mound in the dark. If my aunt had come home from her date, wouldn't her purse be somewhere? Her phone? I glanced backwards at the empty dining table and living room floor. Where were her shoes?

But if it wasn't Karen, then who was in the bathroom?

With Sunny the doorman still downstairs, there was very little chance someone had broken in. And what kind of burglar broke into someone's apartment only to freshen up in the bathroom? No, it wasn't a random thief. And if it wasn't Karen, that meant it probably wasn't her date either. There was only one person it could be.

'Olivia?' I whispered.

Something crashed on the other side of the door, something low and hollow, like a body slumping to the floor. In a split second, the rest of the night flashed in front of my eyes:

Olivia, face down on the tiles, blood pooling underneath her body.

Me, too late.

The flashing blue lights of the ambulance circling the buildings outside my aunt's apartment.

Everyone's faces as they watched me, shaking their heads, disgusted at how oblivious I was, at how I could never do the right thing at the right time, how everybody always died because I wasn't paying attention. Because I never knew how to help them until it was too late.

But Olivia was just on the other side of the door. There could still be time to save her.

'Olivia!' I shouted, twisting the doorknob and shoving the door in. It didn't budge. There was something blocking it from the other side. I leant my shoulder into the solid wood and pushed as hard as I could, pain splashing across my back as the door struggled to stay in place. 'Olivia, just hold on! Please, hold on.'

Suddenly the door gave way, swinging open so quickly I stumbled forward and almost tripped over the crumpled heap on the floor. Blinking into the fog of steam clouding the bathroom mirror, I realized it wasn't Olivia on the floor, just towels.

'What the fuck are you doing?' an incredulous voice said from across the tiny bathroom.

I glanced up, breath trapped in my throat. 'Olivia?' I said.

Olivia, her hair wet and dripping atop her bare shoulders, a fluffy green towel wrapped around her body, stood staring at me with her eyebrows bent. On the floor beside the sink were her wrist cuffs, discarded like snake skin on the hexagonal white tiles. But through the steam of the bathroom, I barely registered any of this. Because all I could see were the pair of gold scissors Olivia gripped in her right hand.

In the heavy warmth of the bathroom, Becky's story about Olivia's mom cut through the steam. Of her one weakness, of Olivia's one weakness. My eyes were trained on the scissors and their shiny gold teeth, glinting in the bathroom light. I had to distract Olivia long enough to get them away from her.

I swallowed. 'How did you get in here?'

Olivia jerked her chin toward the doorway. 'I stole the keys like, the second after your aunt gave them to you.'

'Oh.'

A few beats of silence passed between us before Olivia turned around and faced the small, oval mirror hanging over the sink. 'What're you doing here anyway?' she said, her voice going quiet as we made eye contact in the mirror. 'Shouldn't you be on your way to DC?' Anger crystallized her words, her fist clenching tightly around the scissors.

'I shouldn't have left you in Brooklyn,' I said, shame heating my neck. 'I just – when I saw you with Clark I just, I don't know. I panicked.'

Olivia pressed her lips together and looked down into the empty porcelain bowl of the sink. Her eyes glittered with tears. 'Yeah,' she said, her voice thick. I'd never seen her look so small before, the husk of the once-indestructible Olivia Moon somewhere back on the highway. She let out a low laugh. 'I'm really good at making people hate me. It's one of my many superpowers.'

The towels were still pooled at my feet, probably having fallen from the little white shelf that hung on the wall. 'I don't hate you,' I said as I carefully stepped over them, my eyes fixed on the scissors. If I could just get a few steps closer, I could wrestle them out of her hands.

When Olivia looked up again, a tear slipped down her cheek. 'If you don't now, you will,' she said. 'It's basically in your DNA.'

'What're you talking about?' I said.

'You hate your parents. They made one stupid, really bad mistake while, I might add, saving an entire school bus full of kids. And now, according to you, everything good they ever did is gone. You think I screwed you over, so what makes me different?'

My eyes shot down to the towels at my feet as I clenched my jaw hard. She was right. By that logic, I should hate her. But that logic wasn't actually right.

It was my turn to feel my eyes filling with tears. 'There was no bus or bridge,' I said quietly. 'My parents were—' I cleared my throat. I finally had to tell Olivia the truth. The whole truth. 'They were just plain drunk. They went out for dinner in Virginia, had a bottle of champagne each, got so drunk that my dad drove into a fucking tree, and then they died. The end.'

Olivia turned back around, her mouth open. The truth hung between us like a bright red balloon, one we both couldn't take our eyes off.

After a few seconds of silence, Olivia sighed and said, 'Finally.'

As she did this, I watched her hands loosen around the scissors. Without thinking, I sucked in a deep breath and lunged forward. Olivia let out a surprised yelp as I reached out my hands and groped for the scissors, my fingers closing in around the circular handle, but before I could wrench them out of her hands, my shoe got tangled in one of the towels and I lost my footing. Momentum tugged me down, yanking the scissors across the palm of Olivia's hand.

'Ow, you dick,' she shouted as she clutched her hand to her chest.

As I crashed to the floor, my forehead connected with the lip of the sink before I collapsed on to the tiles, numbness spreading slowly across my skin.

Then, everything went black.

When I woke up, my head was clouded in a fug of pain. I

blinked my eyes open, the image of Olivia's face hovering over me obscured by flashes of bright white.

'What happened?' I said.

Just over my left eyebrow, my forehead pounded to a steady beat. I reached up to touch it but as soon as I put any pressure on my skin, pain pulsed out to meet my fingertips.

'Don't touch it,' Olivia said, gently guiding my hand back to my chest. 'God, I thought you were dead.'

'I thought *you* were dead,' I mumbled. The image of the scissors boomeranged back to me and I tried to sit up, but a wave of dizziness patched my vision with black. 'Oh god,' I said, groaning.

'Let's get you on the couch,' Olivia said.

With her arms tucked under my armpits, Olivia tugged me up to my feet with surprising ease. She dragged me over to the couch and propped my head up with three pillows, my legs sprawled out over the cushions in sharp angles. I closed my eyes as Olivia rummaged around somewhere far off. When she returned, she had changed back into her gorilla T-shirt and shorts from before. In her arms, she was carrying a white plastic box with a red cross that she clicked open on the edge of the couch. A first aid kit.

'You went down hard in there,' she said as she soaked a Q-tip in a clear liquid that smelt like the doctor's office. 'And this is coming from someone that used to fall down the stairs for fun.'

She lifted the Q-tip up to my forehead and dabbed it

gently along my eyebrow. A searing pain rocketed through my head, sending my vision blurry again.

'Sorry, sorry, sorry,' Olivia said under her breath when I hissed in pain.

'How long was I out for?' I asked.

'About a minute,' she said back. 'You should probably go to the hospital. I think you're gonna need stitches.'

She produced a little bag of cotton balls from the first aid kit and stuck one to my forehead with a long, gauzy strip of medical tape. That's when I saw the wad of toilet paper stained with red that she clutched in her hand.

'What—' I started to say as I reached over and pried open her fingers, ignoring the pounding in my skull. A perfect slash mark was cut into Olivia's palm, drips of bright red blood trailing down her wrist. But how could that be? It wasn't possible. Only her wrists could get hurt. 'Why isn't it closing up?' I said breathlessly.

Olivia's eyes were locked on her hand. 'I–I'm not sure,' she said.

'I thought it was only your wrists that could get hurt.'

She squinted her eyes at me for a split second, confused, but then rolled them as it dawned on her who must've given me part of this information. 'I thought so too,' she said eventually. 'But now I'm thinking maybe I was wrong the whole time. Maybe it's not a part of my body that makes me vulnerable. Maybe it's a feeling.'

I frowned. 'What do you mean?'

'My mom,' Olivia swallowed, her face level with mine as she crouched down on the floor next to the couch, 'her moods were always so up and down my whole life. But like, a sort of regular up and down, where if she was sad, we just hung out on the couch and watched our favourite movies and then she was happy again. But right before she died, it was a different kind of down. A permanent one, where nothing could bring her out. I'd make her strawberry pancakes and read her books in bed, and when that didn't work, I got mad. I got *so* mad. I would scream and cry. She could heal her body up every other way, so why couldn't she just change this? She wouldn't tell me what was wrong – I don't think she even *could*. So, I just assumed it was me.'

Olivia stared down into her broken palm, but by the way her eyes glazed over, I could tell she wasn't really here.

'Right before she died, she hadn't gotten out of bed for an entire week. Her bedroom smelt like dried sweat and old food from all the dirty plates shoved under her bed. It was like she was just a hollowed-out version of herself, like the universe had carved out everything that ever made her *her*. And then when I came home one day, she was really gone.'

Tears dropped from Olivia's eyes, leaving wet tracks down her face. Without thinking, I reached up and brushed them from her cheeks. At the feeling of my fingers on her skin, Olivia looked up.

'I used to think she spent all day trying to figure out what would kill her. But now,' she glanced down at her hand, traced the groove of the cut with the tip of her finger, 'I think it only took one try. Because it wasn't her wrists that made her vulnerable; it was her mind.'

My memories flashed back to Olivia just before I accidentally sliced the scissors across her skin. She'd looked so small and empty. Nothing like the fearless version I'd grown so used to, the one that made me feel stronger just by standing next to her.

'And that's why your hand didn't heal. Because you wanted to die.'

At this, Olivia's head snapped up. 'Die?' she said. 'Who said anything about me wanting to die? After screwing things up with you, I just felt broken.'

'But your wrist cuffs were off.'

'I'd just taken a shower,' Olivia said. 'Leather and water don't mix.'

'Then what were you doing with the scissors?'

'I wasn't going to kill myself, I was going to cut my hair,' she said. 'Haven't you ever seen a movie? Whenever a girl has a mental breakdown in a movie, she always cuts her hair.' Olivia shook her head and laughed. 'Jesus, you really do always go straight to apocalypse. Is that why you charged into the bathroom like a freaking SWAT team?'

'I-I . . .' I stammered, but at the sound of Olivia's laughter I couldn't help but laugh too. 'I guess so,' I said.

Suddenly the whole situation felt so stupid and hilarious. Me storming the bathroom like the freaking Rock, wrestling the scissors out of Olivia's hand and then knocking myself out on a sink. The only person who'd made tonight the end of the world was me.

Olivia ducked her head down on to my chest, her

shoulders shaking, as I laughed so hard I could barely breathe. When she lifted her face up, her cheeks were streaked with tears again, but they were the good ones this time.

'God, this is the worst ending ever,' I said eventually.

Olivia swept the hair off my forehead and smiled sadly. 'Did it ever occur to you that this might not actually be an ending?'

With that, I remembered the moment just before I fell, what I'd said to Olivia. What she'd said.

'When I told you about my parents,' I said, swallowing, 'you said "finally". Did you know I was lying the whole time?'

Olivia shook her head. I could see the thoughts running through her mind as her eyes darted around the room.

'I didn't at first,' she said eventually. 'I mean, the school bus thing seemed kind of insane, but I was willing to give you the benefit of the doubt. But when you said they drove off the Woodrow Wilson Bridge, that's when I knew you were lying. I've been on that bridge before; there's no way you can drive over those barriers unless you've got a ramp or something.'

She was right. The barriers were waist-high and solid concrete.

'Why didn't you say something?' I said. 'You just let me look like an idiot.'

Even though anger was prickling my fingertips, I knew it wasn't directed at Olivia. It was with myself for coming up with such a dumb lie, for getting caught.

'Because I knew why you were doing it. You said so yourself; you needed to give your parents a better ending, and I didn't want to take that away from you. I knew you'd tell me the real story eventually, and if you didn't, you'd probably have a good reason. Like me ditching you for Clark, for instance.' She glanced up at me, her eyes refilling with tears. 'Nothing happened with me and Clark,' she said quietly, her gaze falling again. 'I promise. But it would have, if you hadn't shown up. And maybe that's just as bad.'

'It doesn't matter any more,' I said.

The hurt I felt at seeing Clark with Olivia was still lingering underneath the surface of my skin, but I knew it was irrelevant now. Besides, I'd done my fair share of shady shit this weekend, too. I tucked a chunk of hair that'd fallen across her face behind her ear.

'I just—' I started to say. 'I think I always knew deep down, somehow, that my parents weren't terrible monster-humans, but when we found out they were drunk when they died, everything about it just felt so intentional in how stupid it was. When you're a parent, you're supposed to do everything you can to make yourself OK, so you can take care of your kids. Right? So, if my parents cared so little about themselves that they would drink two entire bottles of champagne and then get in a car, it made me think, did they ever care about me at all?'

After they died, I pored over every memory of them, every 'I love you', holding it up to the light. What if I'd misinterpreted all of it? That where I thought they were just weirdo hippies with excellent taste in music, who would do anything for anyone and loved me and my sister more than they loved Marvin Gaye and The Temptations combined, they were actually someone else? Was our chaotic house just a conveniently eccentric pair of clothes hiding a scabby body underneath? Was that whole thing with the Buzz Cuts at the baseball game just my dad's attempt at being a big, macho dude or impressing those girls instead of simply doing what was right and showing me how to be a good person?

Where my parents once were, in my mind, became a cut-out of their general shapes, the insides just an echoey cave. And sometimes in my darkest moments, the ones where I lay in bed until the sun came up, staring at my ceiling and feeling nothing but a cold, featureless fear, I had no trouble filling in the blanks.

'Nothing about their endings made sense,' I said. 'If they were saving some kids or deciding to die together like that scene in *Toy Story 3*, you know, the ending part where—'

Olivia nodded. 'I know the part.'

'Right, OK, like that. If they had endings like that, I used to think maybe I wouldn't be so messed up over it. Maybe it wouldn't be so bad. But to just slam so hard into a tree that the actual dashboard wrapped around it?' The memory made me flinch. 'My parents weren't bad people, or stupid or reckless. It wasn't like they were constantly drunk or whatever. I mean, at least I don't think they were.'

That was another part about doing a post-mortem on memories of my parents. I thought obsessively about their drinking, about every glass of anything. They sometimes had a glass of wine at dinner and they could go hard on special occasions, like my cousin's wedding or Ellen's graduation. But what if it was something more? Something darker? Were they secret alcoholics and I was just too wrapped up in my stupid friends and school and everything else to see it? What if everything was in front of me the whole time, and I was too blind to notice? And what did that mean for me and alcohol? What if drinking a whole bottle of champagne and then crashing into a tree was in my DNA?

'But after they died, the way they went − it was all I could think about. It was like nothing else mattered, and I started to think yeah, OK, maybe they were secretly these terrible worm people and I was too stupid to see it. Because otherwise, what kind of person does that? People who are broken, people who are reckless.' I curled my hands into fists. 'Maybe, actually, I was the one who got it all wrong, and I only figured it out at the end.'

'But even if you had, so what, Hugh?' Olivia said. 'What does it matter now? Your memories of them are what matters, not how they died.'

'You wouldn't care if you thought you were lied to your whole life?'

'You weren't lied to your whole life,' she insisted. 'When are you gonna see that it's you that's putting these thoughts in your head, the one that's judging the way your parents died and letting it ruin every good memory you ever had of them? I mean, yeah, there are probably assholes out there that would have something to say about it, but not the people who actually knew your mom and dad.'

'But that wasn't how they were supposed to go,' I said. 'They weren't ever supposed to go.' I bit down on my lip, my eyes blurring with tears. 'They died before I even realized they could. Before I realized anyone could. That *I* could. Suddenly everything felt like chaos. Nothing was guaranteed. You can live this amazing life with love and success and happiness and then you make one wrong move and you're dead. That's it. What if that happens to me?' Olivia was so still, I wasn't sure if the sound of my voice was lulling her to sleep, but I couldn't stop now. Not when I was finally admitting the truth. 'All this shit with endings – I was thinking about it while you were in the Cabinet. You were right. It's not just bad endings I hate, it's endings in general. Even when I gave my parents this cool ending where they saved a bus full of kids, I still hated it, because they were still gone. But that's not even all of it. My parents dying was the first time I woke up to the fact that one day I'm going to too and I don't know, it was terrifying. It still is.'

Olivia smiled softly. 'Of course it is,' she said. 'You're human. We're all scared of big, giant things we don't understand. Why do you think so many people hate Facebook?'

I laughed through my nose. 'But instead of just like, confronting that fear, I took it out on *Interstellar* and *Buffy*.

I became this giant dork that used all that as an excuse not to go outside. Because if I judged everything on the ending, maybe that's how everyone else would remember me too. I do not want to be the guy that died doing some stupid YouTube challenge.' I groaned. 'God, this all sounds really, really lame when I say it out loud.'

'It's not lame,' Olivia said. 'I know way too well how good it feels to distract yourself from your actual problems. I used to think if I just changed my clothes every couple months, nobody would ever see how lost I was. But I just ended up becoming a cartoon character.'

I lifted my hand up to meet Olivia's, which was resting on my chest. We both flexed our palms against each other so each finger lined up.

'I'm sorry about what happened with Clark,' she said. 'I just – I was so scared that after this was all over, you would leave. So, I thought if I could make things work with Clark, I could leave you first and it wouldn't hurt so much. I don't know, it was stupid.'

'I'm sorry I lied about my parents. Again.' Our fingers locked and dropped on to my chest so Olivia and I could meet eyes. 'It wasn't part of some great big plan of deception, or whatever. It just never occurred to me that you wouldn't know how they died and, I don't know. It seemed like a good opportunity to rewrite the past, so maybe not everybody around me thought my mom and dad were these disgusting drunks.'

'I don't think that,' Olivia said. 'And I'm pretty sure nobody else does either.'

I nodded. 'And I know what you mean about Clark, even though I still maintain he's a giant demon baby.' Olivia smirked. 'It's like with my parents. I know it's way more complicated than I made out, but it was just so much easier to look at it in black and white. After they died, I didn't know what was real any more.' Tears pushed at the back of my eyes as my voice dropped to a hoarse whisper. 'Even though they had a shitty ending, they were good people. They took care of me and my sister.'

Olivia nodded. 'They can be both,' she said quietly.

'Yeah,' I said, clearing my throat. 'And I think I always knew that somehow, in a way. But maybe now I can actually admit it out loud.'

Olivia unlaced her fingers from mine and stuck out her pinkie. 'No more distractions and no more lying?' she said. I nodded and cinched my pinkie finger around hers. 'Not to each other and not to ourselves.'

'Deal.'

She lifted my hand to her mouth and kissed it, her lips lingering against my skin as she started to smile. If I hadn't been 99 per cent sure it would result in me barfing spaghetti all over myself, I would have sat up quickly and kissed her for real. It was the only thing I wanted, to just be close to her again, to be happy and together not in spite of all the shit we'd been through that weekend, but because of it.

I was trying to manoeuvre myself into a position where this would be somewhat possible without all the puke just as the front door to my aunt's apartment swung open.

'Kids, do not eat oysters on a first date,' my aunt Karen said as she peered into her purse and rummaged around for something at the bottom. 'Take my word for it when I say there's no sexy way to slurp down—' At the sight of me struggling to push myself on to my elbows, of the bloody toilet paper wrapped around Olivia's hand, Aunt Karen froze. 'Oh my god, what happened to you two?'

A fresh wave of pain crashed through my skull. 'Minor misunderstanding,' I said with a wince. 'I think we might need you to drive us to a hospital.'

Olivia nodded. 'Sorry in advance about the blood.'

25

SIXTEEN CANDLES

Posted in MOVIES by <u>Hugh.jpg</u> on November 8 at 8:19 p.m.

I'm like super happy Molly Ringwald gets her dream dude at the end of this movie, but can we just talk about how this is the same guy that, a few hours earlier, swapped his drunk ex-girlfriend for some underwear?

After we came out of the ER at the Columbia University hospital the next morning, my forehead sewn back together and the slash on Olivia's hand glued shut, the two of us sat on a bench outside the hospital while my aunt took care of the insurance paperwork at the reception desk inside.

'If we're starting fresh with no lies, then there's something I have to tell you,' Olivia said suddenly.

I turned to look at her, but she was staring out at the darkened street, which was still busy despite the early morning hour.

'Is this the part where you—' I started to say, but she didn't let me finish.

'I broke your sister's truck,' she said.

An ambulance wailed its way on to the street, the siren going flat as it disappeared into an underground parking lot. Olivia's eyes were still trained forward, set on the line of trees across the street as the watercolour blues of the ambulance's flashing light passed over her face.

'You . . . what?' I said.

'I jiggled the wires when you were in the phone booth at the gas station. I know it's stupid and I shouldn't have done it, but I was scared. I knew once we got my mom's stuff back, everything would be over. So, I tried to make it last as long as I could.'

'But you fought me on it so hard,' I said, remembering our argument in the New Jersey motel room.

She shrugged. 'I had to make it look real.'

'You didn't have to do that,' I said. 'I told you, I'm not going anywhere.'

'Yeah, I know that now. But I was worried you were gonna be like everyone else.' When she finally glanced over at me, her eyes were shiny with tears. 'I'm sorry I didn't trust you,' she said. 'And I'm sorry the idiot had to come up and fix everything. I'll pay for the parts, or whatever.'

I shook my head. 'It was actually good that Dan came up. Our throw-down was long overdue.' Shrugging at Olivia, I said, 'Dan's "the idiot".'

She laughed quietly. 'Yeah, I got that.'

It was almost two o'clock in the morning, the ER waiting room filled with mostly drunk people and

304

teenagers. It wasn't even half as interesting as *Law and Order: Special Victims Unit* would have me believe, mostly quiet except for one of those weird game shows where people fought each other with foam noodles over water the colour of toothpaste playing on a TV behind the reception desk.

'So,' I said, my voice echoing against the concrete surfaces that surrounded us, 'what next?'

When I said it, I was obviously joking, so I was surprised when Olivia said back, 'I think I need to stay here.'

I frowned. 'What're you talking about? You can't stay here.'

Olivia shook her head. 'I can't go back to DC, to an empty house.'

'You don't have to,' I said. 'Come stay with me and my sister. Our house is basically a giant thrift store, but I'll put a sheet over my parents' collection of antique porcelain clowns and you won't even know they're there.'

She cracked a smile. 'You and your sister have a lot of shit to work through,' she said. 'We said no more distractions, remember?'

'But where are you gonna stay?'

A long breath streamed from her nose. 'My grandparents live out in the Bronx,' she said. 'They're my dad's mom and stepdad, but they've always been really good to me. It's been a long time since I've been around my family and . . . I don't know, I just think it's a good idea right now. I called them when you were with the doctor and my grandma practically peed her pants. She should be here in an hour.'

The memory of a chihuahua in a gold party hat emerged in my mind. 'Grandma Reggie?' I said.

'The one and only,' Olivia nudged me with her elbow and added, 'you giant stalker.'

She leant her head on to my shoulder and settled into my side as we watched another taxi weave down the street. I didn't want to admit it, but lingering with the warmth of having Olivia so close was fear. Things were only just getting back on track and now I was losing her again. But I couldn't deny that staying here was a good thing for her. We both knew what it meant; she could finally have a family again.

As if she could read my mind, Olivia laced the fingers of her good hand with mine.

'Chill out, Ending Boy,' she said softly. 'You're not getting rid of me that easy. Next semester, you'll get into some cool indie film school in New York and we'll go to weird restaurants in Brooklyn every weekend and eat salad out of tin cans or something stupid.'

I rested my chin on the top of her head and smiled into her hairline. 'I'd rather just post a cardboard box up outside your grandparents' house.'

She laughed quietly from underneath me. 'You do realize you can apply for college at literally any point in your life, right? It's not like the 1800s, where you turn sixteen and basically become a spinster cat lady.'

I shrugged. 'I'll cross that bridge when my box is under it.'

She tipped her face up and kissed me, the combination

of painkillers and the feeling of Olivia's hand reaching up to my cheek leaving my body feeling warm and light. Even though she'd insisted I wouldn't be able to ditch her, all I could think was that I was the one she'd need to get rid of.

Razz was sitting on his porch, swinging the keys to his mom's station wagon around his middle finger as my aunt pulled up to the kerb in front of his house. At the sight of us, he didn't stand. He just watched as Karen and I said goodbye before I unlocked his front gate and slowly made my way up the steps, hands shoved deep in my front pockets.

'You look like a mob boss,' I said.

His feet, resting against the top of the porch railing, kicked up to let me through like a bridge making way for a boat.

'Please, my son,' he said in his best mafia voice, all scratchy and with an accent that was probably supposed to be Italian. He gestured to the chair beside him with gnarled fingers. 'Have a seat. PS, there's no such thing as the mob.'

After Olivia's grandma came to pick her up, I finally called Ellen and explained the whole night's debacle to her. She promised to call Razz, who then assured her he wasn't going anywhere. Still, I'd felt nervous the whole drive home, as though I'd arrive at his house and find the entire place empty with 'FUCK OFF HUGH' spray-painted across his front door.

Groaning, I sat down. Even though I'd been sitting for the last five hours, my body welcomed the ease of pressure so much, I could practically feel my bones giving each other a high five. As my aunt Karen drove me back into DC and neared the exit for Georgia Avenue, with Marvin Gaye keeping us company from the speakers, streets I'd known my whole life sprouted up around me. They looked brighter in a way, tweaked with that warm, goldish glow your hometown gets after you've been gone. I'd only been away for two days, but everything felt different somehow. Familiar, but unfamiliar. Mine, but equally everybody else's, too. I loved DC, had been there for ever, but instead of being everything, it just felt like home. The bottom level of something more, in a way I couldn't put my finger on.

For a few minutes, Razz and I watched the cars come and go down his street. His neighbourhood was more or less identical to mine, just with different faces underneath the porch awnings.

'This is the last time you'll have this view until Christmas,' I said quietly.

This view he'd had almost every single day of his life. It was a strange thought, but one that didn't bum me out as much as I expected it to. Razz just nodded.

'Do I even need to say how sorry I am, or can you tell by the way I'm breathing?' I said after a couple more seconds of surprisingly easy silence.

Razz bobbed his head from side to side, weighing his options. 'It'd still be cool to hear,' he said finally.

I turned in my chair to face him. 'Dude, I'm so sorry,' I said. On his black T-shirt was a snake wearing a bloody crown. It was flicking its tongue into wisps of smoke, daring me to say the wrong thing. 'I screwed up so badly, kiss-and-make-up is like a distant blip on the forgiveness radar.'

Razz's body slumped as he tucked a chunk of hair underneath his purple beanie. 'It's fine,' he said with a sigh.

'No, it's not fine,' I insisted. 'You're my best friend and I ditched you on our last night together before you move across the country. It's the exact opposite of fine.'

'Hugh, it's fine.' Leaning forward in his chair, Razz gripped his hands on the plastic arms and looked me dead in the eye. 'Seriously. All this stuff with Olivia – I was annoyed, yeah, but I know why you did it. It's why we're best friends in the first place.'

'Because I'm the world's biggest douchebag?' I said.

Razz snorted. 'Sure, Hugh. You're the world's biggest douchebag.'

'I know this sounds stupid but – god, I can't believe I'm saying this.' I swallowed. 'I think you were right. I did pick Olivia over you, but it's not because I think she's cooler, or whatever. It's because maybe, I don't know, I was afraid we'd stop being friends when you moved to California. So if I went with Olivia, maybe I'd have something to focus on when you were gone.'

Sitting there next to him, I felt so vulnerable and small, like if he wanted, he could squash me into nothing.

'What?' Razz turned in his seat. 'Please tell me you

don't actually think that. You're literally my only friend.'

'Yeah, until you move to California and everyone sees how rad you are.'

'Hugh. You were the only person in high school that would talk to me. The only. Person. You've always been there for me,' he waved his hand around, 'obviously minus this weekend, but we're moving past that. You seriously think I'm just gonna forget that because I might meet some badass climate change activists in California?'

I squinted at him. 'Is this supposed to make me feel better?'

'I'm joking.' He punched my arm lightly. 'You're my best friend, dude. Three thousand miles isn't going to change that.'

He smiled at me. There wasn't much Razz and I didn't know about each other. All those days walking home together, skateboard slung over my shoulder because Razz had terrible balance and couldn't stay on his without falling flat on his face, dinners at his house, movies on the weekend, concerts off U Street. Even compared to the guys I'd been 'friends' with from elementary school until my parents died, nothing touched how close I was with Razz.

'Olivia told me about Becky Cayman and what she did to you in tenth grade,' I said suddenly. My voice was so thick with guilt I wasn't even sure I could get the sentence out. Everything I said dropped to a whisper. 'I actually defended her to you,' I said. 'I made you listen to me talk about her like she was this great person, and I'm so, so sorry.' A tightness squeezed my chest, so strong I felt almost breathless. 'How could you still want to be friends with me?'

Razz's jaw set as his eyes darted around the porch. The tension was obvious in his arms and by the way he started to nervously flick his fingernails together.

'But it's not just that,' I said. 'You told me so many different times and in so many different ways that you didn't like her and I just kept pushing her on you. I should've listened. I should've asked.'

'You trust people, Hugh. That's not a bad thing.' Razz let out a long breath. 'OK, at least maybe not most of the time.'

'But I trust you more than anyone. That's what makes this so particularly shitty.' I swallowed. 'I promise I didn't know what she did. I really didn't.'

Another sliver of hair fell across his nose. This time when he blew it away, it just landed in the same place.

'Why do you think I went to the counsellor at Mount Luther for so long?' he said, tucking the stray hair behind his ear. 'It's not because I was obsessed with Mr West. Homeboy smelt like straight-up blue cheese.'

This thought landed straight in my chest, punching the breath out of my throat. 'I thought you were going because you were transitioning,' I said quietly. 'Why didn't you tell me it was because of Becky?'

'Because you didn't *ask*.'

A plane coming out of Reagan airport crossed over the trees and buzzed above us. I squinted up into the sunlight to watch it pass, cutting through the cloudless blue of the sky, as my throat tightened. Razz clenched his hands around his knees and sighed.

'Like, obviously I knew you didn't know about what Becky did to me,' he said. 'And do you know why I thought that? Because you're not a butthole.'

I glanced down at my lap. 'This weekend would suggest otherwise,' I said quietly.

'OK, so you picked your fantasy girl over me on what was supposed to be my last night in DC. That sucked. I'm not gonna lie. I spent the whole night watching all *The Hobbit* movies by myself, and that's a sacred tradition I wanted to share with you. It's over now, though.' He clapped his hands together. 'But do I think, for one second, that you're the type of person that would know Becky Cayman basically tried to ruin my life and then shove in my face how amazing she is?' He cracked his knuckles. 'Absolutely not.'

'Then why didn't you just tell me I was being an asshole?'

He barked a laugh. 'Because I was embarrassed. Do you think I want to reminisce about the time I went to school one morning and everyone suddenly acted like I had herpes?'

The thought settled over me, and I nodded.

'It's like, I know you're a good person,' he continued. 'But just because you're a good friend and a good ally doesn't mean you know everything about me. Sometimes it felt like, because you care about me, you thought you couldn't do anything wrong.'

'You're right,' I said. 'I should've asked, and I'm really sorry. If it makes you feel any better, I don't think me and Becky are friends any more.'

'Yeah, that's what I hear,' Razz said.

'What?'

He pretended to smooth down the wrinkles in his T-shirt but I could see the way his fingers hesitated over the fabric.

'Becky called last night and apologized for everything. She actually sounded pretty genuine for someone that's been lobotomized.'

My jaw must have been hanging open wider than I thought because Razz laughed.

'I'm serious,' he insisted. 'It's whatever now. I mean, it'll never be whatever, but that was so long ago, and I just want to move on and not let that be my story any more. You can even keep hooking up with her and I won't—'

'Wait, what?' I could feel the colour of my face going so red it was almost purple. 'You knew about me and Becky?'

Razz gave me a bored look. 'Dude, nobody likes Becky Cayman *that* much, at least not without a really good reason. And your reason just happened to be, you two were getting it on. You're like the least subtle person ever.'

I leant back in my chair, stunned. 'I can't believe you knew and didn't say anything,' I said eventually.

'What was I supposed to say? Please stop boning the hottest girl in school because she humiliated me two years ago?'

'Yes,' I exclaimed. 'Exactly that.'

'Well, I'm not that guy, OK?' Razz rolled his shoulders backwards. 'If you want to be friends with someone, you do you. I really don't care. It was a long time ago, and I know she hasn't done anything to you, except weird voodoo rituals on all the dolls she keeps in her Hugh shrine.'

My eyes widened and Razz shrugged.

'I mean, I just assume that's what she does on weekends,' he said.

I sighed through my nose. 'Even if I wanted to keep hanging out with her, I don't think it'd be the same,' I said. Part of me still thought I did know the real Becky, but that lingering doubt, the fact that I had gotten something so important about her so wrong, still hurt. 'Maybe one day we'll be friends again. I don't know, we'll see.'

Razz scooped up an open can of BBQ Pringles from his feet and offered me one.

'I can live with that,' he said. 'So, about this whole grand theft auto thing. On a scale of one to dropping the H-bomb, how pissed is Ellen at you? When you said you were road-tripping to New York with Olivia Moon, you failed to mention it included *stealing* your sister's most prized possession.'

I grabbed a chip from the stack and dropped it carefully into my mouth.

'I don't know,' I said, chewing. My mouth was still sour from all the neon-orange Cheez-Its Karen and I picked up from a gas station outside of Manhattan and scarfed on the drive down. 'At first, she wanted to behead me, but now I'm not really sure. She was supposed to have this crazy-big meeting today with the manager at Giant to see if they want to stock Killer, but I kind of, you know, screwed everything up by stealing her merchandise.'

Razz whistled. 'Diabolical,' he said.

Ellen hadn't wanted to talk about the meeting when I called from the hospital. All she wanted to know was whether or not I was alive, if my giant fail of a fall had given me brain damage. We'd talk about the rest when I got home.

My body slumped forward so my forehead rested on my knees. As birds chirped overhead in a low, blurry murmur, I realized how nice it was outside. Not humid or sticky, but sunny and calm. The kind of calm that made the air feel like water. There was even a breeze ruffling the trees, which meant fall wasn't far away.

'So,' Razz said quietly. 'Where's Olivia?'

I chewed my tongue and hesitated. Our goodbye was still fresh in my mind, on a constant loop for the entire drive to DC. Razz watched as sadness and hope flickered across my face.

'She's OK,' I said eventually. 'She's gonna live with her grandparents in New York for a while.'

Razz nodded, then looked at me slyly from the corner of his eye. 'And you guys . . . did you . . .'

'Did we what?'

'Are you gonna make me say it?'

I gave him a look.

'Fine,' he said. 'Are you boyfriend–girlfriend?'

'Oh my god.' I shook my head against my legs. 'Are we boyfriend–girlfriend? What are you, four?' I sat up straight and adjusted the brim of my hat. I could feel Razz's eyes on me, his breathing quiet as he waited for my answer. 'OK yes, fine, I kissed her,' I said all at once.

Razz let out a squeal. 'I knew it. You're so freaking predictable.'

'Can we not make this about how I'm obsessed with it-girls, which, by the way, I still dispute.'

'No, I was being a dick about that.' Razz bit into another chip. 'I'm sorry for making you seem like some thirsty bro. I was just mad. In all seriousness, I approve this message. Olivia was never one of Becky's spineless lemmings, she was always weirdly cool. And I genuinely think you can learn something from her versatile fashion sense.'

I laughed and shoved his shoulder. 'I hate you.'

Inside his house, Razz's mom was pacing around and packing a snack box for their trip. I could hear her footsteps crossing through the kitchen and dining room, her shouts to Razz's dad filtering out through the open front windows.

'Did you really like me in tenth grade?' I said suddenly.

Razz made a sound that was a cross between a groan and a laugh. 'Of course I liked you,' he scoffed. 'Our high school was practically a Hugh Copper fan club, and Becky was our fearless leader.'

I tilted my face in his direction. 'Do you still like me?' I asked, eyebrows raised.

Now, he gave a full-on snort. 'Dream on,' he said. 'Unless you're Chris Hemsworth dressed as Thor, I'll have to give you a hard pass.' He emptied the can of Pringles on to his lap and picked through the dust. 'Actually,' he said slowly, mulling the word around in his mouth, 'I've already sorta been talking to this guy at Berkeley. He's gonna be a freshman too. We met on one of those freshman Facebook groups. He's from Florida and his name is Juan. He's Cuban.'

A shard of light caught Razz's cheeks as he moved his face toward the sun, all so he could hide the fact that he was blushing.

'*Muy caliente*,' I said, exhausting what little I could remember from high school Spanish. Razz and I had never talked about guys before, at least not in a romantic way. We were tiptoeing into new territory. 'So, when you say talk, do you mean you play Words With Friends together, or are you like, Snapchat bros?'

Razz rolled his eyes. 'We're texting. He wants to take me out for Cuban food when I finally get to California, which, no thanks to you, will now be a day later than planned.'

'My condolences,' I said, despite the tooth-heavy grin spreading across my face. 'Dude, that rules, though. Are you gonna let me meet him?'

'Duh,' Razz said. He brushed the Pringle crumbs from the tops of his legs, creating a blank midnight-black slate. 'Once you get over your baby-life crisis you can come out and eat tamales with the big dogs.'

Epilogue

MARVIN GAYE

Posted in LIVES by <u>Hugh.jpg</u> on August 29 at 8:47 a.m.

Marvin Gaye had a weird life. I get it. Sometimes I'm still not sure if his songs are about people or drugs. But there's no denying he bled soul. He was one of those musicians where every note of his hits you hard. Yes, he slipped up at the end – and a bunch of times in the middle – but he kept trying for better until the very last heartbeat, and his songs will always mean more than any bullet ever could.

I hadn't been back to my parents' graves since their funeral. Even then, I wasn't actually there. In my head, I was somewhere off in the Lincoln Theatre listening to Marvin Gaye sing, anywhere that could bring me even a decimal point of comfort.

But when, after waking up the first morning post–New York, Ellen asked if I wanted to go with her to Prospect Hill Cemetery on the other side of the McMillan Reservoir, I didn't hesitate. After everything I'd been through over the last few days, what once was impossible now seemed like the only logical thing to do.

The Prospect Hill Cemetery was a German-American cemetery, one that'd been around since the 1800s. When Ellen said that was where our mom and dad were going to be buried, I thought she was joking. We were Swedish. But Prospect Hill was the only place with new plots in DC Ellen could find, and besides, Mom and Dad would probably think the whole thing was funny. In the end I agreed, but mostly because the only other option was actively participating in the decision of where to bury my parents, which was not something I was willing to do.

The grass of the cemetery was still green from summer, but the leaves on the trees that shadowed the grounds were already starting to yellow. A few had given up and fluttered to the floor, where I crunched them underneath my shoe in an attempt to not look up. Other than that, the grounds themselves were empty except for an old man with a basket full of dead flowers and a woman speeding around in a golf cart.

Ellen, Dan and I walked to the north section of the cemetery in silence. Everything my sister and I needed to say to each other had already been said the night before.

Yes, she'd been mad about the weekend.

Yes, she had already gotten over it.

Yes, she'd rescheduled her meeting.

Yes, it was all gonna be fine.

Yes, I could still live at the house.

And yes, she still loved me.

She didn't ask any questions about Olivia or the

specifics of the weekend and I was grateful. There were times when I thought about bringing it up myself. Ellen would stare at me, her eyebrows raised and waiting for the rest of my sentence, but each time I stopped short, unable to bring myself back to the weekend and the lies that had finally caught up with me. Not because it was something I couldn't bear to think about or discuss. I was over that person, over the deliberate silence and the useless avoidance. It was because I had a new beginning to think about, one where I acknowledged my parents out loud and remembered the good along with the bad. The one where Olivia had a family and I had her.

'Here we go,' Ellen said, stopping short before two squat gravestones. She let out a long breath through her nose.

I'd already walked past them, caught up in my game of squishing as many crunchy leaves as I could at the exact right angle of my shoe. I rounded back and paused beside my sister. Together we stood shoulder to shoulder and looked down.

Janet Copper, Beloved mother and wife

Harold Copper, Beloved father and husband

Grinding my toe into a twig shaped like a slingshot, I bit my lip and let out a whistle of a sigh.

'Hey,' I said to the air.

To my parents.

Their graves were much smaller than I remembered. They were grave-shaped, made of a dingy grey marble, and had little carvings of doves next to their names. At the foot of the shiny slabs were two bouquets, their petals dried and brittle. Ellen leant down and scooped them up, dropping the crispy fragments into a plastic bag Dan pulled out of his pocket.

'Have those been here since the funeral?' I said.

Ellen shook her head. 'I brought them last week. I'm surprised they died so quickly, though. Each bouquet was like ten bucks.'

'You came here last week?' I said.

Keeping the surprise out of my voice was almost impossible. After our parents died, Ellen would ask me every so often if I wanted to visit their graves, but when my monotonous 'no' eventually turned into silence, my sister dropped it altogether.

'I come here every week,' Ellen said. She looked around at the empty cemetery. 'They have like two groundskeepers here, and they don't have time to maintain every plot, so I come and put flowers down and make sure everything looks nice.' She swiped Dan's shoulder. 'Dan brings his lawnmower to keep the grass neat.'

Dan shrugged, not saying anything. Since I'd got back, we'd been tiptoeing around each other, but not because we were mad. Our silence felt more like a truce, like a neutral bookmark until we could figure out how to be in the same room normally. But so far, I hadn't made fun of him and he hadn't pouted, not even when Ellen ate the last of the Cocoa Puffs this morning. It wasn't much, but it felt like progress.

'Oh,' I said, braving a glance at Dan. 'Thanks.'

He smiled with just the corner of his mouth.

'I'm sorry I haven't been back here in so long,' I said to my sister.

Ellen bumped me with her hip. 'I knew there'd be a day when you were ready. I was playing the long game.'

The sound of wind sweeping through the trees crested overhead. I bit the inside of my cheek and stared down at the ground. My sister opened her mouth to say something else but seeing it, Dan wrapped his arm around her shoulder and tugged her lightly in the direction of the truck.

'I need coffee,' he said into the top of her head. 'Across the street, there's a—'

'If you say Starbucks, I'll throw up,' Ellen said.

'You know I'm gonna say Starbucks.'

'There are literally eighty million better coffee places in DC,' Ellen said, 'all of which are within four feet of this cemetery.' She threw a glance at me as Dan guided her past the next row of headstones. 'But what about—' she started to say.

Dan's hold on her shoulders was gentle but firm. 'Hugh can meet us when he's ready.'

He and I met eyes again, except this time it was my turn to give him a half-smile.

More leaves crunched underneath me as they both turned away and I dropped to my knees, settling in beside my parents with my back resting against my dad's gravestone. I stretched out my legs in front of me so they sat perfectly underneath a sliver of shade cast from a crooked tree branch. There was a breeze again, scattering the fallen leaves and causing the stray hairs poking out from my hat to tickle the sides of my face.

'Well,' I said to the air. To my parents. 'I feel like we have a lot of catching up to do.'

Then, head leaning atop the curve of my dad's gravestone, I told my parents about the last two years. About Spoiler Alert, about ditching Becky Cayman, finding Razz and then eventually Becky Cayman again. Driving around in the truck, Ellen's meeting at Giant that she'd rescheduled for next week and was going to nail, because that's what Ellen did, and I was OK with this.

'God, I was such a dick about her meeting,' I said to my parents. 'You would be so mad at me. Remember that time Ellen broke her arm, and I was so annoyed when you took her to the hospital and left me with our neighbour that I broke all the legs off her Lego people? This was like that but eight million times worse.'

But I was already trying to make amends. In between apologizing five hundred times for stealing the truck, for standing in the way of her dreams and more or less destroying all of her stock, I promised Ellen I'd stay up with her all week filling in any gaps in her ice cream supply. I'd even offered to take her and Dan out to Shake Shack next weekend, my treat.

I told my parents about Olivia. I spent what felt like hours on Olivia, describing every detail of the ride up, every shade of blonde in her hair when it caught the sun. Colours I didn't even know existed. And how all this led me to what felt like the most important decision I'd made in years.

I was moving to New York.

'Aunt Karen says I can have the spare bedroom as long as I promise not to say anything when she gets home at midnight reeking of garlic butter,' I said. My throat was dry and scratchy from talking so much, the fall air leaving cement cracks in my vocal chords. 'I don't really know what I'm gonna do once I get there, but I figure I can get a job at a movie theatre or something.'

Anything seemed like a better option than hiding in my room. I was finally ready for something else, to move forward instead of a million tiny steps to the side until I finally just reached the same Hugh-sized set of footprints right back where I'd started. I'd keep Spoiler Alert, but I was already taking things in a new direction. Just that morning I'd started a new section of the website, this time talking not about endings, but middles.

'So, I know this is kinda weird, but I wrote you guys something.' The Spoiler Alert post was printed out on a wrinkled piece of paper. I pulled it from my back pocket and flattened it against my thighs. 'Don't worry, I didn't post it or anything,' I said, clearing my throat. 'It's just for me. And you.'

JANET AND HAROLD COPPER
Drafted in LIVES by <u>Hugh.jpg</u> on August 29 at 7:19 a.m.

My parents were a mixture of puzzle pieces shaped like cuckoo clocks, dusty books, me, my sister and yes, champagne. What's important is, they weren't defined by just one piece. My mom loved garage sales, David Bowie and her family. My dad loved reading in the backyard, baseball, rainstorms, my mom and us. They're more than the way they died. And just because it was in a way I wish I could take back doesn't mean I'd take back everything about them. With them and most other things, the ending doesn't really matter. It's everything else that does.

By the end, I was crying like an idiot.

'I'm sorry I tried to change your ending,' I said to my parents as I swiped my eyes with the back of my hand. 'I mean, if you've been paying attention over the last weekend. If you haven't, then now you know. I used to think the way you died defined everything else about you, but now I realize it was just the fact that you died that screwed me up so much.'

I remembered what Olivia had said the night before, when she called me from her grandparents' house. She was the one that'd come up with the idea to add the 'LIVES' section to Spoiler Alert, and together, we were compiling a list of all the people I'd eventually add. Yes, she'd insisted, everyone had an ending, but it's what's in the middle that's important.

'And like, I'm not saying bad endings don't exist,' I said. 'Because they obviously do. There is no way anyone will ever convince me that Keanu Reeves *needed* to fly away at the end of *The Matrix*.' I breathed out a long sigh through my nose. 'I'd also just like to point out that I'm not moving to New York for Olivia,' I said. 'Does it help that she's there? Obviously. But would I go there without her? I don't know, maybe. Probably.' My hair fell in my eyes as I rolled my head from side to side. 'I'm not really building a solid case here.'

I scooped up a handful of leaves and squeezed, letting their jagged pieces slip between my fingers. By the time I stood again, the sun was on the other side of the trees, peeping through the leaves and casting speckled shadows on the pavement a few gravestones away. I paused, facing my parents, and traced my fingers along their names.

'I miss you guys,' I said quietly. 'I'll come back and see you next week.'

Ellen was waiting for me in the truck at the bottom of the hill. 'Dan's bringing us coffee,' she called out to me as I trudged slowly across the grass, carefully slinking between gravestones. 'I told him I couldn't set foot in that unspeakable pit, not when pumpkin spice latte season is upon us.'

It was only the beginning, but I felt lighter already, the weight of my conversation with my parents releasing some pocket of air I didn't know I was holding on to. I didn't feel this big, incredible sense of closure, but that wasn't really what I was expecting. Sometimes endings were left completely open, and you just had to believe things would carry on like you wanted. What actually happened next was up to you.

As I neared her, Ellen smiled and tossed her phone into her lap.

'You OK?' she asked.

I nodded. I'd never really believed in happy endings before anyway. This one wasn't perfect, but for once, I didn't mind.

Acknowledgements

Olivia Moon has existed in my head for considerably longer than she has on these pages, and I owe a lot of people a lot of gratitude for helping her make that transition.

First and foremost, I owe a giant thank you to my parents – in addition to providing years of love, support and Scholastic Book Club subscriptions, you both never once questioned my English degree, and for that I am forever grateful.

I wouldn't have made it through the production of this book as even a fraction of the shell I am if not for my agent, Chloe Seager. Thank you for your ever-patient responses to my essay-long emails and for believing in this story as much as I did.

Nothing shocked me quite so much about publishing this book as the enthusiasm from the team at Chicken House. Thank you to my editor Kesia Lupo and Barry Cunningham for seeing this book for exactly what it was and then making it infinitely cooler. And for helping in a pinch, an emphatic thank you goes to Marti Martinez and Jack Athans for bringing Hugh to life.

I'm lucky to have had a number of amazingly talented writer pals on my side throughout this process. Michael Garvey, Anna Pook and Bikram Sharma, thank you for your sharp eyes, your wisdom and your friendship. And to my workshop crew, Abby Erwin, Dani Redd and Rowan

Whiteside, your feedback, talent and humour are nothing short of inspiring to me. I look forward to being on your future acknowledgement pages.

To all my friends and family that ever asked how writing was going over the years, thank you for accompanying me on this weird journey. Anna Lavezza, Caroline Parry, Becky Nissel, Mary Sollosi and my aunt, Nancy Chambers, you're particularly amazing. Elfijn Goddard, I will forever appreciate your feedback on a very early draft of this novel, even if you 'hate YA'.

I also owe a massive thank you to Rachel Chiarotti, Ali Wigg and Mercy Yates for their support and all the library meet-ups with our toddlers these past few years. You are great friends and incredible mothers.

My sister and I have a very similar sense of humour, and I can't help but think our relationship helped provide the basis for Ellen and Hugh. Emily Morris, thank you for always being one of my biggest cheerleaders. I'm sorry I threw your backpack down that hill.

To Adam Jackson, my husband and best friend, for all the times you put our daughter to bed when it was my turn so I could write; for always being my first reader; for that time you covered our flat in Post-it notes reminding me I was a good writer, thank you. This book genuinely would not exist without you.

And finally, to my daughter, Margot. Your kindness, curiosity and love are an endless source of comfort. You make me want to be better.